ALSO BY JULIE BUXBAUM

Tell Me Three Things
What to Say Next
Hope and Other Punch Lines
Admission

YEAR ON FIRE

JULIE BUXBAUM

DELACORTE PRESS

This is a work of fiction. Names, characters, places, and incidents either are the product of the author's imagination or are used fictitiously. Any resemblance to actual persons, living or dead, events, or locales is entirely coincidental.

Text copyright © 2022 by Julie R. Buxbaum Inc.
Jacket art copyright © 2022 by Gia Graham

All rights reserved. Published in the United States by Delacorte Press, an imprint of Random House Children's Books, a division of Penguin Random House LLC, New York.

Delacorte Press is a registered trademark and the colophon is a trademark of Penguin Random House LLC.

Visit us on the web! GetUnderlined.com

Educators and librarians, for a variety of teaching tools, visit us at RHTeachersLibrarians.com

Library of Congress Cataloging-in-Publication Data is available upon request.
ISBN 978-1-9848-9366-6 (hardcover) —
ISBN 978-1-9848-9368-0 (ebook) —
ISBN 978-0-593-48705-1 (international ed.)

The text of this book is set in 11-point Berling LT Std.
Interior design by Andrea Lau

Banana emoji by Twitter/Twemoji is licensed under CC BY 4.0, https://creativecommons.org/licenses/by/4.0/legalcode

Printed in the United States of America
10 9 8 7 6 5 4 3 2 1
First Edition

Random House Children's Books supports the First Amendment and celebrates the right to read.

Penguin Random House LLC supports copyright. Copyright fuels creativity, encourages diverse voices, promotes free speech, and creates a vibrant culture. Thank you for buying an authorized edition of this book and for complying with copyright laws by not reproducing, scanning, or distributing any part in any form without permission. You are supporting writers and allowing Penguin Random House to publish books for every reader.

For Megan Dempsey,
who talked me through my own year on fire

CHAPTER ONE

Immie

A single kiss had blown up Immie Gibson's life. How strange that two people's lips touching—not even Immie's lips, mind you, but *two other people's lips* and for no more than thirty seconds—could be the reason why, on this first day of junior year, Immie sat sweating in her linen shirt. That's how long Arch had said the kiss with Jackson had lasted: *thirty seconds, tops.*

On reflection, maybe it wasn't that strange. After all, Immie had never been kissed, not properly, not in the way you see in movies, with eyes closed and a sudden, lurching passion.

Maybe everyone else knew that kissing bent the space-time continuum and validated chaos theory and also could indirectly make your best friend low-key hate you.

Maybe this kind of thing happened every day.

"Bad idea," Paige said, pointing to Immie's shirt. "Linen always wrinkles." Her button-down had somehow, during the ride to school, turned from crisp and optimistic to defeated. Crumpled, like her mood.

"Do I have sweat stains? I feel like I have sweat stains," Immie said, pretending she didn't notice the new way Paige liked to throw tiny darts in her direction, how it was not yet eight-thirty a.m. and her torso was made up of a million microscopic seeping wounds.

"Say that a little louder. I think the boys in the back didn't hear you," Paige said.

"You do not have sweat stains," Arch said. "Relax, Im."

Paige had been Immie's best friend since seventh grade, when Immie arrived at Wood Valley Middle School feeling nervous and overwhelmed, a donkey in a field of ponies. Middle school was supposed to be filled with awkward kids—braces and acne, an inability to move smoothly through the world, like you hadn't yet been given the map. Wood Valley, on the other hand, was packed with the well-mannered, the well-groomed, the already slick. The girls even carried cute pouches—canvas and pink polka-dotted and monogrammed—to hold their new menstrual products, like puberty was adorable and fun.

Even at the horrific age of thirteen, Immie knew: these people were *born* with maps. The rules didn't apply.

Also, her period was horrifying.

At their very first assembly in the auditorium, the headmaster stood on the stage and told the gathered mid-pubescents that their admittance to Wood Valley and this important first year of seventh grade were the start of an "illustrious career."

Paige, who was sitting to Immie's right, as she would many times after that by choice, but whose appearance that first day seemed like nothing short of a miracle, sneezed into her hand the word: *bullshit*. Immie thrilled at the transgression. Archer, Immie's twin brother who always sat to her left, who had sat there since pre-K, probably since the womb, wrote down the words *illustrious career* in his shiny, new composition notebook in neat block letters, and then underlined it twice. Arch was born first, by four minutes, so they were always Arch and Immie, a single unit. Or Archer and Imogen, if their dad was angry. They had never been Immie and Arch (or, worse, the matchy-matchy Immie and Archie), which sounded like a crime-fighting duo in a kids' chapter book.

Sometimes things are set in the beginning.

That's what it felt like when Immie found herself sitting in between her brother and Paige on that first day of seventh grade, like the ground was firming beneath her feet, right there at the *start of their illustrious careers* or this *bullshit*, depending on your perspective. They would be Arch and Immie and Paige from then on.

Immie's premonition had been right, or maybe it wasn't a premonition. Perhaps she'd willed it. Either way, they soon became a threesome. Paige had rolled up like seventh grade was just seventh grade. No big deal. Later, Immie would learn Paige could do pretty much anything she wanted and not get in trouble, that sneeze-cursing was the least of her transgressions. Overconfidence and a sly sense of humor were Paige's superpowers, and once Immie understood that about her best friend, she wondered if maybe she hadn't been the one to will their connection—Paige probably had.

But that beginning was a long time ago. Middle school angst had given way to high school comfort—or at least, if not comfort, routine—and so today wasn't supposed to feel like seventh grade all over again. And yet, Immie felt the familiar flutter of panic, the rush of wetness under her arms. If there weren't sweat stains a moment ago, there were now. Paige claimed to have forgiven her, but this was, to sneeze-quote Paige herself, *bullshit*. If Immie had been in her position, if she had thought Paige had kissed her boyfriend, though of course Immie had never had a boyfriend for Paige to kiss because she was a normal living on a planet full of mermaids, she would have been livid. Immie believed in clear lines.

Now, though, if Immie somehow miraculously found a boyfriend, she'd pass him right over to Paige and make them even.

Here, kiss him and hurt me. I miss us.

Of course, neither life nor boyfriends actually worked that way. And Immie hadn't kissed Paige's boyfriend (well, ex-boyfriend now), Jackson, in the first place. But Paige would never know that, *could never know that*, and so Immie was stuck permanently in the aftermath of this ridiculous, self-destructive lie. She was also stuck in this wrinkled linen shirt that gave off a cardboard smell, in this school where she didn't fit in, in this life that made her long desperately for college, as if she had to wait two whole years to pull the emergency exit lever.

That was what she was thinking about—the kiss and her earlier inexplicable optimism and her tiny wounds and their invisible droplets of blood—when the new boy walked in. Later that night, she would tell Arch that the new boy had smelled of smoke, that when she saw him she immediately thought of campfires and s'mores, and so he might be the arsonist. Arch, like a runner throwing a baton, would pass this information to Paige and plant a tiny seed of suspicion. They all felt badly about that later.

But Immie was wrong. The new boy did not smell like smoke. Fires can be a lot like kisses: they can confuse your chronology and leave no reliable witnesses.

Before the alarm went off and they were evacuated to the fields, Immie looked up and saw the new boy, took in his British accent and his sweet brown eyes, and felt an entirely different kind of wound, this one larger, more pointed, possibly fatal. Like someone had put out a cigarette on her heart. (Is that why she thought she smelled smoke? Had her subconscious transformed the image in her mind into something literal?)

Paige, who Immie had thought had gone to the bathroom, but was now sitting next to her again, a tiny bit breathless, tapped her on the arm.

"Dibs," she whispered.

The new boy seemed conjured from her imagination, like that morning Immie had handed God a list not unlike the one she was putting together about herself for those future college applications, and God had handed her this person right back. This feeling was altogether new, and not, if she was honest, entirely pleasant.

"Apologies for my tardiness. Got a bit turned around on the motorway. Total chockablock," he said to Ms. Lee, and handed her the slip of paper in his hand. "Also, you drive on the wrong side of the road here. Bloody confusing, it is." He had tousled hair and brown skin and the sort of accent that conjured up the image of a monarchy. He turned to the class, sad-eyed and wry-smiled, and cocked his head to the side, puppy-like, as if waiting for someone to point to an empty seat and invite him to sit down.

Immie sucked in that *bloody confusing, it is* as if through a straw. She wondered if the new boy was intentionally using as many Britishisms as he could. Like he had decided on the plane ride over the Atlantic that this would be his bit—all Britishisms all the time. Maybe someone had told him that American girls liked that sort of thing.

We do, Immie thought. *We do*.

"It's a freeway, not a motorway," Jackson called out from the back of the room, reminding Immie again of Jackson's existence, which is something she generally tried to forget. Immie had claimed the kiss with Jackson as her own, had reached out and grabbed it, like catching an air kiss blown across the room at someone else. There was no denying she had protected her brother at the expense of her best friend, which, even now, ten days after it all went down, while she was still stewing in the aftermath, felt like the right call.

What surprised her most about the scandal was not the lie itself and how easily she told it; it was how easily Paige believed Immie, as if she had been waiting to be betrayed by her this entire time.

Arch, Immie's twin brother and her better half, her favorite person since birth, had betrayed Paige and kissed Paige's boyfriend, Jackson. Sometimes Immie repeated it to herself—*Arch kissed Jackson and I said I did it*—because it still seemed like a bizarre dream.

Arch liked to joke that he was the first out of the womb because Immie had pushed him. That might have been true. Immie's mom often told the story that when they were babies, Arch wouldn't settle unless Immie was placed beside him in the bassinet. That might have been true too. The point is: Arch and Immie predated Arch and Immie and Paige.

The two of them had never discussed the myriad other possibilities: Arch coming out and claiming that stupid kiss himself. Or maybe separating this particular kiss from some bigger statement about Arch. They didn't even discuss the possibility of him trying what Jackson had managed through the years—cultivating an ambiguous sexual identity. No one would have been surprised to hear that Jackson sometimes kissed boys; he had long ago hinted at his bisexuality or maybe pansexuality, seeming to be above any concerns about labels. But Jackson was like Paige in that way: he was given the single gift of adulthood early—there would be no delay in him getting to be exactly who he was.

Arch was the absolute last person you would think

would ever kiss their best friend's boyfriend. Not because people thought he was hetero, but because he was Arch. Goodhearted, reliable, loyal Arch, who told you if you had toilet paper stuck to your shoe and left his test answers unguarded by his arm when he knew he was nailing them in case the person next to him needed some help.

Arch had come to her crying that night, covered in snot and guilty tears—Paige was his best friend too, after all. As they sat on the bottom bunk, Immie folded her arms around him.

She decided then, in the loneliest hours of the night, when her resoluteness felt like it could slip away by morning, that she'd be the one to take the fall with Paige. This was for reasons far more complicated than sexuality or identity. Or maybe it was for reasons far simpler. Immie and Arch's father was unpredictable and a little scary, and neither of them wanted to explain to Paige the impossible tightrope they walked at home. How the slightest shift—a birthday, maybe, or friends coming over for dinner—could cause him to erupt, and how afterward, they were unsure how to trace back the unraveling. Their father wouldn't rage about the birthday, of course—you couldn't blame someone for having a birthday. Still, a target would always be found: how their mom made the cake, how their mom arranged the cake on the table, how their mom had forgotten their dad hated flowers made of frosting. Immie and Arch's father was likely not homophobic, but that was irrelevant to this sort of inexplicable calculus.

And explaining this to Paige, when they could barely

understand it themselves, would require a certain kind of strength and clarity neither of them possessed.

The new boy took the only open seat, which happened to be next to Arch. He had fidget hair, Immie thought, and when he reached up and nervously tugged on his head and twisted a strand around his finger, she silently groaned. She felt her eczema flare in her inner elbow, a burn that needed cooling.

"You must be Rohan, I presume?" Ms. Lee, the English Honors III teacher asked, and for a minute, her voice too had taken on the British accent, because the gentle lilting was charming and contagious and it seemed she couldn't help trying it on for size.

"One and the same," Rohan said, which made Immie want to turn to him and say something idiotic like *Mind the gap* or *Have you met Prince Harry?* Or maybe just: *You.* "Though everyone calls me Ro. Sorry again about the interruption." He slid out a spiral notebook, which was covered in band stickers, none of which Immie recognized. Ro wore a black T-shirt with a cartoon of a mohawked chicken, tight cuffed jeans, and gray Nike high-top sneakers. His teeth were straight and white, and though, as a true Anglophile, Immie was Team Crooked Teeth, she forgave him this imperfect perfection.

Immie shivered and realized she was no longer sweating. Instead, she was covered head to toe in goose bumps, because his name was Ro, which seemed exactly what the boy of her dreams should be called. Something catchy and to-the-point. Im and Ro.

"Yum," Paige whispered, another single-syllable follow-up to her earlier *dibs,* and the word landed in Immie's gut, like a stone sinking in water. Of course, she wasn't even a little surprised when Paige claimed what was always going to be hers, what Immie would have given her, had he been, against all odds, Immie's to give. That's how badly she needed Paige's forgiveness.

Still, this boy, whoever he may be, was a person, not a penance to be given. He was not a figment of the imagination or even, Immie realized, anything more to her than a person, a stranger transmogrified into a feeling. If it had been a month ago, even, Immie might have made a joke about how you can't call dibs on a boy the way you call shotgun for the front seat. But it wasn't a month ago. It was the first day of junior year, and the kiss had just happened, like a lit match to the dry forest floor, and there was no pulling it back.

All she wanted was for them to be Arch and Immie and Paige again.

There was no such thing as Im and Ro.

Still, Immie rubbed at her chest, right where her heart lived. The material felt rough, unrefined. Paige was right. Linen was a bad choice. She smudged the embarrassing pain away.

And then, for real this time, she smelled the faintest hint of smoke.

CHAPTER TWO

Ro

Ro was angry at the sun. At home, everything was gray. The air was solid and wet, and so he didn't mind so much when he was stuck inside all day at school, because there was nowhere else to go. Might as well huddle up with his books or mess around in the halls with his mates, and wait till the last minute to burst out the front door to catch the bus. He loved London and all the things that made Londoners expert whingers—the weather, the other nine million people who bloody well should watch where they're going, how it was an inhumane place teeming with humanity. He loved emerging from those long escalators leading out of the Tube stations and taking that first gulp of air, knowing that later, when he blew his nose, there'd be soot on the tissue.

On the street, he loved walking with strangers, all of them hunched and nestled under large black umbrellas, hands jammed into their pockets. It reminded Ro that his place in the universe was small and insignificant, and that was a good thing, one's own insignificance. It meant that all the messing-up everyone around him seemed to be doing lately didn't matter. Nothing mattered. Only the forward momentum of gray history, of those gray buildings still standing, of the gray rain forever failing, of even the gray Thames, continuing to churn its sneaky way through his city.

Los Angeles, on the other hand—or at least the little he had seen during the drive yesterday from the airport—was a blindingly bright landscape full of fast-food joints and mini-malls and billboards advertising movies starring exceptionally jacked bald men.

So this was America, he thought.

Ro felt lost. He had no idea where he was, other than in the hallway of a random private school in the city of Los Angeles, in the state of California, on the far West Coast of the United States, following a swarm of students out the emergency exits presumably because someone had pulled the fire alarm. He was walking with a pretty girl named Paige who wore leather riding boots up to her knees even though it was a balmy thirty-one degrees Celsius, and she seemed utterly unconcerned by the blaring electronic voice that kept repeating "Fire. Fire. Fire."

"Some kids here are rich jerks, but not everyone," she said, apropos of nothing . . . or maybe he had missed a solid chunk of their conversation. That was entirely possible, given that they'd found themselves at the end of the hall, and he had no recollection of walking there. He smelled smoke suddenly, but for reasons he couldn't explain, it didn't frighten him. His brain filled with innocent explanations: A science experiment gone wrong. A cigarette not properly put out. He knew with uncharacteristic certainty he wasn't going to die today, and so he continued walking slowly, unworried, following the people in front of him.

"Sorry?" He kept his tone light. It wasn't this random girl's fault he was knackered and jet-lagged and so filled with a volcanic rage that it took all his willpower not to punch one of those steel lockers. He really didn't have the energy for this crap.

Later, when they stood outside and watched part of the east wing burn, he'd wonder, for a moment, if maybe he had caused the fire somehow, inadvertently, without his knowledge, his anger manifested. Like in the movies when a misfit discovers they have a secret superpower. He went so far as to examine his fingertips for evidence of a flame. They, of course, turned out to be normal, boring fingertips.

"You know, the private jets, the sweet sixteens have like, Grammy winners performing, Oscar swag bags. It's pretty gross," Paige said, and then swept her hand under her hair, picked it up into a large undulating ponytail, and then dropped it again. She seemed to be performing in some way, like there might be a reality TV camera behind Ro's shoulder capturing her every movement.

"Oh. Okay. Right." Ro only recognized half of the words she'd spoken, but that was at least partly because he was only half listening. He'd been wondering why he had Advanced Theater on his schedule, given that he'd never taken a single theater class in his life, and how long it would be till he was outside, breathing fresh air. If things had been different, if he were here in this strange, neon land of his own volition, if he hadn't been distracted by the smoke and the alarm, he'd maybe have tried to be charming. Paige was gorgeous, if a little fussily dressed, and he couldn't be sure, but it felt like she might be flirting with him. He could imagine overplaying his accent in response—his best friend, Arun, promised him the girls in the U.S. would love it—and even asking Paige to guide him through the rest of the day, assuming they'd all have to go back to class eventually. But he wasn't here on his own volition. Flirting took energy and a lightness, neither of which Ro could muster.

"Tell me about you," she said.

What was there to tell? He was angry, sure. Also, confused. Lost. Sad. The tiniest bit wheezy. He thought about his three duffel bags, filled with an assortment of clothes that were, he realized now, weather-inappropriate, and how he hadn't bothered to open them, not even to take out his sketch pad or Blue Bear. The bags were still sitting next to the door of his new room, which used to belong to a little girl. For the next two years, he'd be sleeping under a dainty pink lace canopy because his dad had let the place fully furnished.

"You don't mind, do you?" his dad had asked last night, and the truth was, Ro didn't. He minded a lot of other things—the being there in the first place—but the girl's room, with its purple border of doodled fairies, was strangely comforting. It made him think of his older sister, Kiran, and how when she was little, she would prance around their flat in a battered pair of fairy wings and Peppa Pig pajamas. Now she was at Oxford, and her room had a poster that said *Keep Calm and Smash the Patriarchy*, and he probably wouldn't see her again until next summer.

"I don't know. I'm from London. I can say with one hundred percent certainty I've never been given a 'swag bag.'" He coughed a little.

"Yeah," Paige said. Ro looked around to marvel at the sea of mostly white faces, a new experience for him. Ro knew that Wood Valley wasn't going to be like home, where everywhere you looked, there were other brown people. But still he hadn't anticipated this level of *whiteness*.

Ro didn't get to think about it for long, though, because he felt the pressure of being squeezed from behind and the quickening of panic.

"Run! The school is on fire!" someone yelled from behind them.

Fifty kids in front of him, hundreds behind.

All filtering out through a single set of double doors.

"Shut up and chill!" Paige screamed to the freaked-out boy behind them. "Here, hoist me up," Paige said to Ro, and then, without waiting for an answer, she jumped on his back. Paige climbed till she was on his shoulders, like Kiran used to do in the pool at the David Lloyd Leisure Centre on Sundays, when they were little and would chicken fight Kaia and Arun.

"Look, the windows are open, and the doors are right there." Paige cupped her hands around her mouth and, though she was yelling, she sounded calm, even reasonable.

The pressure behind him stilled. "We're all safe. Do not push. Do you understand me? Do not push! If we all wait our turn, no one will get hurt, I promise. Out the door, four at a time. I repeat: the windows are open. Everyone will be fine."

Amazingly, people listened. Slow and steady they filtered out through the side doors, taking deep grateful breaths once across the threshold, and followed the swarm until they reached the far field. From there, the teachers organized them into classes and took head counts, though no one was sure of the numbers. A few kids sucked on inhalers, passing them around to the other asthmatics even though they were supposed to wait for the paramedics. Ro was amazed by the friendly, nervous camaraderie. He couldn't imagine anyone at his old school offering up their inhaler, no matter the circumstance.

The counting was tricky. It was the first day of school, and so the routines had not yet been set. Had Adrien Oh been in first period with Mr. Ames or Ms. Morley? Of course, soon enough, Principal Hochman arrived with the roster, and names were checked off, and a phone tree was activated—whatever that meant—and it became clear, if not certain, no one had been seriously injured. There was a collective feeling of relief, tinged with an indecent disappointment. For a minute, school had been exciting.

Ro imagined his father getting a phone call on his mobile (or would they call his mum in England?), a robotic voice letting him know that his son's new school was on fire. Seemed about what he deserved.

When, a few minutes later, his own mobile lit up with a text from his dad, *you okay?!?!?*, he waited a few beats to write back. Which was cruel, he knew. But so was his father lately.

Fine, he texted. Ro wouldn't give him more than that.

Instead, he stood next to Paige, who, it turned out, was something of a real superhero. Together they watched the east wing burn.

CHAPTER THREE

Arch

"You like him," Arch announced over the hiss of the milk steamer. Arch and Immie worked at Espresso Yourself on Ventura, on a rare block full of independently owned stores, all with punny names. Next door was Book Down Below!, which was Arch's favorite place on Earth, even now, long after the hot guy who used to work there went off to college. The twins' dad's best friend owned the coffee shop, so he threw them shifts for cash, always at the same time because they shared a car. Today they got to work early, because someone had set Immie's favorite bathroom at Wood Valley on fire and so they had been freed long before the last bell.

"I didn't even meet him," Immie said.

Arch hadn't had to mention Ro by name. They both knew who they were talking about.

"But wasn't it sort of weird when he walked in? It felt like Christmas came early for you. I mean, he's adorable and *so* your type, with that accent." Arch fanned himself dramatically, and then wondered why talking about a guy's attractiveness was so natural with Immie and had to be so hard with everyone else.

"You like girls, right?" Paige asked Arch a few years ago. He'd nodded and she took him at his word because why would he lie? LA was a land of rainbow flags and Pride parades, where everyone knew what every letter of LGBTQIA stood for. They had plenty of friends with two dads or two moms and who themselves identified as queer. Often he wished he could go back in time and correct the record, because he'd always known that, for him, it was boys. His was not a slow realization that he was gay, but a consistent understanding.

And yet, he had lied to Paige. He told himself it was because of the many uncontrollable variables. Okay, one uncontrollable variable. He'd tell his father eventually—of course he would, he had no plans to hide forever the person he was proud to be—but he'd done the math. It seemed safer for everyone, him in particular, to wait till . . . when? He didn't know. College, maybe. When he had his own place outside the blast zone. When he could do it over the phone. When he could give his mom ample warning that she might want to take a vacation to see her parents in Minnesota.

But still, that didn't explain why he hadn't told Paige.

The truth was, it felt too late for that. Too late and too early.

Because telling her meant explaining why he couldn't come out at home, and he couldn't explain that. Not really.

This was the way he thought about it: The first rule of Fight Club is you don't talk about Fight Club. First rule of the Gibson household is you don't talk about what happens in the Gibson household.

"That accent. Oh my God," Immie said now about Ro, her face reddening. "The new boy and then the fire? What a weird day, right?"

Before Ro even opened his mouth that morning, Arch knew his sister would be a goner. He knew this not because they shared some weird twin-tuition—unlike their mother, he didn't believe in that mystical crap. Arch and Immie simply had an overlapping genetic code and had spent every single night of their lives together in a tiny, shared bedroom, with the exception of the time she had her appendix out, and even then, Arch had slept in the hospital cot that had been brought out for their mom.

Arch knew his sister even better than he knew himself. It was easier to be clear-eyed about other people's vulnerabilities than it was to be clear-eyed about your own.

Last summer, Immie forced Arch to binge this show about a conniving British royal family who were also secretly vampires, and he knew that's what his sister was thinking about when Ro opened his mouth: that Ro sounded like Jax, Immie's favorite character, who was the fictional second son of the Prince of Wales. When Arch brought up the fact that the real British royals would never name a future prince *Jax*, Immie said, "*That's* your believability issue? Not the fact that they, you know, drink the blood of commoners?"

"I like to think of that as a metaphor," Arch said.

"Two double oat-milk lattes, shot of vanilla in one," Immie called, now at the other end of the bar at the register because some customers had arrived, and Arch went to work steaming and pouring. He couldn't see or hear from this side what was happening at the front, so he had to rely on his sister shouting out the orders. They worked like that for a solid half hour, a well-oiled machine.

"One iced coffee," Immie said, and with the slightest of pitch changes, she tipped Arch off. Not a normal order. Jackson was here. Of course he was here, because he had to be everywhere these days—because God forbid anyone dare try to live in a Jacksonless world. God forbid Arch try to forget those perfect thirty seconds.

Arch could smell him from across the coffee shop, some distinctive spice that undoubtedly came from an expensive bottle you bought at a fancy department store. Arch likely smelled like the soap you bought at CVS, and he couldn't help thinking that even his body odor made clear where he stood in the social hierarchy. Arch bent down and pretended to grab some milk, and instead wiped his sweating face with the steamer rag, which was disgusting, but desperate times and all that.

When he looked up, Jackson was smiling, because Jackson was always smiling, which was one more thing Arch found infuriating about him. Immie was laughing at whatever charming thing he was saying—Jackson always had something charming to say—and Arch thought: *Traitor.*

Immie was supposed to hate Jackson. It was in the twin code.

Jackson was six foot two and sturdy, and though Arch knew for a fact that he'd never played football in his life, he looked like someone who threw balls around on Sundays with a weathered father figure who, afterward, patted him on the back and said *Nice throw, son*. Arch hated Jackson for many reasons—for the way he'd infiltrated his dreams, for messing everything up for Immie—but the way Jackson filled what looked like a tailor-made T-shirt with accidental muscles came in a very close third. Given Jackson's family—his dad ran a talent agency and his mom was a former supermodel—it's entirely possible he did have all of his clothes custom-made.

Let's be honest: the world didn't really need boys like Jackson. Who walked into every single room as if he already belonged in it. Who turned nouns into verbs to show off his casually perfect life: *boated, partied, clubbed*. Whose entitlement ran so deep into his being, it clung like enthusiastically applied cologne.

God, Arch *hated* Jackson.

Arch realized that if kissing Jackson was the biggest mistake he had ever made in his entire life, it was only because he led too small a life. A kiss—no matter how magical or how wrong or, in this case, *both*—shouldn't feel like a first domino, or like one of those butterfly wings that causes a tsunami. A kiss was just a kiss, after all. Something small and insignificant. An indiscretion, not a murder. And yet, if it hadn't happened, everything would be fine right now, or, at the very least, a slightly more normal normal.

Of course, because Jackson was Jackson, he had suffered no consequences, except for Paige breaking up with him, which he didn't seem to have minded. For the record, and the record seemed important in this case, *Jackson* had kissed *Arch*, not the other way around. Yes, Arch had kissed him back, and maybe he kissed him some more after that first kiss, and maybe he returned his kiss in a way that, in retrospect, felt embarrassingly eager, but the point was Jackson started it.

He *definitely* started it.

"So who do you think the mystery arsonist is?" Jackson asked him, as if they were midconversation already. "I was telling your sister I have twenty bucks on the new kid. He shows up late, and a few seconds later the school is on freakin' fire?"

Jackson smiled again, or maybe he had never stopped flashing his bright expanse of teeth, like this was all a joke—not only the fire, but the fact that they had kissed and Immie had taken the blame and now they couldn't be friends anymore. Then again, Arch wasn't sure if they had ever been friends. Jackson had been Paige's boyfriend, and so they hung out sometimes. But friends? Not really.

Jackson and Arch were from different species. Jackson was Wood Valley royalty, and Arch was the son of Wood Valley faculty, and that, besides the vast expanse between who they were as people—Jackson loud and in-your-face,

Arch quiet and private—meant they'd never really be friends.

"I don't think so," Arch said. "Who said it was arson, anyway?"

"What else would it be? Spontaneous combustion?"

Spontaneous combustion. Wasn't that what happened at the party? A bizarre, sudden chemical explosion? When he thought of it that way, Arch felt marginally better. The betrayal had not been his fault. It was science.

Jackson might be able to go around kissing whoever he wanted and no one thought anything of it, but Arch was not afforded that same privilege. Jackson also got to wear fedoras and, once, a bandanna around his neck and plaid pants hemmed above the ankle. Occasionally, he played with eyeliner.

Life wasn't fair.

Arch couldn't imagine what that would be like, to feel comfortable enough in the world to so consistently draw attention to yourself. Immie and Arch and Paige had once spent two hours discussing how the world could be divided into two kinds of people: the ones who could wear red lipstick and not spend the day thinking, *Is everyone staring at my mouth?*, and the ones who could not. Paige was in the first category; the twins were both decidedly in the second.

"Arch?" Jackson asked, and so Arch looked at him, as always too responsive. The eagerness around Jackson was Pavlovian. What did he expect Jackson to say? *I'm sorry? It was all my fault?*

Maybe.

An *I'm sorry* would be nice, actually.

Arch dug his fingers into his palms so his eyes wouldn't fill with tears.

"Yeah," Arch said, and then started stacking cups that were already stacked. Stirred milk that didn't need stirring. Anything not to look again at Jackson's face, which was long-lashed and full-lipped and unfairly pristine. He looked exactly like who he was, which wasn't true of most people. Arch believed an entirely different person lived under his own mediocre pale skin. He'd always loved the Hulk when he was little, the conceit of an outrageous, larger-than-life alter ego bursting to be set free.

Maybe the fire had been arson. He wondered if everyone at Wood Valley, even the overly privileged idiots who had nothing to complain about, also burned with anger. His mom once confessed that she had hated being a teenager—that she found that last bridge from childhood to adulthood the most treacherous one to pass—and that's why she'd chosen to teach high school. To help others navigate it.

Firsts are beautiful, sweetheart, but they also tend to sear.

"Can I get a splash of milk?" Jackson asked. So, no apology. Right.

Arch took back the drink and fiddled with the plastic lid, and because it was filled right to the top, he poured a little down the sink drain. The ice made a jarring rattle. Arch added the milk like he'd done a thousand times to a thousand cups of coffee, and still his hands shook.

"Thanks. See you around?"

"Sure," Arch said, because of course he'd see him

around. Arch and Jackson had five classes together. Six, if you counted lunch. "Whatever."

This *whatever* was a nasty afterthought—it had been a strange, rough day—and as soon as it was out, Arch wished he could reel it back in. Smile instead. Or at least fist-bump. Maybe even offer his own guess about the arsonist. He pictured them as someone who wore their anger on the outside because they needed everyone else to see it. Like that girl Katy Flore, who dyed her hair black and had piercings in places that looked like they hurt, and snarled if you said hello.

"Okay," Jackson said, and took his drink, and knocked on the counter twice with his knuckles. No one would ever accuse Jackson of arson.

He wasn't messy like that.

As he left, Arch tried very hard not to watch him walk away.

"You okay?" Immie asked later after they had closed the shop and piled into their car; only then could they smell how much they reeked of coffee beans. Arch worried that it followed him and Immie everywhere now that they were working most afternoons and that Paige was too polite to tell them. Maybe smelling like CVS would be an upgrade.

"Course. Why wouldn't I be?" Arch asked, and Immie didn't say anything. "It's fine. Really. I think this whole thing has gotten overblown."

"Paige is still weird with me," Immie said in a rush, like a confession, and Arch wanted to tell her that she was imagining things, that Paige was just Paige, but he couldn't lie to his sister, especially not after she had lied so boldly for him. "She didn't even want to hang out this afternoon. It's not like she could have had anywhere she needed to be. We had, like, a once-in-a-lifetime get-out-of-jail-free card because of the fire."

"Right." For a minute, Arch tried to picture Immie striking the match and setting the bathroom ablaze. Impossible and yet still too easy to see in his mind's eye. Her own frustration manifested. Surely she must have regretted taking the fall for him. Surely she'd want to find a way to deflect the darts Paige had been throwing all morning.

No. Ridiculous. Of course Immie wasn't an arsonist.

"When do you think it will get better? Because Arch, I miss her so much," Immie said, and though she wasn't crying, he could feel that she was on the edge of tears. The car felt humid with them.

"I'm so sorry. If I had thought for one second, if I had stopped and thought about it, I never would have—"

"I know."

"I didn't think. It was like *spontaneous combustion*," Arch said. Immie let out a bark of a laugh.

"I know what you mean," she agreed. Arch didn't actually think she did, but that was okay. He was certain that one day she'd have a kiss like that, and afterward she'd call him and say *I understand now*.

"I think Paige'll come around," Arch said, and he told himself he believed it. "She definitely will." The three of them had been friends for so long, their dynamic well established. One kiss—and a lie on top—couldn't ruin that. Some things were too set to be unraveled by that sort of accident.

"You know what my first thought was when I saw Jackson? Not, *Holy crap, Arch, Jackson's here—quick, wipe your face.* It was, *Paige better not see me talking to him,*" Immie said. "How silly is that?"

"Was I that sweaty?" Arch asked.

"Arch!"

"Kidding. Not silly at all. You are allowed once in your life not to think of me first."

"I just want things to go back to the way they were," Immie said.

"I'm sorry, Im," Arch said.

"Stop apologizing."

"Maybe Paige is just stressed and taking it out on you? About junior year." All summer, when Arch and Immie went over to Paige's house to swim after work, they'd found Paige, who was on track to be their valedictorian, studying stretched out on a chair in her bikini. As soon as they joined her, she'd read them the SAT problems she had been given by her private tutor. Immie was convinced that whatever Paige was learning for two hundred fifty dollars a session had to be better than the materials they had from the chain test-prep place near their apartment. Paige had always been happy to share.

"You like Ro. So that's one good thing. Maybe focus on that," Arch suggested.

"Paige was flirting with him in the field. Anyway, she called dibs," Immie said.

"You can't call dibs on a person," Arch said.

"Still," Immie said.

"Crap," Arch said.

CHAPTER FOUR

Ro

Ro had never imagined what his own personal hell might look like, but now he guessed it might be something like this: him, on a stage, with a group of American kids, holding hands and chanting. The teacher, Mrs. Gibson, stood in the middle of the circle and banged on a drum that hung around her torso, like a baby carrier.

The school had been declared safe, though Ro swore he could still taste the smoke in the air. It turned out neither of his parents had been particularly bothered by the robocall they'd received the previous day. Ro's mum said it had made the fire sound like it was no big deal. That they were only letting the parents know out of courtesy. He didn't have the heart to tell her about that moment in the hall, how he felt that push at his back before that girl Paige stepped up and stopped a stampede.

"Feel that beat, people. Let it move you," Mrs. Gibson said. She had long frizzy blond-gray hair tied into two low pigtails, and her feet were bare, toenails messily painted a glittery gold. She looked nothing like any teacher he'd ever had. If anything, she resembled a cult leader, or if Ro were feeling more charitable, a yoga instructor.

"Close your eyes!" she commanded. "Use your other senses."

Ro sniffed the air and picked up the scent of patchouli. He pictured his mum in their kitchen in London lighting scented candles. She'd be just home from work, and would have slipped off her heels at the door, and put on her comfy pants and fuzzy slippers. Ro's mum's black hair was cut in a sleek bob that had one swoop of silver that stretched from root to tip. It looked intentional, a whimsical nod to high fashion, but she'd always had it. When Ro was little, he drew a comic book for her called *Skunk Mum*, and it told the story of Mummy Skunk and her two little baby skunks who fought crime by stinking up the bad guys. His mum had loved it so much she'd had it laminated and reprinted and gave out copies to all their relatives.

"Go to your happy place," Mrs. Gibson called out. He pictured his mum pressing the buttons on the microwave with her knuckles, reheating the daal she made over the weekend. Actually, since he and his dad weren't there, it's possible she hadn't bothered to cook yesterday. She could be eating a bowl of Coco Shreddies for dinner, standing over the sink. No doubt tonight she'd watch *Big Brother* season quintillion on the telly because both Ro and his dad hated that program. Maybe her entire life would be better because they were gone.

That was, after all, sort of the point of him coming here,

even if no one said it out loud. His mum had taken a promotion that would put her in Paris four nights a week. His dad had taken a miraculously timed two-year fellowship at UCLA. Ro hadn't taken anything, except a non-optional flight to LAX and a melatonin.

Ro was far, far away from his happy place. His eyes burned and he bit down hard on his lip. He would not *cry*. It's not like his mum was dead or anything. Arun's mum had died three years ago, and that was awful. Ro's mother was just on the other side of the planet—fully reachable by WhatsApp or FaceTime. Still, he didn't like thinking about the time difference—that his mum lived eight hours into the future, nine when she was in Paris.

"Don't forget the purpose of this class," Mrs. Gibson bellowed. "We're going to explore the self and the soul. We are going to hone your *craaaaaft*."

She sang the last word, like that Oprah meme where she tells her audience "You get a car! And you get a car!" And if Ro wasn't so depressed, he'd laugh. He'd never once considered *honing his craft*, because he didn't have a *craft*. He wondered if it would be rude to drop his classmates' hands—they were both soft, and hinted at dampness, like the girls on either side had both recently applied lotion. He felt a wave of repulsion, and let go. If he held on for another single second, he was afraid he might not be able to keep himself from making a run for it.

"Are you on the beach riding a wave? Feeling the breeze ripple your hair?" Mrs. Gibson asked.

Ro's phone vibrated and he slipped it out of his pocket.

Everyone had their eyes closed, even Mrs. Gibson. No one would notice.

Kaia: Miss you handsome. Who am I supposed to snog now?

Ro felt his body sag with relief. This place might be unfamiliar, but he had a magic device that still tethered him to his old life. Kaia must have used her Spidey-Sense to know he was in trouble. He typed a quick *xoxo*, then discreetly tucked the phone away, but that was enough to keep him for a while. He closed his eyes and thought about his real happy place. Not with his mum and, no, certainly not with his dad. Not some imagined beach either. Instead, he pictured himself with Arun and Kaia in Arun's bedroom, sitting on the floor under that peeling black-and-white Jimmy Hendrix poster that Arun had picked up in Camden, passing a family-sized packet of Walker's Prawn Cocktail crisps between them. They must have done that a thousand times after school, not one of which, taken in isolation, was particularly memorable, but the sum total of which made Ro ache with nostalgia.

Mrs. Gibson stopped beating her drum.

"Now please open your eyes," she said. "Open them wide, friends. Take a look at the world around you."

Ro blinked, glanced right and then left. Everything was bright and foreign and filtered with dust motes. He tried to calculate how many miles stretched between him and home.

CHAPTER FIVE

Paige

"So tell me: what do I need to know to survive here? Other than to take the fire alarm seriously," Ro asked in a mock whisper, like he was James Bond on a secret mission.

It was cute. *He* was cute.

"Like what?" Paige asked. Now that they were juniors, she and the twins had decided to eat lunch near the Koffee Kart, all snuggled up in the comfy chairs toward the back. More civilized over here, without the fluorescent lighting and the screech of chairs on linoleum in the caf. Paige had invited Ro to join them, and so they were four. A new, unfamiliar configuration, one more recent realignment.

"Right, well, for example, if you came to my school in London, I'd warn you to stay away from Simon Snortenbottom because he's a sociopath. If he went to Wood Valley, I'd say with one hundred percent certainty he was the arsonist," Ro said.

"I don't buy that it was arson," Paige said.

"You made that name up. Snortenbottom," Arch said,

and handed a ham sandwich to Immie—which was so Arch and Immie, because *who, other than the twins, ate homemade ham sandwiches after the age of five?* Paige wondered if they noticed that they always sat in the same way, like a married couple who took the same side of the bed. She knew after this they'd split a Snickers bar and then share a single can of Coke, pass it back and forth like a joint.

The twins looked alike, both sweet-faced and round-cheeked, like their mom still made sure they drank a glass of whole milk every morning. Immie's brown hair was long and curly, while Arch's was straight and cut short, but when they talked, their hands tended to move in tandem. So many shared details embedded in their genetic code.

Their smiles featured the same overbite, like their front teeth were winning a race against their molars.

Immie ate some of her sandwich and a piece of ham clung to her upper lip. Paige debated not telling Immie, a reflexive cruelty that was new to her since the kiss, and she felt hot with shame. She quickly did the hand signal for Immie to wipe it away. Paige did not get food on her face and did not occasionally wear her pants inside out and not notice until fifth period, like Immie sometimes did. Paige wondered what it must be like to move through life so carelessly.

"Snortenbottom's real. You'd think with a last name like that his parents would know to avoid alliteration, but nope. His sister's called Sylvie. A tragedy, it is," Ro said. He ate a chip from a bag in his lap, but as far as Paige could see, he had packed no other lunch. "On a happier note, he's actually twenty-seventh in line for the throne. His dad is Earl Snortenbottom of East Sandwich."

"Come on," Paige said, and used her chopsticks to eat her avocado roll. She liked how her lunch looked in her aluminum bento box, the sushi a whole compartment away from her baby carrots, bright and distinct like a staged Instagram photo with the contrast turned up.

"Okay, I made up the East Sandwich bit. But Simon's dad's an earl, truly, and they're both knobs. Seriously though, what do I need to know about Wood Valley?"

"Can't think of any sociopaths offhand except for Paige," Arch said. "And maybe the arsonist."

"Arch!" Immie said, and Paige felt another flash of annoyance. Ever since the stupid kiss, Immie tiptoed around her. Before, it had always been the other way around. Immie had been the one they worried about—with that face that was like a teleprompter of emotion: Red when Im was embarrassed; purple when she was angry; splotchy when she was anxious. Paige was a badass. She could take some gentle teasing, for God's sake.

"You don't look like a sociopath," Ro said, and Paige felt his eyes sweep over her. She liked how he started with her face, then fanned down and back up again. Not pervy. Considered. Paige knew she was beautiful. She felt it was a gift that she could enjoy her looks now, instead of only later, on reflection, when the world will have moved on. Screw that. Women were forced to live within such a small range of allowable behavior. Cry and you're called weak. Yell and you're called shrill. Ask for anything and you're called a greedy bitch. Dare to one day turn thirty and you're suddenly past your sell-by date, as if women were like milk, inevitably curdling.

Paige didn't have patience for any of it.

Her mom had been gorgeous—Paige had seen pictures of her at sixteen, the age Paige was now, on the beach in Miami in a tiny string bikini, hair windswept and loose—and though Paige still thought her mom beautiful at almost fifty, she carried with her a strange invisibility. When the two of them went out together, glances would pass right over her mom and go straight to Paige's chest, her long legs, her face, and then, finally and only sometimes, they would turn to her mother, where there'd be the slightest glimmer of recognition from her mom's regular stints as a talking head on cable news. Paige's mother was legitimately *famous*—a civil rights attorney who'd become known for representing women involved in the #MeToo movement—and still, for the men of Los Angeles, this took a back seat to Paige's jailbait cleavage.

"We sociopaths prefer to hide in plain sight." Paige smiled wickedly.

Paige was pleased with her choice. Ro'd known them all of a day and he already seemed comfortable. Charming. Loose. Paige didn't really know how to do loose—no matter how hard she tried, everything she did reeked of effort—and so she admired the quality in others. Ever the star student, Paige watched and memorized how Ro held his arms, casually aloft on the sides of his chair, his legs crossed at the knee, an occasional light shake of the ankle.

"I realize I'm new to this place, but I have an arsonist theory. You know the Advanced Theater teacher?" Ro asked.

"We do," Paige said, trying her hardest to keep a straight face. She could feel Arch smiling next to her, Immie shrinking in shame. She loved nothing more than when the twins were on different pages.

"Well, she's the worst," Ro said.

Paige knew she should cut it off now, but that would ruin all the fun.

"Why?" Paige asked.

"She made us chant."

"No," Immie said, and smacked herself on the forehead, like a cartoon character. Paige always watched in wonder as Immie let her emotions play out for all to see. Paige had mastered setting her jaw to a rigid placidity. She'd spent hours practicing in front of a mirror in eighth grade, and she gave away nothing unless she wanted to. She thought about shaking Immie by the shoulders. *Three hours, Immie. That's all you need.*

"Yes, she did. I'm not joking," Ro said, and Paige looked to Arch and Immie and they all cracked up in that way they used to before—the three of them on the same wavelength, even though Immie still wore her *I want to die* expression. Embarrassing or not, Immie had to agree it was hilarious.

"What'd I say?" Ro asked.

"Mrs. Gibson's our mom," Arch said, and motioned between himself and Immie. "That's how we get to go to Wood Valley. Free ride."

"She's your mum?" Ro asked, eyes wide. "You're having me on."

"It's true," Immie said.

"I've been here five minutes and I already put my foot in it. I'm so sorry. I'm sure she's lovely, your mum. It's just the chanting."

"It's the worst," Arch and Immie said at the same time. Already back to their shared script. Of course. They were never out of sync for long.

"She's their mum? This is not some sort of piss-take?" Ro looked to Paige, desperate.

"She's their mum. Well, mom," she confirmed. "I hate to say it, but she'll make you chant every single day for the rest of the year."

"She claims it's her brand," Arch added.

"But what if my brand is . . . not chanting?" Ro asked. He was adorable, Paige decided. She had a weak spot for adorable.

"Give me your schedule," she demanded, and Ro handed her a piece of paper, still warm from his back pocket. At the top: Rohan Singh. She said the name to herself a few times in her head: *Rohan Singh, Rohan Singh, Rohan Singh*. She liked how it sounded, its roller-coaster cadence. "You should probably keep your afternoon intact, because that's when you hit most of your reqs. Keep it simple. Just switch out second period. Come to AP Bio with Arch and me. We're going to dissect a pig."

"*That's* how you big it up? With a porcine dismemberment? No thank you, mate."

Paige echoed the *mate* in her head, then *porcine dismemberment*. Ro seemed a definite upgrade from Jackson, who liked to punctuate his sentences with a fist bump.

"Don't tell me you're squeamish." Paige let her voice go flirty.

"Of course I'm squeamish. I'd rather chant than chop up poor Wilbur, and I really, really hated the chanting. No offense to your lovely mum." Ro nodded at the twins. "What unique torture do you have on offer then?"

"Women's studies," Immie said.

Paige watched as she pawed at her elbow. Poor Immie and her eczema.

"Women's studies?" Ro repeated and grinned.

"Yup."

"Like studying women?"

"Um, sort of?"

"Where do I sign up?" Ro asked.

Paige looked from Ro to Immie and then from Immie to Ro.

Nah, Paige thought. *No way.* Ro had literally seen Paige save lives and look hot while doing it. He couldn't be interested in Immie. Not like that.

The kiss had turned her paranoid.

CHAPTER SIX

Immie

The next day, Ro plopped down in the seat next to Immie in women's studies. He was so close she could smell him: honeyed almonds with a hint of coconut. Funny, she hadn't realized how much desire approximated hunger. People used the word *thirsty*, but that didn't feel quite right. Immie didn't want to drink him like a smoothie; she wanted to wolf him down whole. For the first time in her life, she felt predatory.

"So I have a lot to learn about this particular topic," Ro said, and gave her an impish grin.

Immie hadn't yet grown used to his accent, or to his face, which was so handsome she felt like crying. This, she realized, was a weird reaction to handsomeness in general. But her reaction wasn't to his handsomeness in general. It was to his handsomeness in specific.

Ro was wearing a different T-shirt today—this one vintage, with a Live Aid logo—and jeans, and there was faded writing on his arm, though she already knew what it said—*WTF is a #2 pencil.* Arch had spotted it earlier and immediately texted her. He was always collecting other people's particulars. Perhaps this was why he was so private about his own life. He erroneously assumed everyone was as curious about him as he was about them.

If Immie were Paige, she'd say something to Ro like, *I find that hard to believe,* and then touch his arm or something. But Immie wasn't Paige, and Immie couldn't be interested in this boy, no matter how obviously very interested she was. In fact, she had almost convinced herself that her interest was only *because* she wasn't allowed to be interested. She had a streak of minor masochism. Of course she liked the one boy she wasn't allowed to like.

Four years at Wood Valley, and she hadn't had a single crush, had never even before considered the validity of that gross word: *thirsty.* A British accent shouldn't have the power to change that.

Immie spent too much time looking forward to college, which felt like a far-away beacon of wonder and joy and independence. The place where she'd finally get to unleash her inner weirdness without fear of judgment. In college, there'd be men, not boys. First, though, she'd have to open herself up to evaluation by gatekeepers, allow her life's limited accomplishments to be transformed into data and sent away to be judged, which she imagined would feel not unlike the first time she went to the gynecologist and stretched her legs into stirrups.

She decided that this crush must be related to the fire. Shortly after Ro walked into class that first day, the alarm had gone off and her adrenaline spiked. Now those two things were forever connected—that frisson of energy, and his face. Her feelings were a neurotransmitter mix-up. That was the entire basis of the *Bachelor* franchise, after all: an extraordinary situation that tricked the contestants into thinking a plain vanilla person was exciting.

"Heh," Immie said, because words apparently were going to be difficult around Ro. She pointed to his wrist, stuck with simple facts. "Um, number two pencils are a kind of pencil with a certain lead. They work for Scantron sheets."

"Apparently I have a lot to learn, not just about women but about American school supplies," Ro said.

Did she die a little? Maybe she did. She closed her eyes and opened them again. Took a deep breath. He was just a person, like Arch, or Jackson, or all the other people at school she had never taken a second look at. Just because he sounded like a vampire royal did not mean she should puddle at his feet.

His accent felt like swimming in the ocean. Refreshing and disorienting, and surprisingly powerful—it could rip you away from land if you weren't paying attention. It didn't seem fair that millions of people got to walk around and sound that way. It led to unearned conclusions about the speaker—that they were more mature, more refined, certainly more charming. His voice felt like a scam that an entire country was in on.

"So what brought you here?"

"Here to women's studies?" Ro asked and grinned, like he had said something clever. Immie wasn't sure he had said something clever. She was a beat behind. "You did, so thanks for that. The rest, me being at Wood Valley, and in LA: my dad's fault. Long story." Immie noticed that he wasn't smiling anymore.

"Don't get me wrong. There are worse places to end up. But I miss my mates. My mum," he said.

"She didn't come?" Immie asked, and as soon as the words came out she regretted them. They felt forward and prying, the sort of thing Paige would ask and that Arch would know not to. They'd been well trained not to ask too many questions about other people's families. It made it easier for them to not have to reciprocate and talk too much about their own. "Sorry. None of my business."

"Nah, it's okay. She has a great job at home, just got a cool promotion. Didn't make sense for her to drop everything. Again, long story," he said, and Immie nodded, let him leave it at that.

"For what it's worth, I feel lucky that I get to go here. Most people don't take women's studies in high school." Immie hadn't meant to sound so passionate, but she had wanted to take this class since seventh grade. Paige's mom was a feminist hero—she was so controversial, she had to have her mail screened at a special facility—and Immie loved when she'd catch Ms. Cohen on CNN being interviewed about her latest case. Immie often thought about the framed photo of baby Paige that sat in the foyer of the Cohen-Chen house, how it felt like Paige's mother had cast a prophesy: Paige with a tiny fist held aloft in the air, wearing a *Future President* onesie.

"All right, let's get started," Ms. Stein said, and the class quieted. "As I mentioned yesterday, we'll be talking about women's history and the fight for equal rights. We'll explore the construct of gender. Trigger warning: we'll be talking about rape culture, so if you need special accommodation on that topic, please let me know privately. We have a lot to cover and only a year to do it, so I want to hit the ground running. By the end of the week, I want your proposals for your independent-study projects. This year, I'm asking you to pair off so you have someone to dialogue with. I encourage you to think big, and then, think bigger. The goal is to make an impact in the real world."

Immie liked projects with clearly defined expectations. If, say, Ms. Stein asked her to write a hundred pages about the Equal Rights Amendment, that would have been okay. But this—*make an impact in the real world*—felt terrifying.

It was true that when Immie thought about her future, she dreamed big and then, just as Ms. Stein had asked, dreamed even bigger. But in her mind, future Immie was someone totally different from current Immie. Someone better equipped. After college, this current version of herself would molt. She'd Russian-doll herself inside the new and improved Immie, and the memories of how she used to be, now a smaller, less relevant version hidden within, would propel her forward. Shame could be a powerful motivator.

Immie looked around the room. She knew the names of every single person in this class; in fact, she knew the names of every single person in *all* of her classes, and yet she couldn't imagine turning to any of them and saying, *Hey, want to be partners?* Where was Arch or Paige when she needed them? Maybe she should have taken AP Bio instead. She wasn't scared to dissect a pig. She *was* scared to take too many AP classes and then not get fives on all of the exams, which she needed if she wanted her pick of the UC system. Unlike most of her classmates, expensive private college wasn't an option.

"What do you think?" Ro asked at the end of class, and it took Immie a second to translate his English to her English and realize he was talking to her.

"What?" she asked, feeling slow, again, a head bobbing in water.

"Fancy partnering up? I realize you probably have your pick of the room, but you, Immie, are one of only three people I know in this entire country," Ro said, and for the first time, she looked straight into his eyes. Before, she worried it would be like staring at the sun or worse, at an eclipse, like looking at him could do permanent damage. As she met his gaze, this still felt true.

His eyes were brown, like hers, and warm and a little sad and a little angry, which wasn't something she knew you could see in someone's eyes. Not with this amount of certainty.

He had eyes like her face—too revealing. Something they had in common.

They were just eyes, she told herself. Nothing more significant. Certainly not a connection between them or a bridge to dance across. She ignored the sound in her ears—her heartbeat mixed with static.

"Sure," Immie said. "Why not?"

"Really?" Ro said. "I promise I'm a good student."

"I never had any doubt."

"It's the accent. Heard it fools everyone in the States."

"It is dangerous." Immie only heard the words afterward, as if she had not been the one to say them out loud. She'd tunneled into herself.

Immie wondered if it was possible to become someone else entirely. To not Russian Doll yourself, but to re-skin. Shed the prior version altogether.

"I'm not one of those jerks who's going to make you do all the work. I'll do my fair share. In fact, I'll do extra to make up for institutionalized sexism and misogyny," Ro said. "See, I even know some of the lingo."

"You don't have to convince me," she said, even though she wanted him to keep convincing her. If Immie could, she'd stay in this moment of him talking to her forever.

Partnering up with Ro was a terrible idea and also inevitable. She liked the way this felt: the irreparable burning of her retinas, even that internal, staticky hum. Her mind blurred by some unseen white-noise machine. The being allowed to look at his details without it being weird or creepy.

He had a small, raised scar between his thick, wiry eyebrows, and she wondered how he got it. She pictured him taking a hit from a cricket bat, which made no sense because she didn't even know what a cricket bat looked like.

His jaw was strong and his cheekbones sharp and his skin mostly clear, except for a few humanizing pimples at his hairline.

What was in the water in England? Would all the boys there do this to her? Tonight she'd spend some time on the Oxford and Cambridge websites, and the thought—school in another country, school across an entire ocean—felt like the unraveling of one of those inflatable airplane ramps inside her soul. A bouncy escape.

Immie couldn't do that to Arch. Go that far and leave him behind. A different kind of molting altogether.

And yet.

"You're the best," Ro said, and though she knew he didn't mean it, not really, she couldn't help herself. Her insides grinned, which meant her traitor face probably did too.

CHAPTER SEVEN

Ro

"So how was it? Did they catch the arsonist?" Ro's dad asked. He was sitting at the kitchen table with a glass of champagne from the bottle their new landlord had left as a welcome gift and the packet of crisps Ro had bought at Heathrow. Ro would have snatched the crisps back—they were roast chicken-flavored, his favorite, and if the Wood Valley store was anything to go by, unavailable in the United States—but the bag, much like the bottle, looked already emptied.

Greedy selfish bastard.

Ro didn't let himself linger on the words *Welcome home!*, which felt like the landlord's note had animated and slapped him in the face.

"We're not going to do this," Ro said to his dad as he opened the fridge, which was giant, like all the other appliances in the flat, and looked into its cavernous, off-smelling insides. He closed it again.

"Do what? Have a chat about our day? Come on, Rohan. We live here now."

"Nope."

"You're going to have to talk to me eventually. I admire your stubbornness, though. You get that from your mum."

"Don't." Ro's eyes watered and the back of his throat burned, and he wondered if somehow the smoke had stuck to him and had done permanent damage.

"This is a once-in-a-lifetime opportunity for us to spend real time together before you go off to uni. If you talked to me, you might even discover that your father isn't all that bad."

Ro had never seen his father drunk. He didn't trust the look on his dad's face, a sneer loosened by alcohol into a smirk, nor the fact that he was talking in the third person—but for the first time, it occurred to Ro that his dad might be equally devastated about their mutual exile. This realization came with no attendant sympathy. "Thank you for asking, my new job went really well today. I have a lovely office and a lovely new assistant and my first class is tomorrow. Freshmen, so not much older than you. And the library is lovely. Everything . . . just lovely."

"I didn't ask," Ro said and poured himself a glass of water. It tasted cleaner than the water at home and felt cool on his raw throat. Finally, a tiny point in favor of Los Angeles.

His father wore his hair combed straight back, and it was thinning enough that you could see the parallel teeth lines. As if to compensate for the lack of hair on his head, he recently had grown a ridiculous goatee.

Ro would never understand how his dad had gotten a twenty-two-year-old graduate student to sleep with him.

"I'll have more time for my research. This will be good. For both of us. Wood Valley is one of the finest schools in this entire country. When it's not burning down." Ro's dad laughed, as if the fire had been funny. Ro thought about the push he felt at his back, the weight of Paige on his shoulders, that first sniff of smoke. According to the kid sitting behind him in seventh period, the police had no leads. "Your cha-cha pulled some serious strings for you. You should write him a thank-you note."

"Will get right on that."

"Sarcasm doesn't suit you."

"Adultery doesn't suit you," Ro said, and then went to his bedroom and slammed the door, which was made of a flimsy cork and barely made a sound, which defeated the whole purpose of slamming it in the first place. It wasn't even his bedroom, but some random seven-year-old girl's, who was at last measurement three-foot-nine inches tall, as marked on the doorframe with pen. His mum used to measure him and his sister on the back of the hall wardrobe. When was the last time she did that? He most certainly had grown since. This past year, while he slept, his shins and biceps ached, as if his body were being stretched on the rack.

"Tacos?" Ro's dad called from the other room. "When in Rome . . ."

Ro didn't answer for a minute.

"I'll do carryout," his father called. "Apparently there's a place right around the corner. It has a sign in the shape of a cactus and world famous—"

"Fine," Ro called back, cutting him off, because he didn't want to hear his father babble, as if everything was the way it used to be, when the two of them hung out on the nights his mum worked late and his dad picked up fish and chips and they ate them drenched in salt and vinegar and ketchup. When he hadn't known his father was the type of person who was capable of a casual betrayal.

Ro thought about the arsonist, and what it must have felt like for them to light that match. He could picture both the blast and the shiver, could almost, almost understand the intoxication that would come from burning the school down.

Despite his rage, or maybe because of it, Ro was ravenous.

CHAPTER EIGHT

Paige

The night of the party, Paige had slipped a condom into her pocket. She and Jackson had talked about sex, the ifs and the whens. Though she hadn't been sure she was ready, Paige had been the one to bring it up. Jackson, for his part, seemed unconcerned and not in a rush, approaching the discussion with his usual equanimity.

If Jackson had asked—though he didn't—why Paige felt unsure, she wouldn't have been able to answer. Possibly, it was Jackson himself, who she genuinely cared for while also being aware that those feelings were likely temporary. Or maybe it was the before and after of sex, how once it was done, she would forever check her virginity off on the master precollege to-do list. Or it could have been as simple as the mechanics or the risk or the concept itself—Jackson and Paige. Together. Naked. Vulnerable.

But the night of the party, the one that she'd later think of as "the party that had ruined everything," the condom had found its way into Paige's pocket anyway. A secret possibility. She hadn't even told Immie and Arch, but knew that if she were to turn that maybe into a yes, she'd confer with the twins first. Probably in some tucked-away bathroom at the party. They'd know even before Jackson would.

Jackson had invited a few people over because his mom was in Cannes with her infant boyfriend, and having a few people over turned into the entire incoming junior class plus some kids from Brentwood. Someone rolled in a keg and someone else said the price of entry was a bottle, and before they knew it, the place was raging.

Paige had wandered around the party, beer in hand, condom in pocket, and watched Christa Hernandez destroy Adrien Oh in beer pong. Arch was nowhere to be found, and Immie was trapped talking to Roxie Greene, whose favorite topic was Model UN. Paige couldn't find Jackson. He wasn't in the kitchen, which had been ravaged, nor in the living room, where the pair of Jackson's mom's Victoria's Secret wings hung framed over the fireplace, or in the foyer, which had been turned into a makeshift dance floor.

She wound her way up the stairs and down the hall to Jackson's bedroom. She felt light and happy, excited at the prospect of throwing off the shackles of childhood once and for all. Maybe she had decided. Immie and Arch always teased her about her premature maturity; they joked she'd been Freaky Friday'ed with a forty-five-year-old Congresswoman.

Jackson's door was closed, and she knocked once before entering.

"You okay?" Paige asked when she saw Jackson lying on

the bed, staring at the white ceiling. Had he taken something? The party was swirling down below, and Jackson, who usually was in the middle of everything—this tendency was, more than anything, what attracted her to him in the first place—had sought out the quiet. She didn't know, not yet, that he had been mere moments earlier exchanging saliva with her best friend. She was, as of that moment, still his girlfriend and still blissfully unaware that Immie was capable of that sort of backstab.

She was thinking about the condom, and how strange that something that looked like a slimy balloon could have so much power.

"Yeah. I'm fine," Jackson said, but he held his body still, like moving would break some sort of spell.

Jackson's room always struck her as childish, like it had been decorated once when he was eight and then never touched again. He was the president of their class, arguably the best-looking guy in school, he was *cool*, and yet he slept under a navy blue Star Wars comforter. Stacks of books littered the floor, some reaching as high as her waist, and only one poster hung on the wall: Baby Hope being rescued on 9/11. She felt a visceral revulsion from that picture; it was the opposite of an aphrodisiac. She wondered idly what Baby Hope was doing now, if she was, at that exact moment, wandering around some high school party in New Jersey.

"You sure?" Paige asked. What could Jackson have taken? He didn't do drugs. None of her closest friends did. But his eyes were glassy and far away, and when they turned to her, finally, they widened as if coming to. A realization about where he was.

"Paige, I have to tell you something," he said, a hint of panic.

"Okay." She had seen some kids vaping on the lawn, so maybe he *was* high. She expected him to share a random fact, the sort of thing that would only seem urgent to someone baked: like how she should stop eating octopus because they were as smart as human toddlers.

"I kissed someone else. I'm sorry."

Oh.

Paige felt it in her gut first. A twisting.

She looked around the room again. Paige let a sneaking suspicion overtake her. She cared about very few people in this world; it could be a relief that Jackson was now no longer one of them. She would put that condom right back into its box under her bathroom cabinet. It was dangerous to add people to your care list. They could do things like this to you, and then throw out a casual *I'm sorry* for the betrayal.

Jackson still hadn't risen from the bed.

"Who was it?" she asked.

"Doesn't matter." Paige didn't press the point.

"We're done," she said, her face blank. She tucked away the seething anger and the vague humiliation. She'd examine the sting later when no one was around to see.

Jackson nodded. "Okay."

One word. That was all he thought she deserved? She hadn't expected him to agree so easily. She thought again about the condom in her pocket, which had felt like Chekhov's gun, so omnipresent in her thoughts all evening. She wondered if in some parallel universe she was living out an entirely different reality. The gun discharged. She being the one to give him that faraway look. Him holding her afterward, letting his fingers tangle in her long, silky hair.

Paige walked out of the room, and then she did what she always did when anything happened to her, big or small: she texted Immie and Arch. She asked them to meet in the living room under the Victoria's Secret wings.

But by then, the twins were already long gone.

CHAPTER NINE

Ro

Ro had woken up his mum with a text. He'd figured she would be at her office, wearing that headset she wore for conference calls, and that she'd be happy to hear from him, as always. But it was the middle of the night in London and he'd sent her into a panic. Crap.

Ro: Sorry! I forgot the time difference. Didn't realize it's 2am there!!!!

Mum: 3 actually. In Paris. You alright? Please tell me no fires today :(I can't stop thinking about what happened. You could have died

Ro: Mum! It was no big deal! Go back to sleep!

Mum: Are you eating enough?

Ro: GO TO SLEEP. Everything's fine. I love you

Mum: Love you too. Eat those chewy vitamins I stuck in your duffel!

Ro had no idea what his mother was going on about—chewy vitamins?—but he suspected he'd figure it out if he unpacked. Which he wasn't going to do, because that seemed like accepting he was staying.

Instead, he tried to sign into Netflix, but the show he'd been bingeing at home wasn't available in the US. He considered hurling his laptop against the wall. Why was everything so bloody complicated in America? When he'd asked Paige about public transport, she had waved him away with an: "Oh, that's not really a thing in LA. It's a driving city." Surely that couldn't be true, and yet the closest tube stop from their flat was more than a mile away and didn't go anywhere near Wood Valley.

No doubt Ro's father hadn't thought through the logistics when he took this job, hadn't realized that Los Angeles was a sprawling metropolis and that as a result, Ro would be mostly housebound. He couldn't imagine his mum and dad discussing how he'd get to and from school, how his dad, who didn't do the cooking or the shopping at home, would manage to feed the two of them, how Ro'd make do with the London autumn clothes he brought in this neverending summer.

Ro also couldn't imagine his mum and dad talking about whether they'd still be married when they went back. His dad's cock-up had been of such epic proportions, the fallout so extreme, that this two-year punishment was framed in terms of giving Ro's mum time "to think."

Why Ro had also been banished and what *he* was supposed to think about, he couldn't say. He'd done nothing wrong.

Ro wished he had gotten Immie's number so he could text her: *how do people get around here without a license or a driver?* Before English III, Paige had grabbed his Sharpie from his back pocket and scribbled her number on his palm. He could try her, but he got the impression that a text wouldn't simply be a text with Paige.

Ro scrolled. Kaia might be up. Back at home, she'd text him at four a.m. and then they'd sneak out and meet up in front of the twenty-four-hour Tesco Express. They'd eat chocolates and snog a little and talk until the sun came up.

Ro: You up?

Kaia: Am now. We miss you! You okay?

Ro: Yeah. Miss you too. It's . . . lonely here

Kaia: Aw, Ro, you're breaking my heart. Come home for Christmas

Ro: There's this group of three kids at school, boy-girl twins and this other girl, and their dynamic reminds me of us. You, me, and Arun. Makes me happy-sad

Kaia: Which two of us are the twins in this scenario?

Ro: Not an exact comparison

Kaia: Arun is a stroppy cow without you

Ro: Tell him I miss him too

Kaia: Will do

Ro: Night K. x

Kaia: Oooh a snog. That one will have to hold me a while

Ro: Bollocks. You'll find someone new by tomorrow

Kaia: Who says I haven't already?

Ro: Is he as handsome and charming as me?

Kaia: Ripped. Your worst bloody nightmare

Ro: Happy for you

Kaia: Sweet dreams love

Ro wasn't sure if Kaia was kidding, but it didn't really matter. They'd been friends first and they'd be friends after; the fooling around had just been for laughs.

She'd be horrified if she saw him right now. All hungry and pathetic and unsure. She was the one to kiss him first, to say, *Don't worry, this means nothing, weirdo, this is practice.* She never took things lying down.

He should write on his other arm: *What would Kaia do?*

Kaia, he knew, would plan and act, though sometimes in the reverse order. Ro clicked over to some fancy department store called Nordstrom, the closest proxy he could find to House of Fraser, and bought some shorts and a couple of T-shirts and even a pair of sunglasses—all of which he assumed looked vaguely Californian—using his dad's credit card number, which had been autosaved by his laptop.

Then he clicked over to Walmart—because what could be more American than Walmart—and overnighted himself a bicycle.

His plan: no way Ro was staying here in LA. He'd be home long before Christmas.

CHAPTER TEN

Paige

Paige and Immie raced down the freeway in Paige's Audi convertible. Paige suspected Arch hadn't come along because he knew that Immie and Paige needed to figure out how to be alone together again. To recapture what used to be frictionless. That kiss seemed to have a bizarrely aggressive grasp, its fingertips occasionally still sending goose bumps down Paige's arms. She wanted to ask Immie why she had run away from the scene of the crime, why she never accounted for all those missing hours after kissing Jackson when the truth hung out there unclaimed. Immie could have come straight to Paige afterward. She could have looked her in the eyes and said "I'm drunk and I did something stupid and I'm sorry." Like Jackson did, but sincere.

Paige, of course, would have hugged her and told her it was *fine, really,* and they would have snapped right back into shape. Nothing would have lingered. In that case, two short words would have sufficed.

Instead, Immie had waited till the next morning, had admitted it all over the phone, even though they almost never called each other. Text, yes. On the rare occasion, FaceTime. But not like this, words poured into her ear, a tearful apology that sounded practiced and perfected overnight.

Paige had forgiven Immie almost immediately, because she had no other choice. What was she going to do? Be mad at Immie indefinitely? Stop talking to her best friend? Paige and the twins didn't do petty high school drama. It was a kiss. Something temporary and disposable. Unlike their friendship, which was supposed to be forever.

Paige turned the music up louder—they could be Paige and Immie rocking out in the car just like old times, like they were a living ad for being young or for LA or for being young in LA. Then she changed her mind, and turned it off. She wasn't feeling it.

"I need a distraction," Paige announced, and Immie did her one-eyebrow-raised thing that always made Paige laugh.

"Are you serious? We already have so much to do. I mean *junior year*," Immie said, gathering the hair whipping around her face into a high ponytail. "My brain already hurts and we only just started."

"Whatever. You're not the one taking four APs," Paige said, and then felt like an asshole.

"We can't all be such a Smarty McSmartypants," Immie said and smiled, and then playfully nudged Paige with her elbow and Paige nudged back, and there it was again, that ease that had been missing the last few days.

"By the way, I need you to do some Ro recon for me."

"Sure. We're pairing up for a women's studies project." Paige hadn't stopped to wonder if Immie liked Ro, because any living, breathing person would like Ro, and also she didn't care. Immie had forfeited the right for Paige to consider her feelings.

"He hasn't texted yet, though he has had my number for close to seven hours and witnessed me being a real-life superhero. So I'm thinking he may have a girlfriend in London. You have to ask for me."

"How do I ask that? It'll sound like *I'm* into him."

Paige signaled to change lanes and started to move over, but her side mirror lit up; a car in her blind spot. She swerved back. She kept her left hand on the wheel and dropped her right to the shift; this made her look cool and relaxed, like that swerve was no big deal. Like she hadn't already imagined her and Immie's bodies tossed out and turned into roadkill on the 405. Paige's brain was whirring at full speed, a conflagration of self-criticism and worst-case scenarios, and she took a breath to rein it in, like her meditation teacher had taught her.

"Just be like, *inquiring minds want to know* or *asking for a friend who isn't me.*" Paige's pulse settled enough that she could shoot Immie a look. "Actually, no, tell him I want to know. By the way, I'm thinking of running for school president."

Paige said this only because the car in front of her had

overlapping political bumper stickers—Obama, Bernie, Hillary, Warren, Biden. She liked to toss random ideas out there and maybe this was actually a good one. Hadn't she just led a couple hundred students to safety during the fire?

She was a born leader.

Ro plus school plus a campaign might equal enough distraction. A way to slow her brain. She'd stop obsessing over the kiss. She'd stop obsessing about Immie. She'd stop obsessing over the ease with which the east wing burned—that black smoke twisting up in the air like some sort of signal to God. She needed to recover her equilibrium.

It was only a kiss. You don't get PTSD from your best friend kissing your boyfriend. She wasn't going to be forty and crying to a therapist about this. Surely her insides would soon be as placid as her face each time she saw Jackson. And as for Immie, in a few months, all would be forgotten, buried under too many other, better memories of them together.

Still, Paige had always marched through her life like she understood things, and now it seemed she'd understood nothing at all.

Maybe her parents would be proud if she ran for president of the entire school. Nah, they had Academy Award nominations to worry about (her father) and that high-profile sexual harassment suit to litigate (her mother). A high school election would bore them as much as all of Paige's previous bids for their attention.

"But Jackson's class president. I know you're mad about

what happened, but he's been doing it for four years. The plan was for him to run unopposed."

Paige shrugged like this was neither here nor there. And it wasn't. Not anymore.

She'd pushed Jackson aside in her mind. A new boy and a potential new item for her college applications. Check, check.

CHAPTER ELEVEN

Arch

Jackson was in the library even though he was supposed to be at basketball. Not that Arch had memorized his schedule or anything, but when you were trying to avoid someone so unavoidable it helped to have an idea about their extracurriculars. Maybe Arch'd get lucky and Jackson wouldn't notice him, or if he did, maybe he'd choose to throw him a peace sign, nothing more.

Arch could use a reminder of Jackson's annoying bro tendencies.

Jackson was chatting with Ms. Goetz, the librarian, and her fingers were wrapped around his bicep, as if to say *Stop it!* Was Jackson *flirting*? Clearly there was no one he'd spare his charm offensive. Ms. Goetz was in her fifties or sixties and had been at the school even longer than Arch's mom had. She had short silver hair and favored giant statement necklaces and wore cigarette pants cropped at the ankle. Behind her desk hung a giant handmade poster that said *We*

Need You Here that listed suicide-prevention hotline numbers and her personal cell.

Whenever Arch looked at that poster, he imagined Ms. Goetz alone in her studio apartment in North Hollywood, sprinkling glitter onto glue to keep her students alive, and honest to God, it made him feel better.

Arch loved Ms. Goetz and Ms. Goetz loved Arch, and her chatting with Jackson felt like a personal betrayal.

"Hey, Arch!" Jackson yelled from across the room upon spotting him—even though they were of course in a *library*, and the last time they had spoken Arch had thrown out that regrettable *whatever*. Jackson air-kissed Ms. Goetz's cheek, and then marched right up to Arch's chair and, without a moment's hesitation or an invitation, plopped down into the one opposite.

"Hey," Arch echoed, but in a whisper, and looked back down at his notes. He was sitting with his ankle crossed over his knee and Jackson kicked his sneaker, forcing him to look back up. "What?"

"What? What?" Jackson said, grinning, like he was disarmed by Arch's crankiness and had decided to indiscriminately flirt with him too. Like Arch was as easy a mark as Ms. Goetz. Arch felt too weary to play that sort of game.

"What are you doing here?" Arch kept his voice flat. He caught himself before asking *Don't you have basketball?* He did not want to talk to Jackson. He wanted to keep reading *The Crucible*, which was boring and made his brain melt.

Still, it seemed preferable to sitting and enduring the awkwardness.

Arch was wearing his dad's old Calvin and Hobbes T-shirt and a pair of Levi's. Jackson was wearing a stiff-collared, slim-fitted cotton shirt, cropped pinstriped pants, and limited-edition high-top Golden Goose sneakers. He had rings on different fingers of his left hand and his hair was messy, but perfectly wax-pomade messy, and he had the faintest hint of stubble. Arch thought he looked like one of those twenty-five-year-old actors on television who played high-schoolers because normal teenagers weren't hot enough or clear-skinned enough or palatable enough to audiences to play themselves.

Or no: he looked like the lead singer in a boy band, with the kind of smug grin that would be on a poster in your little sister's bedroom.

One of his rings was a silver skull.

Arch wanted to punch Jackson in the face.

"I'm being friendly," Jackson said.

"Please stop."

"Why are you being so mean to me lately? I really don't get it." Jackson leaned forward so his elbows were resting on his knees, as if to get into position while he waited for a real answer. Arch didn't really know why he was mean to Jackson, except that it never occurred to him that Jackson was a real person with actual feelings that were capable of getting hurt.

"I'm not being mean," Arch said, and thought *Why are you such a coward?* If Arch was in a store on Melrose and saw that exact ring, he'd pick it up, admire it, and then put it right back down. He was not the type of person who could get away with a skull decorating his hand.

"Yes. You are being mean. And it's really weird because I've seen you do about eleventy billion good things for a million different people through the years."

"I think you messed up your math."

"You *are* nice," Jackson insisted, and Arch reflexively winced. He didn't want to be *nice*, though maybe that's what he was, what he always would be. *Nice* people kept quiet instead of speaking up. *Nice* people were wimps. *Nice* people might stay in the closet because they were afraid of their father punching another hole in the wall two inches to the left of their mother's head.

Nope, *nice* people were afraid of their *friends finding out* that they stayed in the closet because they were afraid of their father punching another hole in the wall two inches to the left of their mother's head.

Arch thought about the arsonist—who, without realizing it, he'd begun to picture as Katy Flore, though he had no evidence it was her—and thought about how no one would ever mistake Katy Flore for nice. Not that he wanted to snarl at his classmates or listen to death metal, but he didn't love this presumption of harmlessness. Of course, it was true. After all, the only questionable thing he'd ever done in his entire life was that one glorious kiss.

"I mean, you're *kind*," Jackson said, reading Arch's face. "And so I think you must be mad at me or something."

Jackson stopped talking, took a breath, and lowered his

voice, so low that Arch had to lean forward to hear him. "If this is about what happened at the party, it was no big deal. It's not like I've told anyone about it." *No big deal.* Arch thought it was sort of a big deal—it had, after all, pretty much destroyed his sister's life—but sure, Jackson, with your heated toilet seats and plaid pants and outrageous jewelry: *no big deal.*

"It's not that," Arch said. His problem with Jackson wasn't about him telling anyone, or being outed, an expression he hated because it signaled shame and Arch felt no shame about his sexuality. He felt vulnerability, maybe, and a paralyzing fear of his father's reaction. Specifically, he imagined the vein that throbbed in his father's neck, bulging and blue. But he definitely did not feel shame.

Arch already knew there would be a time in the future when he would express himself fully and openly and not worry for one single second whether anything about him signaled to other people that he was sexually attracted to boys. Maybe he'd actively signal, come to think of it. He loved the Pride parade every year in West Hollywood. He couldn't wait to march with his own giant flag, maybe in a goddamn rainbow Speedo.

If there was any shame, it was about his family. He wasn't proud to be a member of the Gibson Fight Club and he felt sickening dread at the thought of anyone else knowing what happened within the confines of their apartment. Talking about his sexuality would require an explanation of why he wasn't out at home. He was not, maybe would never be, ready for that.

He wasn't a *nice* person.

"No one is asking anything of you. I'm not," Jackson said. Arch knew Jackson's recent attention was a direct reaction to Arch's decision to avoid him. Jackson couldn't handle anyone—even someone as low on the social hierarchy as Arch—not liking him. It clashed with everything he apparently believed about himself.

"I know."

"Look around. No one would have cared about what happened." Jackson gestured vaguely around the library, possibly to the large painted rainbow on one wall or the poster that said *Trans Rights Are Human Rights*. Like this was a political problem. Or an identity one. For Arch it was neither of those things. His life wasn't going to have the arc of a feel-good coming-out movie.

"Paige would have," Arch said.

"You think she's happier believing it was Immie? Come on. I don't know what you guys were thinking."

"It was Immie's idea. I don't know. It's all so stupid."

"It is stupid!" Jackson said, punching the air, and Arch reached out and pulled his arm down. He didn't want anyone looking over at them. Why did Jackson always have to be so loud? "No one cares. Why are you punishing me? We used to be friends."

"We were never friends," Arch said, and then watched in what felt like slo-mo as Jackson's face took the blow. Being mean to Jackson wasn't like kicking a puppy. It was like spitting in the face of a movie star. They felt equally transgressive.

Arch backpedaled. "You know what I'm saying. We were

friendly. But, you know, you have your crew. I have mine. Paige was our only nexus." He was surprised by how immediately sorry he felt. He was used to saying the wrong thing to Jackson, but not used to this: realizing he said a cruel thing.

"We were lab partners last year!" This was true. Jackson and Arch were randomly paired up by Mrs. Hahn, and so they spent two semesters sitting next to each other on tall stools, pouring liquids into beakers. When Arch thought about chemistry class, he thought of Jackson leaning across him to grab hydrochloric acid, how their knees would occasionally touch and spring apart, how he spent the whole time feeling nervous he'd spill something. They chatted and joked around and wrote notes back and forth, because Jackson was Paige's boyfriend, and as Paige's best friend, Arch thought it his responsibility to get to know the dude.

So maybe they *had* been friends.

Over the summer, they'd hung out countless times, always with Paige as the connective tissue. They never found themselves next to each other on a couch. This summer their knees had never touched and sprung apart.

Had Arch thought about Jackson's knees in the last few months? It was possible he had. They were good knees.

"I . . . I." Arch didn't finish the thought, because he didn't know how. He looked down at his hands, which were chapped from the steamer at work, and at his cuticles, which were bleeding from being picked.

"I'm convinced everyone in the world has one amazing supersecret talent. Want to know mine?" Jackson again used that conspiratorial tone, so cunning in its ability to make you think you were the only one who mattered in the whole world. There was a reason he was class president.

Arch wondered how Jackson could distill his talents down to one thing. Jackson was a good actor, a good student, a good athlete, a good leader. He was funny and confident. Arch once ran into Jackson carrying his half brother on his shoulders at the Grove, and the two of them were giggling and pretending to be a single robot. When Jackson saw Arch, instead of stopping the game, he held their entire conversation in a robot voice to keep the joke going. That's the talent Jackson had—being able to look ridiculous without anyone thinking him ridiculous.

What would happen if Arch burst into tears right here in the library? What would Jackson do?

"I recognize greatness in others. Paige is going to, I don't know, invent some app that makes a gazillion dollars—"

"Again, I think your math might be off," Arch said with a half-smile. He liked seeing Jackson all riled up. He wanted to kiss his face off.

Punch first, then kiss. That order, Arch decided. No, the other way around.

"And you, I don't know what you're going to do yet, but it's going to be something amazing. I want to say I knew you when." Jackson grinned, clearly impressed with himself.

"I want to be a high school teacher. That's it. That's my grand plan," Arch said, and looked directly at Jackson. A dare or a test, likely both.

The fact that Arch's dream—could he call it a dream

when it was more like a *serious option?*—was to be a high school teacher, possibly even at a place like Wood Valley, might be his only secret from Immie. She'd be horrified. Immie had plans, most of which were built on the premise that her life would happen *not here.*

"That's awesome, man. Exactly!" Jackson nodded with a terrifying sincerity. Maybe that's where his inexplicable power came from—his surprising earnestness. You don't expect earnestness to come in a handsome package with pomade-messy hair and skull rings. "You'd make an amazing teacher."

"Thanks."

"When I was a kid, I wanted to be an astronaut and a painter and a fireman and a Rockette. I never understood why I had to pick just one thing, you know? And I guess I still don't."

"Maybe you don't have to pick one thing," Arch offered.

"Yeah, I guess you're right. I'd like to pick one person though," Jackson said, looking directly at Arch, and Arch's stomach landed hard. Jackson jumped up to standing, saluted, which was one of those gestures that made absolutely no sense and yet somehow, as always, worked when it was done by him. "Okay, got to get to practice. The basketball team awaits. Later, friend."

"Later," Arch repeated, a little dazed, and studied Jackson as he walked away. The way his feet seemed to glide along the floor, the invisible drums he played on his thigh, the way he took Arch's insides along for the ride with him.

CHAPTER TWELVE

Immie

Immie's favorite new hobby was reading Ro's arms. Today, on the left: *tire pump?* On the right, *Ask I???* Was this code? And why his arms and not a notebook or his phone? His handwriting was messier than hers and Arch's, quickly dashed off, but also more intricate. She'd bet he was an artist or at the very least a practiced doodler.

They were in women's studies again and Ms. Stein was on a roll.

"Finally, this is not about an innate dispositional difference between those assigned female at birth and those assigned male. This is one hundred percent about cultural learning, about rigid social gender norms," she said, wrapping up class by talking about toxic masculinity. On the screen was a picture of two kids' T-shirts side by side: NASA from the boys' aisle, Future Princess from the girls'. "One thing I hope you do this semester is look inward. Think about how and whether a ridiculous and reactionary binary system of gender plays into your own life, how it does or does not dictate how you behave. What you demand and what you don't and why. Maybe it's something as simple as the girls in your family doing the dishes more than the boys, or being told to brush their hair. Or the boys being told to 'man up' when they cry. Reminder, project submissions due Friday."

Everyone stood and packed up their notebooks. Immie looked at Ro's hands—he had long, graceful fingers—and she blushed. She wondered if she was playing out some subconscious gender role right now: giggling schoolgirl who had never seen a cute boy before. She shook her head, as if to unleash the crush, her shyness, her reflexive attraction to him. She wanted to let it go.

"We should probably get together to come up with an idea," Ro said. He was wearing jeans and the same mohawked-chicken T-shirt from the first day of school. What did it mean? Was it an awesome British punk band that Immie should have heard of? If she were to write on her own arm, she'd scribble *Google mohawk chicken*. "Today after school, maybe?"

"Sorry, can't. Have to work." Immie thought with relief about the long shift ahead. She loved her job and how it required so little of her mind. She could take an order, and run the register, and scream it out to Arch, all while thousands of miles away in her head. She'd always been able to do this—disassociate from the here and now and escape to better, fictional worlds. Both she and Arch were voracious readers, and she was sure part of that had to do with their small apartment and their loud father and needing a way out of the limitations of space and sound.

Immie had hung a map of the world next to her bed and filled it with red pushpins: all the places she intended to visit one day in real life and not only in her imagination. When she finally escaped.

"Where do you work?"

"At Espresso Yourself. It's a coffee shop. Obviously." Ro smiled and nodded, like this confirmed something about her for him. She had no idea what that look meant. Did he appreciate the punny name? When Stu was considering opening up the place, they'd come up with a long list of options. Her vote had been for *When in Foam,* and Arch liked *Eat. Tea. Foam. Home.* For a while, the place was almost called *Bean John Milkovich,* but the twins had convinced Stu that it was too esoteric, even for film-obsessed LA.

Immie had so many questions for Ro, none of which found their way from her burning brain to her slow lips: What did he think of this class? Did he too feel boxed in by gender? Did moving halfway around the world unmoor him? How was Wood Valley different from his old school in London? Had he ever told a really big lie to protect someone else? "Can you do tomorrow?" she asked instead.

"Brilliant. Shall we?" He pointed to her phone. He was asking for her number. *For a school project, Immie.* Still. He was asking for her number. They'd now be connected with another tether, and she felt it click, like when she and Arch and Paige went indoor rock climbing and she'd been clasped into a harness.

She recited her digits. Two seconds later, her phone pinged: *hi this is Ro.* Immie wondered how many times she would read this message and whether, with each time, she'd feel the same mix of longing and guilt. She could picture it: lying on her bed, tracing the letters with her finger.

She really needed to get a life.

This was attraction, which was nothing more than fantasy, when you thought about it. You looked at a person and told yourself a story about how you'd fit together, when in fact you didn't know if you'd fit at all. An empty, untrustworthy, meaningless feeling.

"So listen, I wanted to ask you . . ." Immie didn't know how to ask whether he had a girlfriend, a boyfriend, or a theyfriend. Even if she blamed the question on Paige, it felt like an overreach. Nope, she couldn't do it. If that made her a wimp, well, then, maybe she was a wimp.

Maybe she didn't want to know the answer.

Immie didn't like the idea of some beautiful girl touching Ro's hands, linking hers with his, them fitting exactly right. Some beautiful girl who shared with Ro something bigger and more real than mere attraction and fantasy. Immie didn't understand how people built relationships like that, how you stood on top of a pile of interactions and they somehow added up to the privilege of touching each other. She couldn't imagine love actually happening for her. That was something reserved for the special few, not for the Immie Gibsons of the world. Like running a marathon or getting a full ride to Harvard or having a dad who made you feel safe, not scared. "Um, what do you think of LA so far?"

"It's sunny?"

"Good observation."

"And I took a bus for the first time and it took me two hours to go five miles. I don't have a car. Or a license. I reckon I need both." He looked embarrassed and Immie's body went warm. It was the *I reckon*, two words she'd never heard anyone put together in real life. On *The Vampire Royals*, yes. Not by a guy standing in front of her.

"Where do you live?"

"Hancock Park?" Ro said it like a question, like he wasn't sure. "On the other side of the hills. In what feels like a land far, far away."

"We live right near there. In Koreatown."

"Really?"

"Yeah. LA is weird like that. Kids commute to this school from all over." Immie thought about offering him a ride in the mornings—the twins drove separately from their mom (she liked to get to school a full hour before first bell to prep for classes), and they cut through the leafy streets of Hancock Park to avoid traffic. But giving Ro a ride would mean more time with him, and even with Arch as a buffer, it would put her nervous system on overload.

She already saw him too much. Her eczema was flaring up in angry swathes across her stomach from the stress. Funny how real her delusion about their connection could feel, like she wasn't making up the emotions at all.

This crush had to end, and the only way to make that happen was for Paige and Ro to get together, as was the natural order of things. That would surely turn off this attraction spigot.

If Paige and Ro were together, Immie could go right

back to focusing on what mattered this year: her classes, the SATs, looking ahead to her college applications. Nothing was more important than getting into a good school anywhere but LA. She reminded herself of her constellation of red pushpins.

Ro's phone vibrated and he glanced down at a text. She couldn't read what it said without being obvious, but she saw a name: Kaia. Later she'd describe Ro's face to Arch like this: a collective relaxation, an unfolding, like relief. She wished she could be the one to do that to him. Iron out the sadness.

Immie started toward the door.

"See you later," Ro said, smiling, a raised hand in the air. The smile already felt familiar and warm and like it belonged to her. She knew why. She had already borrowed it in her imagination.

But she also knew this smile in real life was not meant for her. This one belonged to the girl in his phone. The next one, no doubt, would be for Paige.

CHAPTER THIRTEEN

Ro

"Did you know we're biologically designed to be in a constant state of want?" Paige asked. Ever since that invitation on the second day of school, Ro joined Paige and the twins by the Koffee Kart for lunch. He was grateful for the rescue. Otherwise, he'd be eating his sad sandwich alone. "My meditation teacher taught me that."

"That was by far the most Los Angeles sentence I've ever heard," Ro said, and wondered what other sorts of crap people hired private tutors for here. Were they all learning Reiki and doing Pilates after school? He toasted Paige with his La Croix, which was a bizarre flavored fizzy water that he couldn't pronounce and that was ubiquitous enough that Ro suspected drinking it was some sort of status symbol. He missed Lucozade—its bright packaging and medicinal tang. His longing felt physical, a sweaty, desperate wanting, which made him wonder if homesickness was a real disease that you caught in foreign airports, the cure only found when you crossed back through passport control.

"What does that mean? *A state of want?*" Immie asked. She tucked her hair behind her ear and revealed tiny gold heart earrings. Today she was wearing ripped jeans and leather sandals, and her knees poked out as she sat cross-legged on the chair. Ro's eyes were drawn to the gentle slope of her ankle; he wanted to trace it with a Sharpie. Immie'd be interesting to draw. She was all lines below the neck, in contrast with her round cheeks—sharp-elbowed, sharp-shouldered, sharp-kneed—with the occasional unexpected curve. Looking at her made his fingers itch. No, he didn't want a Sharpie.

He wanted to render her in charcoal. Play with its smudging.

"We, as humans, always want *more*, or at the very least, want things to be different than how they are at any given moment," Paige said, pointing at them with a baby carrot.

"Example," Arch demanded.

"Okay. I was just thinking they keep it too cold in here—"

"We learned in women's studies that most offices are set to a colder temperature to make men more comfortable," Immie said, and Ro wondered if this is how he and Arun and Kaia sounded when they sat around and talked nonsense. Like kids playing adults in a stage production.

"Men are always the default," Paige said.

"As it should be," Arch said, and Immie crumpled up her napkin and threw it halfheartedly at his head.

"Okay, better example: I saw Claire's bag, and I was like, I'm going to die if I don't get one exactly like it. So basically, the human condition is to be greedy and insatiable. Which is why I no longer believe in monogamy." Paige reminded Ro of Kaia, though the girls looked and sounded nothing alike. Kaia was half-Jamaican, half-British, plaited her hair around her head like a crown, and wore men's clothes she found at Oxfam. Paige, on the other hand, who he'd learned was three quarters Jewish American and a quarter Chinese American, let her hair crest around her shoulders like a river and her clothes were dainty and expensive-looking. Still, they played a similar game: big, attention-grabbing pronouncements while taking no crap. Just for the fun of it. Kaia once said, apropos of nothing, *Did you ever think about the fact that your parents might be having a wank at the same time you are?* and Ro was so horrified he didn't touch himself for a week.

"Wouldn't it be easier to buy the bag?" Immie asked. "Instead of dooming yourself to a lifetime of polyamory?"

"Bought it online during fourth period. And don't be so judgmental. Deciding not to buy into some monogamous construct is not the same as dooming myself. There are lots of ways to live your life. Right, Arch?"

"Why are you looking at me?" Arch said. "Anyhow, no one *believes* in monogamy. Couples try their best to practice it. Like yoga or your multiplication tables."

"How about you, Rohan Singh? Do you have a special friend? More importantly, do you believe in monogamy?" Paige asked, and he felt the questions pour over him. Paige mimed putting a microphone in his face like a newscaster. She was so over-the-top that it was easy to pretend she wasn't flirting at all. And maybe she wasn't.

"No and yes." Ro thought about how, when he said goodbye to his mum at the airport, she insisted on paying the outrageous car park fees at Heathrow and walking him inside. After he and his father checked their luggage, she had hugged Ro and kissed him and told him to *be good, betté*, and he knew then if he cried, it would only make things harder for her. He held back his tears and resisted screaming *Please let me stay!* He was too late for either; the time for arguments had long come and gone.

Instead, he let himself be carried by the current toward airport security, like this was normal and routine, he and his father, masks already in place, rolling their carry-ons behind them until they flew across an ocean to move halfway around the world. The two of them without Ro's mum didn't make sense, like a doll without its head.

Ro's dad didn't get a hug or a kiss or a *be good* from Ro's mum.

She believed in monogamy. Ro's dad had *tried his best to practice it*.

"Wait, no to which? The girlfriend or the monogamy?" Paige asked.

"I like that expression, *a constant state of want*," Ro answered, not clarifying. "I feel that way, though I'm not fussed about small details. I want big stuff, though. Like, for pretty much everything in my life to be different."

"That's dark, dude," Paige said.

"Not really," Immie said. "That's how high school is supposed to be. We're not supposed to like it. We're supposed to survive it. I can't wait to get the hell out of this place."

"Really? You can't wait to get the hell out of Wood Valley?" Arch asked. Ro enjoyed watching the twins. They seemed to anticipate each other's sentences, and on the rare occasion when they didn't, they couldn't hide their discomfort.

"What's so bad about this place?" Paige asked.

"Nothing. I want to start my real life." Immie shrugged, like this was obvious.

"We're not your real life?" Paige's tone downshifted to anger, and Ro wondered if she was intentionally misunderstanding. Ro knew exactly what Immie meant. In the Underground, he'd see advertisements for package vacations to Crete or Tanzania with pictures of people attached to bungee cords overlooking rickety bridges, arms spread wide as if to gather up something invisible. When he looked at those photos, he'd feel a tightening at his neck, like a dog pulling against its collar.

Ro wanted to start his real life too.

"That's not what I'm—"

"I get what she's saying," Ro interjected, a risky move, since he barely knew these kids. He should have stayed quiet. Let them hash it out. He already ate dinner and breakfast alone; he didn't need to add lunch to his social isolation. "I felt the same way back home and I had the best friends anyone could ever ask for. I was desperate to leave. We all were. And it's even worse now, no offense intended to you lovely people."

"No offense taken," Arch said. "Though I think I might be still offended by Im."

"Come on," Immie said. "You know what I mean."

"I do?"

"School can be suffocating," Ro said, again jumping in.

"Especially when it's on fire," Paige said. "Pun fully intended."

Ro thought again of Immie's ankle, the slope of her hip, and how when you drew someone and then broke them down to their components, they sometimes seemed too vulnerable on the page. An imperfect machine. He thought again of his mum and how she hadn't cried either when they said goodbye, though he was sure she had later, at home, when no one was looking.

"Seriously, you guys never fantasize about getting the hell out of here? For real? Just walking out the door and never coming back?" Immie asked, looking from Paige to Arch and back again.

"I like it here," Arch said.

"I do too," Paige said.

"Right. I get that. It's just that this is not the *only* place in the world," Immie said.

"But it's a good one," Arch said.

"It's still *high school*," Immie said, which to Ro felt like game, set, match.

CHAPTER FOURTEEN

Immie

At three a.m. on the night of the kiss, Immie sat next to her brother on the bottom bunk. She thought about their father asleep in the next room, how his incessant curiosity about their lives mirrored Arch's curiosity about everyone else's. She thought about the terrible year they'd spent in lockdown, the way their dad moved around the apartment like an animal looking to strike. How she and Arch would take long walks and drives to escape. How Paige's backyard transformed into their sanctuary.

Mostly, she thought about Arch's face when he told her what had happened—equal parts devastation and elation. Still flushed and blotchy. She could almost see the imprints where Jackson's hands had been on his cheeks.

Immie didn't need to take the fall. They had options.

The truth, for one. Telling Paige was not the same thing as telling their father.

Or they could keep quiet altogether. Pretend not to know a thing.

No, that felt like even more of a lie.

Immie didn't hold her decision up to the light. She acted with an impulsiveness that was new to her. Immie understood that she'd do this for her brother, and she understood it in the way she imagined Paige always understood things: with an unshakable certainty that Immie had never before experienced.

Decisiveness, it turned out, was comforting. She would take the fall for Arch, and yes, telling Paige would be terrifying, and Paige would be pissed. But soon she'd get past it. The whole thing would be chalked up to a drunken mistake, a meaningless few seconds. They were Immie and Paige, after all, which had always been bigger than Paige and Jackson.

Once the decision had been made, one more thing set, Immie rolled over and fell fast asleep to the sounds of Arch's snoring.

CHAPTER FIFTEEN

Paige

Paige looked at her daily planner, old-school paper and leather-bound, which broke each day down into fifteen-minute increments. She flipped through the pages and looked at all those boxes filled with assignments and extra-curriculars and the minutiae that added up to her full life. Seeing the rows with the tiny, satisfying checks she marked when something was *done* felt almost erotic.

So far today, she had gone to tennis practice, then to extra SAT tutoring since she needed to work on consistency with her math if she was going for a perfect score. She had done three hours of homework, including writing a twenty-page essay for English III on the boring *Crucible*.

Her dad was shooting on location in Vancouver and her mom was in D.C. for a trial, and so other than Marta, who came during the day to cook and clean and also, Paige suspected, send proof-of-life photos to her parents, she was alone.

Paige could feel the empty space around her, all the

empty bedrooms and the empty kitchen and the empty backyard and her empty body.

Alone isn't the same as lonely, she told herself, which was another thing her meditation teacher had taught her.

Paige picked up her phone and scrolled to *Favorites*. Once over the summer, when both of her parents were away, she panic-dialed the private security company because she thought someone was breaking into the house in the middle of the night. Where were her mom and dad again? On safari in Africa? Davos? She couldn't remember. Two guards showed up at the door with guns strapped to thighs in thick polyester pants, and the younger, handsome one drank in Paige in her tank top and short pajama shorts, and said, with surprise, *You're here in this big house all alone, gorgeous?* They searched every room, even the closets, declared the noise to be from the wicked Santa Ana winds, and before they left, the cute one scribbled his private cell on the back of a business card and winked.

Feel free to use this anytime you're scared, he said.

Anytime, he repeated, like a bad line in a movie.

Paige didn't tell her mom—about thinking someone was breaking in or the business card—because her mom would have insisted Marta start sleeping over again, like she used to do when Paige was little. No doubt she would have also gotten the security guard fired. Marta had her own life and her own kids and Paige was old enough not to need a babysitter anymore. She wasn't sure if a hot security guard winking at an equally hot minor should be a fireable offense. Truth be known, she might have kind of liked it, had felt that wink somewhere between her legs. She didn't like the gun, though, which in ways she couldn't articulate, made her feel powerless.

Tonight, the wind was quiet, and Paige wasn't scared. She was lonely or alone or whatever. After exhausting her online Rohan Singh stalking—turned out there were a few too many of them for it to be much fun—she decided to text Immie.

Paige: Ro asked me to marry him and have all of his glorious babies

Im: Wow. He moves fast

Paige: Right? I mean the baby making part at least sounds fun

Im: Slut

Paige: Don't slut shame me. Have you learned nothing in women's studies?

Im: Term of affection. So I guess Ro doesn't have a girlfriend if he's looking for a wife

Paige: SIGH DID YOU NOTICE THAT DODGE AT LUNCH?

Im: Oh wait, was that like Ro fan fic? Boy didn't ask to make little Ro-Paiges?

Paige: Dude, it would be Paige-Ros, obviously. But yeah, total fan fic, as is my slutitude. You do any extra recon for me?

Im: Not much. We're supposed to meet after school for our project

Paige: ASK THEN

Im: Aye aye cap'n. Will try not to wuss out again

Paige: My parents are away. It's quiet af here

Im: I'd kill for it to be quiet here. Both Arch and I are currently wearing noise canceling headphones

Paige paused for a moment. She felt buoyed by their banter. Ready to scratch the surface of what was bothering her.

Paige: Do you ever wonder if this is all a big waste of time?

Im: What? School?

Paige: All of it. LIFE

Im: You okay? You're freaking me out

Paige: I'm fine! You're the one who said you can't wait to get out of here!

Paige waited as the three dots appeared, then disappeared, then appeared again. How could she tell her best friend that she was afraid of her own insignificance? That if she died, Marta, who she liked but whose last name she had never even knew, would be the one to find her body? What did that say about the value of her life?

Maybe by trying to do everything right she was doing it all wrong.

Im: I didn't mean that it was a waste

Paige: But it kind of is, right? I mean, we do all this stuff to get into a good college and then we do it all over again so when we graduate we can get a good job. And we're the lucky ones! But what if it's all just a big distraction, but not the good kind?

Im: Distraction from what?

Paige: The fact that we're all, one day, going to DIE?

Im: Interesting theory but I'm never going to die

Paige: Amen sister

Im: Maybe it's the opposite

Paige: What do you mean?

Im: What if all this stuff is to make what time we do have on this Earth meaningful?

Paige: You sure are half glass full tonight

Im: P, for real, you okay?

Paige: Of course I am. Why wouldn't I be?

Im: I dunno. Sometimes we just aren't

Paige: I'm always fine

And it was true. Paige *was* always fine. She'd broken up with her boyfriend and been betrayed by her best friend, and still she was *fine*.

She turned off her light and lay down on her bed. She thought about dying in her sleep and how that would mean all the fifteen-minute increments in her planner would be left undone forever. She pictured all the empty boxes waiting to be ticked. She thought about what would happen if she called that security guard's phone number; she'd kept his card in her nightstand drawer, and every once in a while she'd take it out and reread it. *Chase.* Would he come over? What would he expect from her if he did? Sex?

He was an adult, after all. And that's what grown-ups did when they went over to each other's houses late at night, right?

She pictured opening a bottle of red wine from her parents' cellar, though she had no idea how to use their fancy bottle opener. Carefully pouring out two glasses. Civilized. No beer in red Solo cups. She imagined the security guard slipping his big man hands into her hair and kissing her hard against the cold refrigerator door. She'd feel the bulge of the gun at his thigh pressing against her bare leg.

The fantasy stopped there.

Paige was a virgin. With the exception of Arch and Immie and Jackson, everyone at school assumed she'd been having sex for years. In Paige's experience, this was an assumption people tended to make about young pretty girls.

Sometimes Paige would overhear her mom telling her friends that Paige was sixteen going on thirty. Paige took it as a compliment. She looked forward to adulthood. To it finally being age-appropriate that she essentially lived alone.

Still, when Paige actually thought about the mechanics of sex, the fact that it meant that another person would put their own parts inside of hers, she couldn't imagine that level of intimacy, of literal opening-up. She wouldn't have gone through with it at the party. Not with someone like Jackson, whose Star Wars duvet made her feel like they were children getting together to play with Legos.

She was not capable of that kind of surrender.

No, Paige wouldn't call the security guard. What would she even say? *Remember me?*

He would, of course, remember her. People tended to.

Still, the idea was ridiculous. Dangerous, even. A pathetic attempt to feel more alive. Like cutting or playing with matches.

She threw off her covers and walked pantsless across the room. Her window shades were open. Who knew? Chase might at that very moment be patrolling her gated community on foot. Maybe he'd look up, see her silhouetted in the moonlight.

She liked imagining that: him watching her.

Paige sat down at her desk on one of those yoga balls that worked your abs. She'd write up a campaign plan. A road map to victory. If she was going to run for president, she had to win.

CHAPTER SIXTEEN

Arch

"I thought we had a truce," Jackson said. He had stomped up to the counter at Espresso Yourself, and though Arch felt the usual stirrings of hatred and desire, he also felt giddy. He'd never seen this version of Jackson before, though to be fair, Jackson didn't have many other modes other than suave and unflappable. Right now, he seemed downright tantrum-y. After their kiss, there had been a single wide-eyed second when Jackson had seemed as thrown by the whole thing as Arch was. Then Jackson wiped his mouth with the back of his hand and, with a sardonic smirk, said, "Oops. That wasn't supposed to happen."

For a while now, Arch wanted to ask Jackson what that actually meant: *wasn't supposed to happen*. He had turned it around and around in his head. *Wasn't supposed to happen* made him think of something inorganic, an accident of fate. That didn't seem right. Jackson, after all, in the midst of a heated discussion about the Avengers, had by his own free will grabbed Arch by the back of the head, brought their faces close together, and kissed him. Nothing accidental about that.

"Did you put her up to it?" Jackson asked.

"Can I help you?" Arch asked in his most bored barista tone, as if Jackson was any other customer, as if he wasn't clearly flapped—which likely wasn't a word, but Arch figured it would make a good one. Jackson's hair was pomaded in a million different directions, and this annoyed Arch, like even his hair was allowed freedom that other people's wasn't.

"Why would you do that?" Jackson asked, loud and indignant, arms folded in front of him. Arch looked around the cafe. The place was quiet. The only person around was a guy with his laptop and a cup of coffee and headphones who Arch assumed was writing a screenplay, like every other coffee shop customer in LA. Immie was supposedly in the back taking inventory, though Arch guessed she was hiding out with the SAT prep app.

"Do what? Offer you coffee? It's my job," Arch said. "But if you don't like it, there's a Starbucks down the block."

"Seriously, Arch."

Arch shivered. He had never before heard Jackson use his name, or if he had, it was pre-kiss, pre–Jackson becoming something other than Paige's boyfriend. He felt the word resonate throughout his whole body, like a fingertip tracing a line down his back. One word and it felt like watching an ASMR video.

"I don't know what you're talking about."

"The election? Paige is running for president," Jackson

said, his eyes wide and unhinged. Arch felt his insides unclench. For a minute there, he had thought—what had he thought? That their secret was out? Jackson wouldn't have cared all that much. Why did it feel like Arch, who already had so much less relative to his peers, was always the one with something to lose? "And just like that, my high school future, poof!"

Jackson mimed an explosion with his hands, and it took all of Arch's willpower not to laugh right in his entitled, pretty, melodramatic face. No matter what Jackson did—even if he flunked out of Wood Valley, which of course would never happen, not only because Jackson was smart, but also because his dad had paid for the new auditorium—he would be *fine*. Arch did not understand the mechanics of being rich, but he knew that Jackson had a trust fund, would likely be granted admission to whatever private college he wanted to go to, and wouldn't have to worry about paying for it. Arch imagined that life for Jackson felt like walking around in an Iron Man suit. No one could hurt you.

"Your entire future?"

"I've worked hard these last four years. I've done a good job as president. And she's going to challenge me? Why? Out of revenge? It's not fair. This is my thing," Jackson said, as if he hadn't heard Arch, and maybe he hadn't. He was too worked up. Arch found this both disgusting and adorable.

"Maybe Paige wants a chance to be president. She's entitled to run," Arch said calmly. He turned around and started to make a cup of iced coffee for Jackson, even though he hadn't ordered one and the last thing he needed was more caffeine. Arch needed to break eye contact. It occurred to him a moment too late that Jackson would know he remembered his last order. Dammit. Jackson would think Arch crammed all sorts of Jackson-related information into his brain.

"Of course she's entitled. This isn't about entitlement."

"It's not?" Arch threw this question over his shoulder, and he could feel it land. Good.

"You're an asshole," Jackson said, with surprisingly little malice, seeming to return to his agreeable self after his rant. "You're right, but you're an asshole."

"For the record, I had nothing to do with it. You know Paige. She does what she wants with little input from others." Arch handed him the drink and their fingers brushed.

"You left room for milk this time."

"That will be three-fifty." The words came out too sharp and abrupt, and like every moment with Jackson lately, Arch wanted a redo. He never seemed to get it right the first time.

If he could, he'd instead say *On the house.*

"Remember when we did that lab about chemical reactions, Archer? How if you change one thing, the rate of reaction totally changes? Like certain chemicals just work better with other unexpected chemicals?" Hearing Jackson call him Arch was one thing, but hearing him call him "Archer" was something altogether different. The world went wavy, and Arch gripped the counter, on the underside, to steady himself.

"Yeah." Arch had kissed other boys—four, to be exact—all

at YMCA camp in a thicket of woods behind the cabins. Those kisses resulted in mosquito bites, chafed backs from tree bark, and, in one case, poison ivy. He didn't wonder about those boys, most of whom lived far away, not even late at night or in the shower, when one let one's mind go to such places. In hindsight, those experiences felt like practice for kissing Jackson.

"I think about that lab a lot, is all," Jackson said. Arch looked up and Jackson looked back, always so much braver than he was. Arch looked away. "I don't know. I've been thinking about everything lately."

Arch didn't know what to say to this. Lately Arch had been thinking he'd done his entire life wrong, from the very first second, when he let Immie push him out of the womb. She should have gone first.

"Don't hurt yourself," Arch said, and felt a stab of pride at this line, even though it came a beat late. Not quite up to Jackson's standards, but not bad.

"Heh," Jackson said and then he shook his drink, a final rattle, another exclamation point of a gesture.

After Jackson left, Arch picked up his own empty cup and copied the movement with a flick of his wrist. His didn't make a sound.

On the car ride home, both Arch and Immie felt the hush as they glided down through the hills. The sky fell pink behind them, a riot of color, and Arch set the music to a low, steady hum. They weaved, as the traffic cleared, through what felt like backcountry. They crossed from the Valley to the city and emerged on the other side at the lip of Hollywood—a bizarre alchemy of seediness and eager tourists, the big block-letter Hollywood sign framed in the rearview mirror. The throngs and bright lights and the broken people carrying their homes on their backs left them unscathed; they were hermetically sealed within their 2005 Toyota Corolla and, of course, their own minds. Vine turned to Rossmore, and again the scene changed, like panels on a film set moved by people clad in black. Dispensaries and dollar stores and taco joints gave way to multimillion-dollar mansions, gates and hedges and security cameras with single suspicious red eyes. Still, they kept going, as they did every night and every morning in reverse, and turned east to Koreatown. The sprawling mess of a city reasserted itself. Tall buildings and inset mini-malls, and everything in Korean—characters unintelligible to the twins, except to mean *home*.

They turned onto a street of bland apartment buildings, the type with exterior fire escapes and tired names evoking lunar phases—Crescent Court, New Moon Units—and began their daily scout for parking. Tonight, they were lucky. They only had to walk two blocks.

These commutes felt like losing a layer each morning, until, when he arrived at Wood Valley, Arch was at his essence. And the reverse also felt true—the ride home involved a thickening of skin, one layer on top of the other, as they approached the unpredictable. Most of the time, they wouldn't need the extra padding. Sometimes, though, they would.

As soon as Arch opened the door to the apartment,

he knew it was one of those nights. He knew the air had warped even before he saw his mom on the couch crying, or his dad's face contorted with fury, or even the bag of frozen peas resting on his father's wrist. Arch had already felt it in his joints, like how Immie's appendix scar told her when it was going to rain.

Just like that, one day's story became another.

"Are you okay?" Arch asked. This was, of course, directed to his mother. He was not worried about his father's okayness. He was worried about his father's temperature, whether his mood, ever in motion, was swinging up or coming down. Always better on the way down when his dad descended into cold silence, sometimes for weeks on end, and there would be an awkward peacefulness in the apartment.

Arch saw his father's pumping blue vein in his mind's eye, if not with his actual eyes. His father's head was turned to the side. His neck unreadable.

"Jesus! What do you think? That I hit her?" his dad screamed, as if this was not within the realm of the possibility. And actually, the truth was, as far as Arch knew, and Arch realized his knowledge was limited, though he couldn't say whether this limitation was intentional or not, his dad had never hit his mother. He had pushed her, and squeezed her arm, and once elbowed her in the sternum. Nothing that would leave any permanent damage, nothing other than a small bruise or two, marks that you could, in muddied hindsight, chalk up to accidents, marks that could easily be covered with sleeves or concealer.

Things weren't "call child services" level in their house.

At least that's how Arch secretly thought of it, like he lived with his own terror alert system in his head. Red, orange, yellow. Things had never been bad enough to rise to the level of *abuse*. Which was a gross word, a word that implied that there were *victims* somewhere: black eyes and little kids cowering in a corner while an addict raged and broke furniture. A word that implied the need for an *intervention*.

Arch's father didn't drink or take drugs, he didn't leave them marked or hiding. Arch and Immie were practically adults, and they loved their father, because he was funny and smart and on Sundays made poo-emoji–shaped pancakes.

He had an unpredictable temper and lost control. That was all. Flailed around when he was angry. He'd never actually hurt the twins, would never, not intentionally. He'd thrown things—a glass (at Arch), a vase (at Immie), a book (unclear, though probably at both)—but they'd always dodged, and understanding their father's moods and, more importantly, their own temperaments, they didn't fight back. They retreated to their shared room, locked the door, and put on their headphones. Lay in the dark and let the shame wash over them.

Arch didn't know what Immie listened to during those nights, which, to be fair, were infrequent, maybe a couple of times a year, or maybe a little more frequent than that, but not by much. If he were forced to guess, he'd say maybe once a month, tops, and of varying degrees of seriousness. Maybe every other week. No one could be sure. There were certain things you let slip by without memorializing them.

He assumed, by the slight rattle to the bunk bed, that

Immie must turn to loud music. He'd never asked because he hadn't wanted to know. Arch listened to audiobooks. Usually something long and nonfiction—an old dude sonorously telling him about Ulysses S. Grant or the War of 1812. Something random and obscure and completely useless, borrowed from the library for this one purpose only. The idea was to be anesthetized, a mask laid flat over his mouth.

But tonight, Arch and Immie hadn't made it to their room. They were stuck in the living room, waiting to see how it would all shake out. If refuge would be needed, and for how long. Arch's stomach rumbled.

"You okay, Dad?" Immie asked, her voice calm and controlled. Arch thought that his sister would make a great hostage negotiator. She was tonally reassuring, which was a sneaky way to gain trust. Immie was always the last person suspected of anything and the first to take the blame.

"There are going to be layoffs at Transcom. So, you know, bad day for your father," his mom said. She swatted at her tears, spreading the black from her mascara and turning her cheeks into a watercolor painting. Arch thought of the sunset during the drive home, the layers of color on color, the unexpected beauty of it. He thought of Ro thinking Arch and Immie's mom was the arsonist, and how, strangely, he'd suddenly wished she were. That would mean she had the wherewithal to burn something down.

Arch's dad had worked at Transcom for about a year now, which was a pretty good run for him. He'd be fired or laid off or whatever, and he'd spend a few months stomping around the apartment, and then he'd find something else. This happened with such frequency that the losing and gaining of a new job were the kinds of events that Arch met with neither alarm nor celebration. The only time things had gotten scary was during the pandemic, when finding employment seemed next to impossible. Arch's worries didn't extend beyond this night, and how best to traverse the small patch of carpeted hallway that stretched from the living room to their bedroom, to get to the blissful moment when he and Immie closed their door. That perfect little click, and then the second, even better one: the turn of their lock.

The lock had appeared one day on their door with no explanation, a gift from their mother. *Thought you guys could use a little privacy*, she said, which didn't make sense, since they shared a room. Arch and Immie both understood that it was not for privacy but for their protection. They felt grateful and liberated, a moment not unlike when their mom had one day surprised them with the keys to the Corolla, though this was, they knew, about being caged as opposed to set free.

"We're going to finish up homework . . . ," Arch said, and righted Bert, the overturned plant that their dad had named and had presumably kicked (there was an Ernie too, and a Snuffleupagus next to the shower); what Bert's transgression could have been, no one knew. Then, with one last look at their mother—the slightest check to make sure there was no real danger, and there really wasn't, probably, though Arch suspected some more tears and yelling, his father looked like he still had some more energy to burn—the twins escaped to their room.

Once inside, hermetically sealed and unscathed, Arch on the top bunk, Immie on the bottom, both of them headphoned, Immie scrounged two Kind bars from her backpack and threw one up to Arch. This would have to suffice for their dinner.

Things would be better in the morning, though. They always were.

CHAPTER SEVENTEEN

Immie

When Immie drove to school, she'd weave through the side streets; she thought of it like a video game—bonus points if she dodged a red light. When Arch drove, on the other hand, he was resolute about his route and never wavered, which was why, after his second unplanned right, Immie spoke up.

"Where are you going?" she asked.

"It's a surprise." Arch was probably taking them through that random Starbucks drive-through in Hollywood, assuming she needed a pick-me-up after last night. Lately, he'd been leaving her small treats, tiny, gallant acts of penance, and she adored whatever he chose. Not that she needed gifts to forgive Arch. She'd never been mad at him in the first place.

Immie had woken up today with a bizarre sense of relief. Her dad was asleep on the couch, and her mom had left early for school, and the morning so far had been drama-free. In the life cycle of her parents' fighting, the afterwards were easier than the befores. Escalating tension was replaced by a moment to exhale, and Immie reveled in that unexpected gift of space. During the waiting you were powerless, a passive observer in the worst kind of suspense. Afterward, you were temporarily free. There were no eggshells to tiptoe over once all the eggs had been cracked.

And maybe things were finally back to normal with Paige. She would pick her up a latte, come to think of it. Though she had done nothing wrong, tiny acts of penance were still a good idea.

"The Starbucks is on Highland, not Mansfield," Immie said when Arch took another unexpected turn into Hancock Park. Immie always thought of her mom when they drove through this neighborhood. She loved how the trees canopied the roads and how the houses spliced efficiently into two. Before she had the twins, their mom had lived in a tiny studio garage in the backyard of a duplex, and Immie could imagine a different version of her here—younger, freer, auditioning during the day, waitressing at night, dreaming bigger than the life she ended up with. Finishing her days the good, ambitious kind of tired, not the weary, adult kind she wore now around her neck like a shabby scarf.

Immie watched the world wake up outside her window. A Hasidic mom, long-skirted and beautifully wigged, wrestled kids into a minivan; next door, a shirtless, muscled twentysomething stretched before a run. Immie recognized him: she'd seen him on a recent episode of *Law & Order: SVU*. He'd played a lawyer with a dirty secret.

"Who said anything about Starbucks? Look for number three-oh-six."

"Seriously?" Immie asked when Arch pulled up to the curb in front of one of the duplexes, and Ro was waiting for them on the front stoop. He was wearing a Glastonbury Festival T-shirt and cargo shorts. Until now, Ro had only donned pants, and so seeing his long legs unravel to standing unraveled Immie. He seemed taller and older with his shins showing. "Why didn't you tell me?"

"Because you would have said no."

"You know how I cry every time I hear the song 'Hallelujah'? Especially the Jeff Buckley version?" Immie whisper-asked.

"Yeah."

"Well, that's also how I feel every time I see Ro's face," she said, just before Ro opened the door and climbed into the back seat. She could feel him settling in behind her and the car felt suddenly stuffy. Immie cracked open her window.

"Morning," Ro said, and through the passenger-side mirror she could see his face peering up at her—smiling, open, eager. His hand rested on the seat behind her shoulders, and it took some willpower not to rub up against it, like a cat. He was too close. Should she ask *Who's Kaia?* She had, after all, promised Paige.

"Morning," Immie croaked.

"Thanks so much for the offer of a ride. You have no idea how much I appreciate it. I'm happy to pay for everything.

Petrol, snacks, whatever your hearts desire. I owe you guys big," Ro said.

"It's no problem," Arch said.

"You've fundamentally changed my life," Ro continued, and that's when it occurred to Immie that this wasn't a one-time offer. That they'd be sitting in the car together five days a week for the rest of the school year, sharing this recycled air. His long legs pressed the seat into her back, and she found herself leaning into the pressure. She was going to murder Arch. She thought of the arsonist, who the police said was most likely a disgruntled student, and for a moment she understood how someone could light the girls' bathroom on fire. How life could make you so angry about what you couldn't have, that you felt left with no choice but to take the whole world down.

"The commute with my dad has been—how shall I put this?—hell on Earth? You don't even know. I was considering bicycling, but I can't figure out how to cross the motorway. Freeway. Whatever. The thing with multiple lanes and lots of the giant cars you Americans are so fond of."

"So what you are saying is that we're saving your life," Arch said, and cut his eyes over to Immie. She could hear him in her head: *We're doing something kind here, so no, you will not murder me later. It's just a crush. Maybe repeated morning exposure will help you get over it.*

"You really are. First Paige saved my life, literally, and now you two. Is this a safe space? This feels like a safe space," Ro said.

"This is a safe space," the twins said at the same time.

"Okay, so my dad? He's kind of a big royal arsehole. At the moment, the less time with him the better." Immie felt a tingle in her spine. She'd never said anything like that out loud about her own father, not even to Paige or Arch, though her father was also a big royal arsehole. Movies had made it seem like other people's dads were easy and uncomplicated, if occasionally overprotective. Their role in the family beyond provider was to throw out quips and dish up spaghetti and tell a certain brand of dorky joke. Moms seemed to be more of a problem—cloying and commanding, reliving their adolescence and body issues through their children.

Immie loved her mother, who was and did none of those things, but she often found herself hating her father with an alien fervor. Occasionally, she'd catch herself fantasizing about his death. She didn't kill him in a gruesome or painful way in her mind; she wasn't cruel or a sociopath. She simply disappeared him. Allowed herself to imagine, if for only a little while, what it would be like to not live under the long, fickle grip of his moods and the noxious fumes of his personal disappointments. She imagined it felt like graduation would: a release from prison.

Also this: a release from a consistent, omnipresent shame.

"I hear you," Arch said, and for the second time this morning, he surprised Immie. Arch had worshipped their father when they were little, and had, in more recent years, tacitly agreed to the idea that they'd remain loyal and silent about what happened at home. Immie remembered

Arch used to follow their dad around the apartment with a toy tool belt that matched their dad's and tighten invisible screws a half millimeter to the right of the real ones. Immie's dad wasn't a monster. He had bought his toddler son a toy tool belt, and then later, a real set of tools from Home Depot. When Immie went through a phase of believing in fairies, he'd secretly sprinkled "pixie dust" on the kitchen counters for her to find in the morning, even though the glitter got in everything and drove her mom bananas. Sometimes Immie played with the tool belt and sometimes Arch put on her fairy wings, and no one batted an eye.

It suddenly seemed unfair to judge people by their worst moments.

"So, any car rules I should know about? I understand if you're not morning people and prefer quiet," Ro said. "I can shut it."

"No rules except Arch and I switch off driving every day. And Arch is in charge of music. Always. Trust me, it's not worth fighting him."

"Got it."

"Talking is not only allowed but preferred," Arch said, and Immie risked a glance in the side view. Ro was again smiling at her. She smiled back.

"At home, Kaia wouldn't allow me or Arun to speak before nine a.m. or until she'd consumed at least three flat whites, whichever came first."

"Who's Kaia?" Arch asked, and Immie looked straight through the windshield and gripped the glove compartment as if bracing for impact. Later she'd have to google *how to cure a crush*. Proximity wasn't helping.

"My best mate. It's me, Kaia, and Arun. Kind of like you two and Paige. The three of us have been friends forever," Ro said, and his voice caught.

"So Kaia's not your girlfriend?" Arch asked.

"Not really. I mean . . . no. She's not at all," Ro said, and Immie didn't know what to do with that equivocation. She dismissed her own feelings on the matter, and memorized the answer for Paige, for her to do with that information whatever she wanted.

"You must miss them," Immie said.

"I'm gutted," Ro said. "Truly."

Immie sat with the word *gutted*. She filtered out the charm of Ro's accent, that delightful tacked-on *truly*, and listened. *Gutted* made her think of a knife pressing against the belly of a fish; lonely and dead-eyed and then, ultimately, emptied. *Gutted* seemed a lot like code for heartbroken.

CHAPTER EIGHTEEN

Ro

Later, it was just the two of them: Ro and Immie sitting under a tree behind the cafeteria, brainstorming ideas for their women's studies project. They hadn't gotten very far. Their conundrum was Goldielocksian: everything they came up with seemed either intimidatingly big or unimpressively small. Ro was happy to be outside where there was no need for him to mentally note the location of the nearest fire exit.

"How about something to do with free access to sanitary products for the homeless?" Ro asked.

"Sanitary products?"

"You know. Like women stuff."

"You mean like tampons." Ro nodded. His mum and sister had kept a box under the bathroom sink at home and sometimes he saw the crisp, blue wrappers in the bin. They were things like any other things. He didn't need to associate them with the word *vagina*. He didn't have to think about how they worked—the adverts led him to believe they involved absorption—or how they were inserted, or whether Immie might be wearing one right now. He closed his eyes to blink away the image, which was, as embarrassing as it was to admit, arousing. The truth was, he found most things about Immie arousing. The way her hair refused to stay contained in a rubber band. Watching her face give away too much and mismatch with her words. Even her name, which sounded like a nibble, not a bite. It was a casual, sexy suggestion of a name, like an unexpected slit in a skirt.

If Kaia were here, she'd laugh right in his face. *You have it bad, mate.* Arun had confirmed that Kaia had already found someone to replace Ro for her midnight snogging needs. This confused him. Not the fact of Kaia kissing someone else, that seemed inevitable long before he left, and he felt neither sad nor disappointed on that front, but the idea of the world back home continuing to hurtle forward in his absence. When he thought of London, he pictured everything staying exactly as it was—gray and reliable. Which made no sense, since nothing was the same at all.

"So, like lobbying the government to provide tampons to the homeless?" Immie asked.

"I was thinking more like buying a bunch and giving them out." Ro rested his back against the tree trunk. Immie's cheeks were freckled and pink from the sun and she had a trail of beauty spots down her right arm, like ants marching in a line. Ro enjoyed reading Immie's face. Her eyebrows tightened when she spoke to Paige, eager and alert, ever so slightly on guard. They relaxed when she spoke to Arch, smooth, unruffled, elastic. When she spoke to Ro, they gathered in the middle, like the crest of a wave.

Right now, she lowered the left side of her lip a millimeter, which was the face she seemed to make most often in the car. He assumed this meant she was thinking.

"A tampon drive," Immie said.

"Right. Yeah." It had not rained a single day since Ro'd been in Los Angeles, which was an ominous delight. He'd grown used to the pinch of the sunglasses on his nose, the lazy comfort of only wearing a T-shirt, even the warm bath of the sun. Yet where did the water he drank come from? Would it one day run out? California and its beautiful leisure felt unsustainable. He imagined it breaking off and floating away into the Pacific at some point in the near future.

Ro was gripped by a bizarre longing for a woolly jumper. In London, a rare sunny day set you free to romp around on the grass, to strut outside and gulp the air. In LA, the endless march of them—day after day of that orange ball burning bright in the sky—turned out to have the opposite effect. He found himself feeling slow around Immie. A little sweaty too.

"Though it's not very exciting, is it?" he said. "We could maybe do some sort of art installation alongside the collection, like build a wall out of tampons or something?" Ro tried to picture it—a tower of blue boxes. Or perhaps something with a suspension hanging from the ceiling. He tried to picture an actual tampon but realized he had no idea what they looked like.

"We could do something about destigmatizing"—Immie choked on the words—"period blood."

"If you can't even say it, we can't do our whole project around it!"

"I can say it," Immie insisted. Her entire face was red now, and Ro liked watching her blush, how it overtook her from forehead to chin, a slow and steady saturation. Like an animation being filled in.

"Look at you! You really can't. Try it. I dare you to say it without blushing."

"Period blood. Period blood. Period blood. See? If you say it fifteen times fast, the period fairy comes and takes away your cramps." Immie touched her cheeks, and Ro wanted to do that. To rest the back of his hand and feel the heat of her face.

Oh, bollocks.

"Phew. My cramps have been such a pain in my arse lately," Ro said, and Immie laughed. "Now let's see if you can shout it."

"What?"

"Period blood. Let me hear you scream."

"No way."

"Throw off the shackles of the tyranny of menstrual subjugation!" This was a silly flex, and yet Ro felt he had no choice. In London, Ro was smart and capable; here, he felt like a right idiot, unable to understand basic English or drive a car or cross the bloody street. Or talk to this girl he barely knew without wanting to paw at her like a creep.

"I understood maybe every other one of those words."

"Just scream it! I have faith in you, Immie Gibson."

"PERIOD BLOOD!" she yelled, hands cupped around her mouth, and then she lay down on her back giggling. He held up his palm and she gave him a high five and he could swear he felt that touch zigzag through his body, like an energy shot.

"I saw this article a while back about this Instagram influencer who posted a picture of her . . . your turn." Immie pointed at Ro.

"Period blood," Ro supplied, and then, to his surprise, he felt himself catch her blush.

"Right? It's not so easy. Anyhow, there was this whole uproar. Like, people were disgusted. Which I get, but when I really think about it, it's not really gross. It's natural. And thinking it's gross is all part of the shaming of women. Or to be even more transinclusive and nongender-essentialist, as Ms. Stein wants us to be, the shaming of people with uteruses over the natural functioning of our bodies. In some parts of the world, girls can't even go to school when they have their periods."

It was Immie's turn to flex, and she seemed all lit up, like she was enjoying talking to him as much as he was enjoying talking to her. Ro had never actually thought about uteruses, and when he tried to picture one, he thought of a splayed chicken. He thought about women's bodies, of course, a frightening amount, actually, and not just the obvious bits, but also their toes and elbows and whatever you call the underside of their knees. Right now, he was calculating the distance between his body and Immie's body and how that distance might be closed, whether it would be possible to one day follow that trail of beauty marks with his fingers. What measure of courage it would take for him to say *Would you like to go out with me sometime?*

Like the coins and the power outlets, he had no idea how those sorts of things worked in America. Maybe she had a boyfriend who lived in the OC, a place he knew of only from reality television but made him think of sculpted white tossers with surfboards and coiffed hair and two-word vocabularies limited to *dude* and *chilling*. Could that be Immie's type? Or maybe she had some bookish boyfriend who Ro had not yet seen because he was always in the library studying; maybe he had dark circles under his eyes, and together they drank espresso and talked about philosophy and the misery of human existence. That seemed more likely. He couldn't picture Immie at the beach, and he certainly couldn't imagine her tolerating someone thick.

"So we could center our project on making people less scared of . . ." Ro pointed at Immie.

"Period blood." Ro made an appreciative crowd-going-wild noise. "And yeah, no way."

"But it's a great idea. It was *your idea*."

"Nope. I don't want to be our"—Immie paused dramatically—"supplier."

She shuddered, and Ro laughed.

"Anyhow, I kind of want to do something where we can see a tangible result," she said. "Ms. Stein said to think big."

"Fair enough. Back to the tampon collection idea?"

"Maybe? Let's start by calling homeless shelters and finding out if this is actually a problem and then see where that leads us," Immie said.

"Sounds like a plan."

"Cool."

"Cool." Now they were sitting there looking at each other and things turned awkward. Even more awkward than when he made her scream *period blood*, which in retrospect might not have been his finest flirting moment. How did his father manage to convince an attractive young woman to sleep with him, when Ro could barely talk to one? If he hadn't fallen into the Kaia thing, he might have spent his entire life having never kissed a girl. "Hey, so you said you live in Koreatown, yeah?"

"Yup."

"I was wondering if you'd show me your neighborhood sometime. I read online you can get life-changing bulgogi and that delicious Korean tofu soup. That there were all sorts of cool stores and stuff. I figure while I'm here I should get to know LA."

"Sure. I'd love to!" Immie smiled, and Ro felt an unclenching in his chest. Perhaps he wasn't as bad at this as he thought.

"Great."

"Great," Immie repeated, and then, after another beat added: "We should totally invite Paige along."

Ro stilled his face so it wouldn't betray his disappointment. Clearly, Immie wasn't interested in him. And that was cool. He was not some weirdo stalker who thought about her tampons and the underside of her knees.

And anyhow, none of it mattered anyway. Ro was going back to London as soon as possible. The last thing he needed was a girl getting in the way.

CHAPTER NINETEEN

Paige

"Come on! You handed her that match. I expect better from you!" Paige's coach yelled across the court, and Paige felt the words sting, as acute as a slap. She'd gotten creamed by that Marlborough bitch, who somehow seemed to play directly to Paige's few weaknesses. Actually, her opponent wasn't a bitch at all—they had gone to elementary together and Paige had fond memories of the two of them on the swings—but Paige usually played best from a position of righteous indignation.

Didn't work today.

Nothing seemed to work today.

"Sorry, Coach," Paige said, then threw her tennis bag over her shoulder and ran to her car before anyone could see that her eyes were filling. Earlier she had gotten her very first B in her entire life—on an AP Bio quiz—and she still felt the eighty-five percent twist in her gut.

In debate, she'd been assigned the side of defending a

border wall, and though she normally liked a challenge, this felt wrong.

Paige didn't get eighty-five percent, and she didn't lose tennis matches, and she didn't argue for things she didn't believe in, even for practice.

During the drive home, she let one tear fall, and then she was done with the self-pity. When she pulled up at the security gate outside her neighborhood, Paige looked as she always did: competent, in control. Instead of Chuck, who usually greeted her with a thumbs-up attached to a heavily tattooed arm, today Chase, the security guard whose card she kept in her nightstand, was standing in the little hut. He didn't lift the gate when he saw her car coming, and so she slowed to a stop. For a fleeting second, she thought again about border walls.

"Identification, please," he said without looking up.

"Seriously?" Paige asked, and then Chase looked at her. She was still wearing her short tennis skirt, and she wondered if he could see her tan legs from his perch above. She hoped so.

A slow grin spread across his face as recognition dawned. "You!" he said.

"Me!" she said back, and mirrored his smile. After the monotony of today, broken only by her own failures, she liked this feeling of her pulse quickening, this tiny fissure of danger. Chase wore a gun at his waist. His wrists were thick and he wore a chunky silver watch, the old-fashioned kind, with a little hand and a big hand. She licked her lips, looked down and then up, right into his eyes, like she'd learned from a YouTube video about how to flirt.

Paige's mom loved to lecture her about how girls needed to be more careful in this world, even if it wasn't fair. Of course it was the boys who needed to learn consent and boundaries and no means no. *Still*, her mom had warned, *still, watch yourself. A girl's entire life can be ruined with one small, seemingly insignificant miscalculation.*

Of course, a girl's life could easily be ruined without a miscalculation too.

Paige had seen some of her mother's files.

Was that what Paige was doing right now? Making a miscalculation?

Paige, who moved so carefully—planning and plotting in those goddamn fifteen-minute increments—who kept detailed records of what she ate, of how many reps of weights, of the books she needed to read, of her grades, of the clothes she wore so she didn't repeat too frequently, allowed herself to loosen for one moment.

Screw careful, she thought. For the first time all day, she felt some semblance of control. Of power. Of . . . hunger.

Decision made. Click.

"Well it's nice to see you . . ."

"Paige," she supplied.

"Right. Chase." He pointed to his chest, which was smooth and hairless in the little triangle peeking out of his uniform. "Poor Chuck has the flu. But lucky me. I see a backpack. You're a college student, right? Let me guess. UCLA?"

"Go Bruins," Paige said.

"I have your house on my list for extra patrol. Should I stop by later to make sure all is okay up there?" Chase said, and Paige wondered when she had started calling him Chase, if only in her thoughts, and not "the security guard." Using his name meant that she thought of him as an actual person and not a character in the play she had staged in her mind. She hadn't yet written a next scene, and here they were, setting one up. Rearranging the background furniture, shifting from car and hut to Paige's cavernous living room.

She imagined him sitting next to her on the couch and casually placing his hand on her thigh. In her mind, it was all too easy.

"Sure," she said. The gate lifted and she beeped her horn once, quick and cute, as she drove through faster than necessary.

"So, what happened on the biology quiz?" her mother asked over dinner, which was arugula salad with chicken, a lone, grilled four-ounce breast that Marta had weighed on the kitchen scale and left under Saran wrap. Paige's father was still shooting in Vancouver, and Paige realized she had no idea how long he'd been gone or when he'd be back. She wondered if he thought of her beyond the once-a-week scheduled FaceTime call they had on Sunday mornings which took up a single fifteen-minute slot in her planner. Sometimes less.

"You check Ratiodome?" Paige asked. Ratiodome was

the app where students' grades were posted for their parents to monitor. Since her mother had never once mentioned it, Paige had figured her mother didn't even know the app existed. Paige's parents expected her to continue getting spectacular grades—especially since they had given up on her older sister, Violet, who had dropped out of college to become a ski instructor in Aspen—but they weren't on top of her daily life the way the other parents seemed to be with the kids at her school. Her mom didn't believe in what she called that "helicopter-parent bullshit." Paige was competent and mature, she said. No need to police her activities or her friends.

"Of course I do. Well, I mean, Rochelle does." Rochelle was Paige's mom's assistant, who Paige's mom liked to joke was her "wife." Paige's mom had a receptionist at the office, so Rochelle's job was more about life management: picking up dry cleaning, arranging hair and makeup and Botox for her mom's cable news appearances—practically a full-time job in itself. Ironic that a professional feminist had to pay so much attention to her personal appearance, but as Paige's mom always said, CNN doesn't let ugly or old women or, god forbid, old ugly women talk on-screen. Men, maybe, but never women.

Apparently, part of Rochelle's job was also checking Paige's grades. Rochelle spoke like a robot, in clipped, short efficient words, like she didn't have time to engage on a human level.

"I put a stop-loss order on anything lower than a ninety-three," Paige's mom said.

"What are you talking about?"

"You know how in the stock market you can put a stop-loss order, so if a stock drops below a certain number, it automatically gets sold?"

"No."

"We need to brush up on your financial literacy, darling. Well, Rochelle knows that if you drop below a ninety-three to alert me. That's all."

"And then what happens? You sell me on the open market?" Paige asked.

"Don't be silly. I'll sell you on eBay."

"Funny, Mom."

"So what happened on the quiz?"

Paige poked at her chicken, which tasted like a seasoned deck of cards. She didn't know what had happened on the quiz. All she knew is that she felt vaguely ill from that B. She couldn't decide if she liked that her mom had been keeping tabs on her, which might mean that she cared about the minutiae of Paige's life, or if Paige was disappointed that her concern only stretched to whether she was screwing up. In all the years of Rochelle apparently checking her grades, all those years of straight As, her mom never once came home and said, "Great job on that math exam. Knew you could do it!"

"I'll do better next time," Paige said, because that wasn't up for debate. This B was an anomaly.

"Of course you will. Let me know if you need a tutor. I'm sure Rochelle can find someone helpful."

"It was one B."

"If you want to get into Yale . . ." Her mom let the rest of the sentence dangle. Paige's mom, who had gone to the University of Miami and the University of Miami School of Law, and despite all of her success still wished she had made it north to the Ivy League, wanted Paige to go to Yale and then Yale Law School, and then clerk for the Ninth Circuit, and then, of course, for the Supreme Court. Harvard would probably be okay too, but Yale, for reasons Paige didn't understand (maybe because Hillary Clinton had gone there?), captivated her mother's imagination. Paige had no idea if she wanted to go to Yale or to be a lawyer, but she was on board, simply because it *was* a plan. Paige found nothing more soothing than a plan.

"Right," Paige said. She thought about Chase outside somewhere, walking the neighborhood with a flashlight, keeping them safe from bad guys. Paige liked the idea of pretending to be a college student, the kind who flirted with older men and had casual, insignificant hookups, and who threw away her virginity—let's be real, virginity was a social construct, not a real thing anyway—on a whim.

But she also liked the idea of some delayed gratification. The fun would be in the fantasy, not the actuality, in riding, for a while, that fine line between excitement and fear.

If Chase came over—and he wouldn't, not tonight, at least now that her mom's car was in the driveway—what would they talk about? Certainly not her B on the bio quiz. Would he even expect to talk? Would he check her closets for intruders? Or would he just reach over and try to take off her clothes?

How many spaces in her planner would he take up?

Two fifteen-minute blocks, Paige decided. Maybe three. For most activities, that tended to be enough.

CHAPTER TWENTY

Immie

"What does it matter?" Arch asked Paige. They were all loitering in front of the auditorium after the last bell, killing time before the twins had to get to work and Paige had to get to practice and Ro had to get to wherever Ro went after school.

"I just don't understand," Paige said.

"That I got a hundred percent? Why is that so hard to believe?"

Immie knew Arch wasn't offended. It *was* hard to believe that Arch got the highest grade in the class. If life were a sport, Arch and Immie were playing in the local Little League on Sunday mornings for fun, and Paige was training with a private coach for Olympic gold.

"I got an eighty-five percent," Paige said.

"Maybe you were having an off day," Immie offered.

"I don't have off days."

"Eighty-five percent is still pretty good," Ro said.

"Yeah, no, new boy," Paige said, but she still gifted him with a smile. Immie wondered how she did that: gave someone a cute nickname and comfortably used it straight to their face. Immie had a "gray T-shirt dude" and a "red hoodie guy" who occasionally came into the cafe, though those were monikers she'd only used within the confines of her own mind. It never occurred to her to say them out loud or to give them a flirty spin. "You don't know me that well yet, but let's get something out of the way now: I don't do eighty-five percent."

"You guys are going to have to give me a tutorial on the 'yeah, no' and 'no, yeah' you use, because it's all very confusing," Ro said.

"No, yeah, we'll get right on that," Paige said, and Ro laughed.

"Maybe you need more sleep," Arch said.

"Maybe you need to eat more," Immie said, because come to think of it, Paige was looking both thin and tired and maybe even *fragile*, which was a word that she had never used in the same sentence as her best friend's name. Arch and Immie used to worry that Paige's pace felt unsustainable. Years later, they'd agreed that maybe it was just unsustainable for them.

"Thanks, *Mom*," Paige said, which made Immie think of Paige's family, and how she'd kill to be a member of the Cohen-Chen household. She envied how much room they seemed to have. Not the size of their house—though she'd take that too—but the wide emotional berth they granted each other. She knew Paige got lonely sometimes, especially since Violet moved out; still, that quiet seemed idyllic. Immie's home felt like roasting in a sauna of other people's feelings. "So, what's the plan this weekend, kids?"

"Immie's going to show me Koreatown," Ro said with such a sweet hopefulness that Immie almost groaned out loud with longing. He oozed the charm of the simultaneously confident and unmoored, and she loved the idea of leading him around her neighborhood and showing him the landmarks of her childhood. BCD Tofu House, the cute Japanese notepads at Daiso that her mom always slipped into her Christmas stocking, the giant pears from the H Mart. She wanted to hand him her Los Angeles, which was the sort of place that revealed itself slowly and deliberately, coy about its less flashy but more interesting bits. "Also, we're going to price out some tampons."

"I was saying I hoped you'd come too," Immie added quickly. "Arch is in."

"Tampon shopping? Hard pass," Arch said, and Immie glared at him.

"K-town? Really? Come on, let's go someplace cool," Paige said.

"Ouch!" Arch said.

"No offense," Paige said. "You know I love your apartment. It's supercute."

Immie didn't look at Arch because she didn't need to have her feelings amplified by their mind meld. Paige rarely, if ever, came over to their *supercute* apartment, which of course was code for *small*. Also true: neither of them wanted her there. Her eyes were too sharp. Their home was too revealing. She'd somehow smell the friction.

Based on the handful of times Paige and the twins' father met, if Paige thought about him at all—which Immie guessed she didn't because Arch and Immie didn't talk about him much—Immie imagined Paige thought him funny and charming and probably a bit of a loser. Immie didn't think of her dad as a loser, only because that word implied a certain amount of powerlessness, which wasn't the case. In their small orbit, he ruled like a disgruntled king.

"But . . ." Ro looked to Immie and Arch and then back to Paige.

"I mean, are you also shopping for snail-mucus eye creams? Because other than killer skincare products—all of which are available online now, by the way—there's not much to see there," Paige said and flicked her eyes to her Apple Watch. Immie knew she had tennis practice in five minutes and this break in her calendar was color-coded as: "in-person social." "Let's go to Runyon instead!"

"What's Runyon?" Ro asked. Immie considered her choices. She could defend her neighborhood, which she loved and was proud to show off, or she could defer to Paige. The latter was the path of least resistance.

"It's this awesome hiking trail up in the hills. Amazing views," Paige said.

"Okay," Immie agreed.

"Okay," Ro echoed. "But maybe we can get Korean food afterward?"

"Yeah, no," Paige said. "Too many carbs."

"So not yeah," Ro said. "What you mean is not yeah at all."

"Exactly." Paige slung her tennis racket bag over her shoulder, and as she was walking away, she turned around: "You're getting it, new boy."

CHAPTER TWENTY-ONE

Ro

Ro: How much do tampons cost in London?

Kaia: A couple of quid, I think? I'll check Boots later. Why?

Ro: School project

Kaia: LA is soooo weird

Ro: Yup

Kaia: How's Operation Get Home Fast going?

Ro: Stalled out. Any ideas?

Kaia: Beg your dad? Ask your mum? Book a ticket online, take an Uber to the airport and get on one of those rusty machines that fly through the air and cross the Atlantic? This isn't that hard

Ro: I think my mum would kill me

Kaia: How are things with the girl twin?

Ro: Not interested

Kaia: Daft cow. Her loss

Ro: You'd like her. Actually you'd like all of them

Kaia: I only like you and Arun.

Ro: What about your new bloke?

Kaia: He's more a handy appliance than anything else

Ro: As the Americans say, a tool

Kaia: Yeah, except, I mean it literally. I use him as I would a vibrating appliance

Ro: KAIA

Kaia: WHAT? He keeps my wrist from getting knackered & saves me batteries

Ro: KAIA

Kaia: I think belly buttons might be going out of style

Ro: A body part can't go out of style

Kaia: Read in the Daily Mail that people think Kate Middleton doesn't have one and now we've all gone off them

Ro: I still like belly buttons

Kaia: Ask your fancy LA friends for me. Want to see if this has gone global

Ro: Anything for you

CHAPTER TWENTY-TWO

Arch

At night, when Arch couldn't sleep, he lay on his bed and imagined all the things that were above him: the ceiling; Mr. and Ms. Lee and their bichon frise, Pesky; the roof and its kidney-shaped pool; the sky and outer space and the infinite universe. None of this was comforting. The world was already too big, even when he limited his scope to our planet. All those countries and religions and wars and oceans and melting ice caps and microscopic insects—there was too much of everything. He wished he could shrink the world down to the size of Los Angeles, or maybe even to one-half of Los Angeles, to a carve-out that included K-town and Wood Valley and Espresso Yourself and that was it. Keep things small and simple and controllable.

"Ugh, I can't sleep either," Immie called up from the bunk below. They'd been sharing this setup for so long they could read the slump of their mattresses and the sounds of the springs.

"Yeah."

"I'm so claustrophobic," Immie whined, and the words bloomed in front of Arch in a wistful cloud. What he had been feeling was the opposite of claustrophobic. There should be a name for it: the anxiety of excessive expansiveness. "I want to pack up all of my crap and, I dunno, *go*. Drive somewhere. Get out of this place. See the world."

"I love you, Im," Arch said, because he didn't know how to say what he wanted to say, which was something like: *Don't leave. Stay still.* These words weren't fair, he knew. Arch had burdened his sister with too much already—the stupid kiss, yes, but also so much more. The burden of himself and a conjoined life. The burden of sharing this room and this space and this family. The burden of his wanting things small to stay safe when she wanted them big.

He noticed she didn't put an *us* in her runaway fantasy. He didn't blame her.

"I love you, Arch," she said.

"Is it Ro?" he asked, gently.

"Is what Ro?"

"Why you want to run away?"

Immie laughed an uncharacteristically dry, bitter laugh. Not a laugh at all, more like a smoker's cough, which reminded Arch of the fire. They would, in all likelihood, never find out who set it. And this seemed to be one more thing that kept things too big and broad and undefined. Arch felt that they deserved to know who was that angry at Wood Valley. "No."

"Dad, then?"

"No."

Was this the first lie she ever told him? Arch wondered. It felt like it. Or did Immie have a whole secret internal life that he didn't know or understand? That was one of the many prices we paid to be human: the bitter acceptance that we'd never truly know the people we love best. He closed his eyes and thought of Immie lighting a match and dropping it onto a pile of paper towels. Again, it wasn't as hard to picture as it should have been.

"Is it me?"

"Arch!"

"Sorry," he said.

"Don't you ever just want to be somewhere else? Someone else?"

"I don't know. I guess?"

"Do you think all teenagers are filled with this much *longing*?" Immie asked, and as usual, when Immie asked him a question like this or vice versa, he wondered how people who didn't have a twin made it through the world. What did you do if you didn't have someone else to ask *Is this normal*? Did you google? He and Immie had survived the worst of puberty just like this—staying up way too late and talking their way through. "Like, maybe it's a feature and not a bug of being sixteen?"

"So we *are* talking about Ro," Arch said.

"No! I don't mean for another person, though that too, I guess. I mean *longing*, like wanting more. Wanting everything. I want to eat the whole world and then when I'm done, move on to the planets," Immie said, and tears sprang into Arch's eyes. Genetics was a bizarre thing—they were both looking upward and outward at the same time, contemplating the endless unfolding of the universe, having near-identical thoughts at exactly the same time. But that tiny switch in code, the one that made Arch Arch and Immie Immie, and their thoughts were not identical at all. When you drilled down, actually they were the complete opposite.

"I don't think you'd want to eat Uranus," Arch said, and when he felt the bed shake from Immie's laughter, he was glad he reached for the dumb, easy joke. He again felt so sad for all the people in the world who didn't have a twin. His life was infinitely better because he could throw his T-shirts at Immie and say, *Smell this; can I wear it again?*

"Dammit! DAMMIT! DAMMIT!" Arch's dad yelled, as they heard a loud bang and the sound of shattered glass. Arch quickly assessed. There had been no fight precursor, so it was unlikely anything had been thrown. An accident. No big deal.

"Leave it, Dan. I'll get it," his mom said, and she was using her conciliatory, make-peace tone. His mom knew how to de-escalate; they all did. Let her calm him, let this be another unremarkable, forgotten evening in their long slog of adolescence. Let this be only what it is: a glass slipped out of fingers onto a tile floor, a cleanup, a moving-on.

Sometimes, after his parents would fight, on the worst nights when it felt like morning would never come, Arch would find himself enraged at his mom, not his dad. His mom could placate his dad, and her decision not to felt like a choice. Like if Superman flat-out refused to use his powers of flight to save Metropolis. Arch knew this was misdirected anger. His mother was human, entitled to human reactions in the face of irrationality.

Entitled, even, to her own anger no matter how much she chanted and meditated and preached about finding inner peace.

Still. She was the one who got to decide whether they stayed.

"I think it's fine," Arch whispered. "Broken glass."

"Yeah," Immie whispered back.

"Who do you think set the fire?"

"I dunno. Maybe Katy Flore? She literally barked at me last week. Like a dog."

"Poor Katy Flore. Can't be easy being her. Okay, night, ImIm." Arch used the nickname from their early childhood, the one that only slipped out when he needed extra comfort. He pulled his comforter up to his chin, wriggled till he was tight in his bed. "I hope you have happy dreams of eating all the planets."

"Night, Archie," she said.

"Nom-nom," he said.

CHAPTER TWENTY-THREE

Ro

"Have you ever run away?" Ro asked during the ride to school. This was his favorite time of the day, when he sat perched in the middle of the back seat between the twins and let the car's gentle rock wake him up. A little space before the assault of his shiny new school and its shiny new people and his not-so-shiny new life. He'd grown comfortable with Arch and Immie and their morning routine, and for those forty minutes when he loosened his grip on his homesickness.

"So weird. Immie and I were talking about that last night. She wants to get one of those sticks and hang her possessions off it in a bandanna and, like, hitchhike to Mexico," Arch said.

"What are you talking about?" Immie asked. "Who said anything about a stick and a bandanna?"

"You know what I mean. A bindle! Like in the olden days," Arch said. He was driving today, which meant that it was harder for Ro to see Immie's face. He had to use the side-view mirror instead of the rearview and the angle wasn't quite right. He caught only the hint of her profile. Her cheeks were ruddy and creased with pillow lines, and for a moment Ro imagined that he was twenty-five and not sixteen and that she liked him in the way that he liked her, and that they woke up in the same bed every day. This, he realized, was presumptuous even in fantasy, and what bed, he didn't know. Certainly not his canopied one here or the mangy single bed he'd had in London. A bigger bed, a grown-up bed, a next-stage-of-life bed. A bed that would remind him of those people bungee jumping in the posters he stared at in the Underground.

"What olden days? Anyhow, I don't want a bindle or to hitchhike, though Mexico sounds cool," Immie said. "We've never run away, but I've thought about it. A lot."

"A lot?" Arch asked. "Really?"

"Well, yeah, I guess," Immie said, turning to look at her brother. "You haven't?"

"Nope," Arch said.

"I mean, it's not like I'm going to actually *do it*," Immie said.

"I might," Ro said.

"For real?" Immie asked.

"I know my dad's credit card numbers, so I could buy a ticket home. I guess that's not really running away, though, is it? I'd be going home to my mum," Ro said, and Immie turned her head sharply to the right, so through the mirror he wasn't only looking at the curve of her nose, but he could see her eyes, the upward sweep of her thick lashes.

He didn't know what she was thinking and he wished he could ask.

"That's reverse running away. Doesn't count," Arch said, and the jolliness of his voice sounded forced. Ro hadn't meant to turn the conversation serious, and worried that he'd un-earn this morning ride. As soon as Kaia had mentioned the possibility of him buying a plane ticket, it had seemed less like a suggestion and more like a real, implementable plan. She was right that it could be simple: he could get on a plane, watch four movies in a row, and land at Heathrow. There wasn't anything his dad could do once he was more than five thousand miles away.

"Can I come?" Immie asked.

"Mum, what if I just came home?" Ro asked later that night. They were video-chatting, and only after he'd said the words did he realize his miscalculation. He should have done this when he couldn't see her face. Or maybe he shouldn't have done this at all. Stuck with Kaia's idea. Ambushed her at the flat. She would never turn him away.

"Betté, I love you and miss you so much it hurts, but we talked about this."

"No, we didn't," Ro said. They hadn't talked about much, other than an out-of-the-blue "say no to drugs" lecture his mum had given him the night before he left—the result, he suspected, of her consumption of American teen dramas, and which was a waste of breath because Ro had no interest in drugs or even drink, really. Two of his uncles were alcoholics, and so his parents had long made clear he should be extra careful.

Ro was cautious by nature. When he snuck out to meet Kaia, he always left a note, and he made sure they always went to the better Tesco, not the dodgy one too far off the High Street. If someone told him even six months ago that he'd be contemplating stealing his dad's credit card to buy a thousand-pound plane ticket to travel halfway around the world by himself, he wouldn't have believed it.

The only reason why Ro even knew about his dad's—what was the right word? *affair? dalliance?*—with a graduate student was because Arun had overheard his parents talking about it. Ro's mum and dad knew he knew, though he didn't know how they knew he knew, and he assumed they were nothing but relieved that gossip had done the hard work for them. When one afternoon after school Arun had told him what his father had done, it had almost seemed funny. Okay, not funny, exactly, but ridiculous. The idea of his boring, stuffy dad ruining his life over a shag. That was before Ro realized it would ruin his own life too.

He couldn't imagine, if his mum had chosen to tell him the truth, how the conversation would have gone: *So your dad slept with his twenty-two-year-old student and now has to take some random fellowship in Los Angeles to avoid getting the sack.*

Instead, his mum chose to lie, even as they both knew she was lying. Ro wondered if all families were like this. Too scared to say the truth out loud.

Big news, Ro. Your dad and I got simultaneous promotions!

She said it like he should be happy, like the correct response was celebration and congratulations, like it was inevitable that he would leave with his dad instead of staying home with her. "It's tricky, darling, but we'll WhatsApp or something. We'll figure it out. Better for you to go have an adventure in the U.S."

No one said the word *divorce*. No one even said the word *separate*. She did say that being apart from both of them would *give her time to think*.

If he got on a plane to go back home, would that ruin it for her? Could she not think with Ro around?

Ro wondered what Kiran would say. She'd of course been on their mum's side, had told Ro that their mum hadn't so much as lied as omitted critical information. *Wouldn't you have done the same?* she asked, and Ro had to admit that he would have. He'd never been very good at saying the things no one wants to hear. He hadn't, for example, told his mum that he didn't want to go to Los Angeles, that he was as furious at his dad as she was, that he couldn't understand why she'd banish him halfway around the world *with him*. Didn't she used to joke that Ro was only allowed to apply to King's because Oxbridge was too far? Didn't she used to say that he could live at home forever, even when he was married and had his own kids?

"Are you having trouble at your new school?" his mum asked now, her voice thick with worry. "I thought you were making friends."

"It's fine. It's not that," Ro said.

"Then what is it?" Ro wanted to say *Los Angeles isn't*

home. He couldn't say that though, because he'd spent the last three years talking about how he couldn't wait to take a gap year to backpack around the world. He'd even ordered the expanded passport to make room for all his hypothetical extra stamps. Two years abroad in the States was exactly the sort of thing he would have dreamed about until it happened. His mum probably thought she was doing him a favor.

"Nothing. Never mind. Maybe you can come here for the holidays?" Even as he asked this, he knew it was impossible. He would live in a place his mother would never see, another thing that was previously unimaginable. Again, he was being melodramatic. The same way he'd reacted to the fire. He had become such a baby. "Or I could go there?"

"I'm going to Italy with Auntie Priya and Auntie Beth. Girls' trip. And Kiran is getting a Eurail pass with some friends. I think you should stay put and keep your dad company. We wouldn't want him to be alone at Christmas."

Isn't that what graduate students are for? Ro wanted to ask, but instead he kept quiet.

CHAPTER TWENTY-FOUR

Paige

Paige lost another tennis match and she was pissed. She squeezed her fingernails against her palms, the pain a good way to stave off the tantrum. She needed to be careful, check herself. Paige imagined throwing both her racket and a punch, breaking her opponent's nose, watching the red spill out onto the court like an offering. She wanted to scream at her coach, yell "I quit!" and be done with this nonsense, gift herself six more fifteen-minute blocks a day, five days a week.

No. Tennis was carefully chosen, not because of her interest in the sport, which she could take or leave, but by complex analysis with a college advisor. It rounded her out, the advisor said, as if she needed curves to get into the Ivy League.

Paige bent over, hands on knees. She stared at the ground, which was undulating. Her head throbbed, a beat that churned her gut, and she considered the possibility that she might puke right here in front of both teams.

"You okay?" Coach Kho asked, and jogged over. Paige did box breathing, and swallowed bile. She wouldn't display her lunch; she'd already shown enough weakness.

"Yeah. Just a little dizzy," Paige said, and made her way slowly to a bench. "I'm fine."

"Did you eat today?" Coach Kho asked, and Paige bristled. Why was everyone always trying to assign her an eating disorder? If she ate too little, her friends and coach worried. If she ate too much, her parents worried. That she was careful with food, as she was with everything else, wasn't a problem. It was the opposite. A solution. She did not let her weight fluctuate more than three pounds in either direction, sticking to a number that kept her tight but not skinny.

In control.

"Of course. I'm just tired. I was up late studying." Paige had worked on AP Bio until four-forty-five a.m. and then napped until six-thirty, when her alarm went off. When her mom was asked how she managed to juggle so much for *New York* magazine's "How I Get It Done" feature—her full-time law career, two children, the boards of six different nonprofits, nightly appearances on cable news—she had said, "I'll sleep when I'm dead." And it was true that Paige's mom didn't sleep a ton, though the truer answer, Paige always thought, was *lots of paid help*. Paige's dad was never asked how he balanced his film career and two children, because he was a man and men never got asked such reductive questions. Paige suspected if he was asked, he'd answer with some crap about teamwork. That would have been even less true.

No one ever asked Paige how she got it all done because what she accomplished was fundamentally uninteresting to everyone, including her parents, even if it was impressive in its quantity. Her parents were highly accomplished professionals who were very, very busy doing very, very big things, and the same was expected of Paige one day. (Her sister, who was so very, very busy smoking pot and teaching kids to glide down the bunny slope that she hadn't been home for Thanksgiving in three years, somehow got a pass.) At the twins' apartment, they named their plants, and family photos and framed finger paintings from Arch and Immie's preschool years took pride of place on the walls. Sometimes Paige looked at the clean, giant expanse of her refrigerator door and wondered why it never occurred to her parents to display one of her straight-A report cards. As far back as Paige could remember, she'd never made the cut, not even on the fridge reserved solely for the Perrier.

"You're not yourself lately. Your head's not in the game," Coach Kho said. Paige imagined her mind being something wholly separate from her body, that bizarre divide of self that Immie had once described feeling, and she imagined that could come with a certain amount of freedom and efficiency. It would be amazing if she could cut herself at the neck, one clean slice, and send her brain to the library, her body to practice. Maybe even just her forearms.

"Sorry," Paige muttered. Coach Kho stood in front of her Wonder Woman–style, hands on her hips, and leaned in to take a closer look. Was she checking her pupils? Did she think Paige was on drugs?

"Are you sick, sweetheart?" she asked, and the unexpected switch to kindness and concern in that *sweetheart* made Paige's teeth ache. *Sweetheart* was the sort of word she imagined Mrs. Gibson would use before tucking the twins into bed with a hot water bottle and Netflix when they had the flu. *Sweetheart* was a forgiving word, a surrender of expectation. Paige didn't deserve a *sweetheart*, especially not from Coach.

She'd lost.

"I think I need . . ." Paige didn't finish her sentence because she didn't know what she needed. To have won the match and to score one hundred percent on her next bio pop quiz and to get into Yale and be done. Except she wouldn't be done, of course. She'd be starting.

Her legs felt gelatinous. Coach Kho handed her a small bottle of Gatorade and Paige took a sip, though it was green and filled with artificial sugar and not the sort of thing she'd normally allow inside her body. She took another swig and then greedily sucked the rest of the deliciousness down. Maybe she was thirsty. She normally carried around a Hydro Flask to make sure she ingested the seventy-four ounces a day the nutritionist had recommended in middle school, but she'd forgotten it this morning.

God, she was tired. Could she put her head down right here on the bench and close her eyes? Take a catnap? Would that stop the world from spinning?

"I'm going to call your mom," Coach Kho said, and Paige wanted to protest—her mom was in London for a conference on women's rights and her dad was—*where was her dad, again?*—but her eyelids were too heavy. She slipped into sleep, right there on the bench on the sideline of the tennis court, which later, on reflection, might have been even more embarrassing than puking.

"Thank you so much for rescuing me," Paige said an hour later. Immie had left Arch at the cafe, which meant she'd had to drive back to school, pick Paige up, and drop her on the west side at her house before turning around again. "I'm so sorry. I realize this is way out of your way."

"Don't even worry about it," Immie said, and she didn't look put-out. She looked happy to be doing this for Paige. Perhaps this was more penance, but Paige didn't want to think about that right now.

"Seriously. Thank you," Paige said, and she could hear the warbling in her voice, like she was close to tears. Immie reached out and grabbed her hand and squeezed; this only made it worse.

"What happened? You okay, P? I was super freaked out," Immie said. "You never get sick."

"Coach overreacted. She wouldn't let me drive myself home or Uber, and my mom and dad are away, so . . ." Paige cleared her throat. She didn't mention that she could have called Marta, who was paid to be first on her emergency contact list. "I think it was a migraine. Or dehydration. I'm fine."

They had pulled up to the curb, and Paige looked up at her house. Its immensity felt startling from this angle.

There were eight bedrooms; two had been repurposed for her parents' offices, one had been turned into a home gym, and another was a full guest suite with its own separate entrance. When broken down like that, the size had seemed reasonable and necessary. From the passenger seat of the twins' Corolla, though, it felt oafish and absurd, maybe even disgusting.

She wondered if Chase was doing rounds of the neighborhood, and she couldn't decide if that made her feel safer or more vulnerable.

"You here alone tonight?" Immie asked.

"My mom will be home late." Paige made no move to get out of the car. She knew the longer Immie stayed, the worse the traffic would get, and her drive home, which would normally take thirty minutes, would balloon to way over an hour. Still, Immie didn't seem to be in a rush. She felt Paige's forehead with the back of her hand and she shook her head, as if almost disappointed Paige didn't have a fever.

"What if I can't do it?" Paige asked, again looking out the window, though this time at her lawn, at its impossible green slope and the long winding pathway to her front door.

"Do what?"

"All of it," Paige said and waved her hand around to mean *everything*, starting with the getting out of the car, the walking, the closing of the door to the world behind her. The making her way into the kitchen and then the bathroom and then her bedroom. The homework and the SAT prep and the studying and the school magazine and the running for president. The brushing of her teeth and the washing of her face and the application of her prescription acne cream and then a serum and facial oil on top. The waking up tomorrow morning and starting all over again, ad infinitum.

What if she couldn't do that?

"P—"

"What if . . . I can't keep being me?" Paige saw the truth with a sudden, overwhelming clarity: her aggressive overachieving was a symptom, not a goal.

"Now you're really scaring me." Immie unclicked her seat belt and faced Paige. "On a scale of one to ten, how worried should I be?"

"An eight-point-seven, I think."

"I can work with eight-point-seven," Immie said. "Talk to me."

"What if it all falls apart? What if I keep losing matches and failing tests and . . . I don't know. What if it's all too much?" Paige asked. She put her head on the dashboard, which was dusty and would likely leave her with pimples or a hive. She closed her eyes. Stifled a sneeze.

"That's what this is about? First of all, you didn't fail any tests, and even if you had, so what? And what does tennis matter? It's a game," Immie said. "It has no purpose beyond recreational amusement."

"So what? So Yale."

"Yale shmale."

"Tell that to my mother."

"I will," Immie said, and grabbed her phone from the cup holder. "I'll call in to MSNBC right now and remind her that she has an amazing daughter no matter where she goes to college. Honestly, if I had my choice, you'd slum it here on the West Coast with Arch and me. Screw Connecticut."

"But I look so good with a sweater tied around my neck. It would be a shame to waste that superpower," Paige said, and sat back against the seat. She could feel Immie's relief that she was starting to sound like herself again.

Paige was a good actress.

"Dude, you rock every look. It's not fair." Immie's phone beeped.

"Arch is waiting," Paige said. "You should go."

Paige did not want Immie to go. She wanted the two of them to go inside and pop popcorn and snuggle under the cashmere blanket on the couch and watch a romcom. She wanted to forget about school, about the fact that her mom still hadn't called her back, even though she'd left multiple messages on her cell. She wanted to dissolve into coziness and forget about her own unraveling.

"Arch'll understand." Immie's phone beeped again. And then again.

"You're blowing up. I'm at a three-point-six now. I can manage a three-point-six."

"You sure?"

"Go. Seriously. I'm okay." Paige opened the car door, picked up her backpack, which felt heavier than it had this morning, and then threw her tennis bag over her shoulder.

"I love you, P. Call me if you need anything. You know I'm here, right?" Immie asked through the open window. Paige wondered what that actually meant: that Immie was *here* when she was literally in the process of leaving. Wasn't that the definition of *not here*? Immie was going to go home to Arch and the rest of the Gibson family, to eat dinner around a table with other people who loved her and found her interesting. Immie's dad would whip up spaghetti and meatballs, and her mom would make the garlic bread and a salad, and they'd chat and laugh about their days.

Immie would be *there*, not here. Paige couldn't blame her. If she'd had the choice, she'd be there too.

"Of course," Paige said. "Love you too, Im."

She jogged to the front door, her bags pummeling her back, running for no other reason than to prove to Immie that she could. She went inside, and just like that, she was here, alone, again.

CHAPTER TWENTY-FIVE

Immie

"Do you think she's having a nervous breakdown?" Immie asked Arch that night before they fell asleep. These were the memories of her childhood she knew she'd return to long after they'd left this place. The hours spent in this bunk bed, talking in the dark. The comfort of Arch's voice sinking into her from above like the perfect song set to repeat. The way her fingers trailed longingly on the map.

What would happen when they went off to different colleges? Would he forever be the voice in her head? What if she went as far as New York and slipped away into its towering anonymity? What would happen to them then? She didn't know how far she could travel until the tether that bound them snapped.

"A nervous breakdown? Who? Mom?" Arch asked, which was weird. They were usually on the same page. No additional explanation necessary. Tonight had been good. There had been no reason to worry about their mother.

Since the latest blowup, a calm had settled over the apartment. They'd eaten baked ziti, all four of them at the table, phones put away—their mother's rule—and their dad told a funny story about a sales job interview he went to that day that claimed to be for a medical device and turned out to be for a sex toy company.

"I think I'll stick to insurance," their dad said.

"You were probably *vibrating* with excitement at the prospect of making the switch," their mom said, and the twins cracked up.

"I bet the whole thing was pretty *hard* on you," Arch said, and his dad playfully threw a piece of garlic bread at him.

"I think there were some *holes* in your plan," Immie said, and they traded puns like that for fifteen minutes, until Immie said something about "strapping on" and they collectively decided it had gone too far.

It had been a *normal* night, or as normal as a family that joked about sex toys at the dinner table got. The ease of it made all those other bad nights feel like a figment of Immie's imagination. Like the version of her father in her mind was a fever dream, and this guy, the one who threw garlic bread, not vases, and told funny stories, not yelled curses, was her real dad.

"No! Paige!" Immie said now to Arch. "You didn't see her today. She was . . . different."

"She's not having a nervous breakdown. She's probably sick."

"Paige doesn't get sick."

"Everyone gets sick."

"Not Paige."

"You do realize she's just a person?" Arch asked, and he shifted over, causing the whole bed to shake. Immie wondered if, when she finally had her own room, she'd have trouble sleeping, in the way that people from a city couldn't sleep in the country for lack of noise.

"What's that supposed to mean?"

"I think you idolize her, that's all."

"What the hell," Immie said, and she felt an unfamiliar anger rise from her insides. She and Arch rarely fought. Their mom used to say it was creepy how even as toddlers they willingly shared their toys with each other, never grabbing for whatever the other had in hand. And now as teenagers they lived peacefully side by side, or, more accurately, at least at night, stacked one on top of the other.

"Relax. I didn't mean anything. That came out wrong."

"Paige is *our* best friend. Not only mine. *Ours*. You were the one to blow it all up. Not me." Her voice shook with a nascent rage.

"I know, Im," Arch said, quietly now. "I'm sorry."

"I'm not looking for an apology for that! I don't even care about that anymore." Immie kicked at Arch's mattress in frustration. "But don't make it like it's weird that I'm worried about *our* friend."

"It's not weird. But sometimes you put her feelings or her interests above your own."

"Are you serious right now? Think about what you just

said to me." Immie could hear her own hypocrisy—how she said she didn't care about the kiss and then brought it right back up again—but he was a hypocrite too.

"You're right."

"And what's up with this whole pretending like you aren't as desperate as I am to get out of Dodge, by the way? In the car with Ro? And the other day with Paige? Suddenly you're so happy you want to stay in this little room forever? I can't even breathe in here!"

She felt the world above her, Arch on his mattress, the ever-present smell of coffee, a heaviness in her chest. This place was too small, too tight.

"Im?" Arch leaned over the side of the top bunk, and she could make out his upside-down head in the dark, his hair given over to gravity. He looked at her with a sad smile, which was her smile, because they had the same mouth.

"What?" Immie felt tears rush to her eyes, and she couldn't explain them. She didn't even know who she was mad at. Arch? She didn't know how to be mad at Arch. That would be like getting mad at her own leg. Was she annoyed at Paige? Sure, the drive home was long and frustrating, made twice as long by an accident on the 101 on the way back, but they got to have time together today, the kind of quality time that used to be their normal. Paige getting sick, or whatever had happened, had been an unexpected gift.

Paige could have called Marta, but she called Immie. That meant something.

And the Ro thing wasn't worth tears. She'd never be that girl who cried over the boy she couldn't have. She'd fallen for an accent, that was all.

"You know what I was thinking about earlier? Remember when I came out to you?" Arch asked.

"Yeah." Arch had come out to Immie in sixth grade, and it had been so uneventful that Immie hadn't thought of it as Arch "coming out" at all, until six months later, when he reminded her of the conversation and she realized it obviously had been a much bigger deal to him than it had been to her. On a night like this one, the two of them talking in the dark, he'd said what felt to her like out of nowhere and not out of nowhere at all: *Im, I think I like boys. I think I'm gay,* and she'd said, *Of course you are.* Arch later claimed that she'd said the exact right thing, though on reflection she wasn't so sure. She had known he was gay, had always known, in the same way she'd always known he preferred dark chocolate to milk and liked to sleep on his left side, not his right, and in the way she presumed he knew a million things about her that she'd never have to say out loud. To pretend she hadn't known would be a lie and they didn't lie to each other. Still, she could have waited a beat, acknowledged that this was a *moment*, a turning point, even if she hadn't understood it was one yet. Then he'd said, "Don't tell Dad. Or Mom. But especially not Dad."

"I don't know why I was thinking about that," Arch said now, his head back on his pillow. She wanted to say, *Maybe you're ready*, but she didn't because this wasn't like everything else, where she got to push him forward. And maybe she wasn't sure if she was being selfish. Maybe she was the one who was ready. *Screw Dad. When did we vote and elect him king? He's the one who should feel ashamed, not us.* "But I can still hear the way you said it, *Of course you are*, like it was the most obvious thing in the world."

"I didn't mean it like—"

"No, I know, though even if you had, it doesn't matter. Well, it shouldn't matter. You knew. That's what you meant. You just knew. Kind of how I know one day you are going to leave." His voice cracked, and then they were both crying, silently, staring up at their respective ceilings.

"You're going to leave too," Immie said.

"Nah. I'm not. Not like you are. We've never lied to each other, Im. Not about the big things."

"I know," she said, and she thought of her New York City apartment, the one that only existed in the future in her mind. It would be a tiny studio in a sketchy neighborhood and sometimes when she came home there'd be cat piss in the hallway. She'd be cold in winter and hot in summer and keep her books in milk crates and do her laundry at a laundromat six blocks away. But at the end of the day, she'd close her door and be blissfully alone, the only noises the purr of the city—cars backfiring, ambulances whirring, horns yelling. Impersonal noises. Other people's dramas, not hers. She closed her eyes and saw it, this imperfect fantasy that felt so real it was like stepping into a television set.

She didn't know where Arch was in all this. Somewhere else—in LA, probably. She'd feel him, though, the slightest tug at her back. Perhaps Immie wouldn't understand what home meant until she left it.

"Let's not start lying now," Arch said.

CHAPTER TWENTY-SIX

Arch

Arch looked in the bathroom mirror at school in the north wing and thought about college. He squinted his eyes as if trying to see himself two years into the future, to allow himself the daydreams he suspected fueled Immie's days. What utopia did she imagine welcomed them when they left here?

Of course he should get back to AP Bio—he needed to sketch the life cycle of a fruit fly and hand in his lab report. Apparently Wood Valley deemed it essential that he not go forth into adulthood without first understanding that the egg and the larvae stages spanned eight days. Arch lingered, shaped his hair into a mini-mohawk, and then messed it up again. A pimple was growing on his jawline, and he leaned in to pop it.

And of course that was when Jackson walked in on him, up close at the mirror, squeezing a zit. Five hundred fifty kids in this school, and if any other one of them had walked into this bathroom and caught him in the act, Arch wouldn't have cared even a little bit.

"Can I tell you a secret?" Jackson asked, and if he was disgusted, he hid it well. His voice held that conspiratorial tone Arch envied. Arch suspected this was what got Jackson elected president every year. The fact that he made you want to lean in closer, made you feel like you were in on the joke even if there wasn't one.

When Jackson and Paige went head-to-head, Arch had little doubt who would win. Paige might be powerful, but Jackson was magic.

"Sure," Arch said, stepping back, pretending to have been examining nonexistent lint on his shirt. Being shitty hadn't worked to loosen the kiss's grip. Here was the thing though: if you were lucky, you got maybe a handful of exquisite kisses in your lifetime. The exquisiteness didn't mean anything, didn't stretch beyond a single indelible moment. Still, it was a beautiful thing—a perfect kiss. It was a gift to be revisited in your imagination and in your dreams and to be mined later for texture. The feel of the back of Jackson's head and its surprising soft bristle. His lips, soft and hungry. His eyes, soft and hungry too. Kisses like that couldn't be replicated, and even if they could, repetition would kill the perfection.

It shouldn't have been a surprise that the kiss—the singularity of it—had changed everything.

Arch tried to guess what Jackson might say. *I set the fire. I like you. You catch the Lakers last night?*

"I love popping pimples. Like, sometimes I actually wish

I'd break out so I could pop them," Jackson said. Arch gazed at Jackson's clear skin and something flared in his chest. Jealousy and desire and anger and, most of all, an indefinable, unrelenting sadness. "I realize that makes me a freak."

"Not sure that's the thing that makes you a freak. But yeah, gross," Arch said, with a shaky laugh, and now Jackson was somehow even closer, so close that Arch could feel his breath.

"May I?" Jackson asked, reaching up to cradle Arch's chin. Was he going to pop his zit? No, this couldn't be happening. Their kiss had been ill-fated, sure, but the aftermath did not require this level of unsexy intimacy. If this continued, if pus erupted from Arch's face in front of Jackson, he'd never be able to look at him again, no less kiss him. Is this what other boys did together? Drink beer, and talk sports, and pop each other's zits? Arch had never really done the male-friend thing. He'd been happy with Immie and Paige.

"No way, man," Arch said, and reflexively jumped back, not realizing his backpack was behind him on the floor. The fall, like all epic falls did, happened in slow motion—one foot on unstable ground, the other sweeping upward like a comic book character bested by a banana peel. The hand reaching out to catch empty air, a desperate flapping. And then Arch flat on his ass on the gross, vaguely wet bathroom floor.

"Oh my God!" Jackson yelped. "You okay? That was a wipeout."

"Fine." The ground was slimy, and Arch closed his eyes and resigned himself to the fact that when he stood up, there'd be a dirt imprint on his butt. The humiliation pulsed through his body, a wave-like panic. He opened his eyes to Jackson standing over him, his mouth twitching. "You're not. You better not be . . ."

"What?" Jackson said, and held up his hands in mock innocence. "I better not be what?"

"You are! You're laughing at me."

"I'm not laughing at you," Jackson said, but his mouth had given way to a full smile, and his shoulders were shaking. "Really, I'm not. It's just . . ."

"You caught me popping a pimple. I'm on the freaking bathroom floor. There are fecal particles everywhere. This is like a nightmare."

"*Fecal particles*. You said *fecal particles*. Come on, that's not fair." Jackson was doubled over, hysterical now, and Arch felt the stirring of the laughter's contagion. "Okay, I'll stop. Nope. Can't."

"Jackson," Arch said sternly, though it came out lighthearted, as if he had no control of his lips curling upward.

"You know, you're also sitting in urine."

Arch tried to stand up; his foot slipped on something wet and he fell back on his ass. Jackson was laughing so hard now, tears were streaking his face.

"That was pee, wasn't it?" Arch asked, finally giving himself over to the hilarity of the moment.

"Yes. Yes, it was," Jackson said.

CHAPTER TWENTY-SEVEN

Ro

"I thought we could watch a movie tonight," Ro's dad said. He was lying on the couch with his loafers on, and Ro wanted to slap them off. His mother had a no-shoes-in-the-house policy, and though her strict enforcement used to annoy Ro, at the moment he felt aggrieved on her behalf.

"Homework," Ro mumbled.

"Come on, mate. It's Friday night!"

"I'm not your mate." Ro peeked into the refrigerator, which was still too empty. His dad had bought some basic condiments, and there were some greasy leftovers from the takeaway they'd been eating most nights. At home, his mum liked to cook in marathon sessions on Sunday afternoons. She'd pop on the radio and dance around the kitchen as she fried onions, and then all week long the fridge would be packed with Carte D'Or ice cream containers full of home-made food.

"By the way, I won't be home tomorrow evening, so order yourself dinner."

"Where are you going?" Ro didn't want his dad to think him curious about his life, but he couldn't help himself.

"Out for drinks with a colleague." Was that code for *date*? Was his dad *dating* already? His parents hadn't explained the parameters of their separation—oh my God, was his mom *dating* and that's why she wanted Ro halfway around the world? The word *date* started ringing in Ro's ears—*date, date, date*—which felt like an Americanism. Was that what his mom's Christmas travels were about? He closed his eyes and pictured it: his mum and Auntie Priya and Auntie Beth on the pull. No way.

"That sounds delightful," Ro said, injecting as much sarcasm as he could into the words. He looked at his father, who was wearing his plaid pajamas, the same Marks & Spencer pair he always wore, but here on this American couch in this American flat he looked ridiculous. Not a professor of postcolonial and world literature, but a man-child who couldn't even figure out how to throw together a meal. Pathetic.

It was entirely possible his father was going out for a platonic pint at the pub. Did Los Angeles even have pubs? He knew they had swanky hotel bars and clubs with celebrities and paparazzi and juice places, but where did normal people go to have a proper drink? He'd have to ask Immie or Arch. He wasn't going to overreact. It didn't matter what his father did now. His mum needed two years to think. Of course they were getting divorced, and now this new word, one he was surprised to realize hadn't really formed in his mind before, one that hadn't been weighed or shaped for impact, hadn't before been palpated by his tongue like a loose tooth, bloomed: *divorce, divorce, divorce.*

What would that actually look like? His parents *divorced*. Exactly like this, Ro realized.

"We need to start cooking for ourselves," Ro said, turning to his dad, perhaps the first direct sentence he'd said to him since they'd arrived. He was channeling Kaia again, who'd have cleaned the flat and learned to cook and mastered public transport by now. She'd already have been to the beach and let the Pacific Ocean wash over her toes. Lately he'd been more like Arun, passive, letting the world swirl around him. And though he loved Arun, loved how during exam time he shrugged and said, "All I can do is my best, innit," Ro needed a bit more fire right now. "We haven't had a veg in over a month."

Ro had finally unpacked his bags and found those Costco-sized gummy vitamins his mum had tucked inside. He'd been taking one every morning, religiously, as if she could see him, and at night when he brushed, he timed himself with his phone for the full two minutes, like she had always begged.

"I can make Pasta Bake. Do they have Pasta Bake here?" his dad asked. On second look, Ro's father's face seemed tired and haggard, the gross goatee slipping like it knew to be ashamed of itself. Maybe his dad was suffering too, but Ro couldn't dig up any sympathy. He wanted to lift his father off the couch by his pajama lapels, shake him a little. Also, who wears their outside loafers with pajamas *in the house*? What was wrong with him?

"Take off your shoes," Ro said, pointing at his father's feet. "That's disgusting."

"You sound like your mum," Ro's dad said, sounding wistful.

You are not allowed to miss her, Ro wanted to say.

You did this, Ro wanted to say.

"Put on your clothes. We're going to the shops."

"I bet they don't have Pasta Bake," his father whined.

"We need vegetables."

Ro's father nodded, swung his legs off the couch, and stood up. "Fine, but afterward you're watching a movie with me, then."

"Don't push your luck," Ro said firmly, like his mum would have had Ro asked her if he could spend the night at Arun's during the school week. And then he turned his back to his father and started writing a shopping list.

CHAPTER TWENTY-EIGHT

Immie

Immie's life was full of Ro, a constant drum in her ears and a heightening of senses, so when, on a random Friday night at Ralphs, he was suddenly standing right there in front of her, palpating eggplants no less, she blinked a few times to check whether he was real. She knew you couldn't manifest people with your imagination or, more accurately, your inappropriate lust. And yet.

"Do you know how to tell if an aubergine is ripe?" he asked her, as if they had been mid-conversation, as if they had earlier made an agreement to meet up in front of the produce. She blinked again.

"What?"

"Sorry, hi. I should have said hi first," Ro said, and pulled her into a hello hug. She was too flustered by her body being pulled against his that she didn't have time to feel awkward. She noticed that the back of his hair was wet and curled up and a single ringlet separated from the rest of its pack. She wished she could wrap it around her pinkie and tug. Where did these thoughts come from? Was her reaction to him merely chemical? She'd figured he might be like any other allergy: repeated exposure would lessen the reaction. She pictured herself going to the doctor every week, like Adrien Oh had to for his peanut allergy, and each time getting an injection of his scent. Eventually growing immune.

"Hi," she said and smiled. He smiled back. It was nice to see his face in real life again, under these harsh fluorescent lights, even though it had only been a few hours since they'd last seen each other. It felt a little like that time she stopped at the Arco to get gas and there was LeBron James, filling up a Bentley. "What are you doing here?"

He tilted his head to the left, to the person who was obviously his father, even though they shared few features in common. If Ro hadn't been there and Immie had seen only this man tonight at Ralphs, she was sure she'd still have been able to identify him anyway—something about the pull of his mouth reminded her of Ro. The way he looked around the store disoriented and slightly disappointed, as if he were asking himself, *What did I do to end up here?*

"Shopping," Ro said. Immie internally kicked herself. Of course he was shopping. What else did one do at the supermarket on a Friday night? Cruise the rotisserie chickens?

"Me too," Immie said inanely and held up her basket. He leaned over and peeked inside.

"Huh."

"What?"

"I wouldn't have pegged you as a sugar cereal type.

I'd have guessed you were into something more straightforward. Like Fruit 'n Fibre."

"I'm insulted," she said, but she grinned anyway. She didn't want him to think she was a Fruit 'n Fibre type of person, whatever that was. She'd much prefer him to think she was one of those happy Instagram influencer types who took sexy pictures of themselves in a bathtub full of Froot Loops or something. (Not that she'd *ever* taken a sexy picture of herself, within or not within the vicinity of breakfast options.) Still, she liked that he'd considered her cereal choice at all, and let herself imagine for a minute that maybe he sometimes thought about her.

"Don't be. The world needs straightforward people who also indulge in sugar cereals. Where's Arch?"

"Home. Our apartment's kind of small, and everyone was home, and, I don't know, I just needed to get out for a minute by myself, you know? Get some fresh air."

"Because of course the supermarket is a very natural place to get fresh air."

"We also needed milk." She held up her palm for him to inspect her shopping list, sloppily jotted down in pen. She wanted him to understand things about her, that she also casually wrote on her body like he did.

"It's nice to see your face," he said. Her heart stuttered. She scratched at her elbow. Looked down at his cart, which was empty except for a single cucumber, and then back up again. "Well, that was a weird thing to say. But you know what I mean." Ro laughed at himself, confident, undeterred.

What did he mean? She had no idea. Did he like her face in the way that she liked his—that it brought forth in her a strange, unreasonable fondness? That though she assumed he'd prefer the word *handsome*, she thought him beautiful?

No, he obviously did not mean that.

"Introduce me to your friend," Ro's dad said, saving Immie from having to respond. He reached out his hand for her to shake. "I'm Vijay. You go to Wood Valley?"

"This is Immie, Dad. She and her brother have been driving me to school."

"Oh, Immie!" Ro's dad said, overly performative as if he wanted to signal that Ro spoke of her often, which gave her the distinct impression that he'd never spoken of her at all. "I can't tell you how much I appreciate you giving my son a ride. Why don't you two go get some dinner? Celebrate this moment of serendipity."

Ro rolled his eyes, though Immie assumed that was because he thought his dad was embarrassing.

"You want to?" Ro asked, a little shy. Immie pictured herself passing out on the floor of the produce department, only coming to when the vegetable misters came back on. Her explaining her Ro allergy to the EMT, that she had passed out from overexposure.

"I mean, it's kinda late," Immie said to her high-top pink Converse, though it was not kind of late. It was six-thirty p.m. She remembered, suddenly, that she was dressed like a toddler: an old-paint-stained pair of overalls over a striped yellow T-shirt, the comfy clothes that she liked to throw on at home. She wondered what Paige would have been wearing had she been here instead. Of course, Paige probably had never set foot in a Ralphs—Marta did all the Cohen-Chen family's shopping at a west side Whole Foods—but Immie figured if Paige was going to serendipitously (what a great word!) run into her biggest crush, she'd have been wearing tiny shorts and a sports bra, or a cocktail dress, or maybe even the *Fleabag* jumpsuit.

"On me," Ro's dad said, peeling bills from a roll of fifties from his pocket and handing them to Ro. Would Paige be mad? Having dinner with Ro on a Friday night, despite her overalls, would be the closest thing to a date Immie had ever experienced. Not that this was a date. This was a random, casual hangout, before their group hangout on Sunday, when they planned to hike Runyon. Not everything had to mean something. Not everything had to be looked at with a Paige lens.

"Come on," Ro said, grinning. "We should get out of here quickly before my dad figures out he messed up the exchange rate."

"Okay," Immie said, and abandoned her Lucky Charms right there, next to the eggplants.

CHAPTER TWENTY-NINE

Ro

Ro wanted to ask Immie about the paint, and how it had gotten on her overalls, if it was in pursuit of art or house maintenance. He wanted to apologize for his dad, who, before the whole graduate-student affair, he had thought funny and quirky—who used the word *serendipity* in casual conversation?—but now seemed over-the-top. Forty-five-year-old men weren't supposed to be so animated.

"You okay with this place?" Ro asked for the second time. He was nervous.

They had gone to a restaurant a few doors down from the supermarket, which was fancier inside than it had looked from the window. Dimly lit by candles. Cloth napkins. Classical music piped in. The kind of place adults went out to celebrate wedding anniversaries, not the quick bite Immie'd probably signed up for.

"Your dad did hand over a lot of cash," she said, giggling. So she felt it too. Like being here meant they had gotten away with something. It wasn't only the money, of course, though that level of generosity was completely out of character for his father. Usually, he yelled at Ro to take shorter showers, to turn off lights when he left a room, to be economical. *Money doesn't grow on trees, Rohan. Your mum and I work hard to put those ugly T-shirts on your back.*

"How about we do this right: starters, mains, dessert. Everything." Ro reached out his knuckle for a fist bump, and when she tapped his hand, he felt a shiver down his spine.

"In."

"How many people live in Los Angeles, you think?" Ro asked.

"No idea. Why?"

"Just wondering what were the chances of us bumping into each other tonight. I mean, it's like—"

"—'serendipity,'" Immie said.

"I beg you, please don't ever quote my dad. And please don't tell me he seemed nice. Looks can be deceiving." Ro unwrapped the bread perched in the middle of the table carefully, like he was unswaddling a baby. Handed Immie the basket before serving himself. *Eat to the left, drink to the right, sit down, stand up, fight, fight, fight.* The chant his mum had taught him so he'd have proper manners ran through his head. If she saw Ro right now, she'd be proud of the napkin draped on his lap, that he knew which knife to use for the butter.

"Yup. If you met my dad, you'd be like, *Immie, seriously, this is why you fantasize about fleeing the country?*" Immie said, and then, as if horrified, she covered her mouth with her hand. "I shouldn't have said that."

"Why?"

"Please don't tell Arch I said that." Immie looked stricken. At first Ro assumed it was fear, that she was worried Arch would be mad, but on second glance, it wasn't fear. It was shame.

"Of course not. But you can talk to me. I won't judge. Parents sometimes really suck."

Immie nodded, as if deciding about him. He'd already decided about her. If Immie asked, Ro would tell her everything: his dad's affair, their banishment to foreign soil. He wondered if Immie would care if he hopped on the next red-eye home. Maybe she went to fancy adult restaurants all the time with guys, didn't need to repeat silly rhymes to remember what plate to use, that this night was not remarkable to her in all the ways it was to him.

"My dad . . . he's . . . I mean, listen, I don't even talk about this with Paige," she said. Ro kept quiet and waited for more. He could handle an awkward silence, if that's what she needed to gather herself to speak. He watched in suspense as she undid her ponytail, retied it, undid it again. Her hair fell down her back, unruly. Ro couldn't decide which way he preferred. "My dad's unpredictable. Really difficult, you know? Like, one second we'll all be joking around, and then someone will say the wrong thing—and none of us will know it's the wrong thing—and it's like everything changes. Dr. Jekyll, Mr. Hyde. And when it happens, when he gets angry, I get so angry too. It's like contagious or something, and I swear, it's so embarrassing, and I—"

"Hate him?" Ro supplied, in a neutral voice.

"Yeah, exactly. I *hate* him even though I'm not supposed to. I mean, Arch doesn't hate him. I think he'd consider UCLA if he got in. Meanwhile, I literally count the days before I can leave this place. The fact that Arch is all 'shrug, whatever' about our dad, like living with a monster is no big deal . . . Okay, he's not a monster. I should never have said that. But it all makes me feel even worse. What does it say about me that, I don't know, that I have so much rage?"

Ro did not know if Immie expected an answer from him. She had folded in on herself, in what seemed to be part relief and part exhaustion from her rant. She kept her eyes on her bread roll, and Ro wished there was a gentle way to force her to look at him. The anger he'd been feeling toward his own father poured through him now, he could feel it in his hands, which had, without him realizing, curled into fists. Five smiles indented on his palms. It was possible he despised Immie's dad even more than his own.

"It says you're human."

Immie took a sip of water. Her hair was tied back again. Somehow he'd missed the transition back into a ponytail and he was sad about that. She nodded, as if she believed Ro's words. He was not so naive as to think this was actually possible. That he could say something so basic and important and that she'd take it aboard as true.

"Four million. There are four million people in Los Angeles. I don't know why I pretended not to know that earlier," Immie said. She had lifted her eyes finally, and he allowed himself the not-insignificant pleasure of staring right at her. He was used to his back seat view; this one was so much better.

"Four million is a lot of people."

"*A lot* of people," she said. "Sorry about the venting. I guess I really needed to get that out."

Ro thought of his mum's stovetop pressure cooker. How it gurgled and hissed from a tiny black knob at its center and how his dad was afraid to use the thing, because he was convinced it would one day explode all that steam in his face.

He wanted to say *Maybe I'm here, in America, in Los Angeles, in this random posh restaurant, because I was supposed to meet you and listen to you and absorb your anger into mine.* He didn't want to creep her out, though. He knew it was weird of him to elevate a couple of fantastic conversations, daily dreamy looks at her profile, and this strange certainty brewing in his gut, to the level of fate. It was weird of him to assume their fires matched.

Still. Four million people.

He watched as his hand reached across the table to hold hers, a move that was subconscious, manifested out of yearning, not choice, as if it were not his own hand but someone else's. He already knew what she'd do in response: She'd politely pull her own hand away. Rest it daintily in her lap.

Still, he reached toward her, slow, slow, slow. Or maybe it wasn't slow at all. Being around Immie seemed to distort time. When he finally made it, when his thumb gently stroked hers, she surprised him by not pulling away at all. Instead, she linked her fingers with his.

"Hi," Immie said, as if, finally, they had been properly introduced.

CHAPTER THIRTY

Paige

Paige had no idea when she became the sort of loser who spent Friday night home alone watching her mother yuk it up on MSNBC. Her mom had always been busy, but in recent years the #MeToo movement had put her career in overdrive. The second a high-profile actor/director/producer/lawyer/chef/Muppet was accused of harassment, Alexandra Cohen was there to swoop onto a cable news program wearing a red pantsuit and opine on the allegations. Tonight she was talking about the horrific new rules set forth by the Department of Education to better protect students accused of rape. Her mom had a single strand of hair sticking to her sweaty and enraged face, and she must have been making a good point because the other panelists were nodding. Paige liked watching her mother this way. All fired up and on mute.

Of course, Cricket, a senior from the tennis team, was having a get-together at her house near the beach, and though the twins didn't want to go because it was too far west for them,

Paige could have made the effort. She had other friends who would likely be there. Okay, not friends, but acquaintances. People she could have texted beforehand, sent some cute *Are you going?* gif, and then met up with them. She could take and post some selfies at the party, and later she would have come home feeling like she'd done *something*.

No. She needed to focus on bio. She flipped through her notes. If she wanted to get back on track, she needed to double down. Summon her focus. She was used to performing, never understood the kids who had to resort to snorting Adderall or hiring tutors or, worse, that girl Chloe two years ago whose parents paid for her SAT score.

Just do the work, she'd thought. *It's not that hard*.

But a wobbliness had descended on her brain, and her muscles felt heavy and brittle, and every morning when her alarm went off, she'd squander an extra ten minutes she hadn't set aside in her planner to stare at the ceiling.

What could she do to make herself *feel* something? Paige knew all about cutting and vomiting and drugs and the myriad reckless ways teenagers self-soothed. She also knew intuitively those outlets weren't for her. Too icky and dangerous and embarrassing.

She'd have to be more creative. Paige played with the cigarette lighter she kept in her desk drawer for her candles. Flicked it on and off, a nervous habit. She liked the metal scrape against her thumb.

She put the lighter down and called security.

"Tell us what happened again. Start at the beginning," the tall man, Leon, said. He had a curiously eyebrow-less face despite a full head of hair, and a pink scar, like a centipede, on his chin. She didn't need to see his badge, which wasn't a real badge but a plastic toy made by the security company, but he had insisted when he first entered the house. Leon was enjoying a cold glass of iced tea with a lemon slice at her kitchen island. Chase sat next to him, eyes roaming over Paige like a warm bath.

She was wide awake now.

Leon and Chase had already searched the house, every last room and closet, guns raised and pointed at the air. They had made Paige wait behind them until they shouted "Clear!" like in the movies. It had been awesome.

"I was upstairs studying, and I heard a noise. Like a loud bang. I thought I should call you guys. Just in case. I was freaked out." Paige shrugged, in a move she hoped looked coquettish, like she was sorry to have wasted their time, even though they were getting paid to be here and it was literally their *job* to check on her.

Paige was wearing an ivory silk pajama set—long sleeves, long pants, and the shirt kept slipping off her shoulder. She wished she had changed first before making the call, put on something that showed a bit more skin, and she would have had she thought any of this through beforehand. Instead, she had dialed on a whim, and now they were here, and she wondered what was going to happen next. She couldn't remember the last time she felt such anticipation.

"That sounds scary," Chase said like he meant it. A little

paternal. She looked at his hand. No ring. He might actually be someone's father.

"Yeah, it was." She wished she'd poured herself a drink. Nothing alcoholic, in case later they found out she was underage. A cup to wrap her hands around, a prop to add gravitas to her charade.

"Where are your parents?" Leon asked.

Paige held up her palms, and at least this wasn't an act. It was impossible to keep track of them.

"I could check the calendar." On the side of the fridge, Marta kept a calendar that color-coded her parents' travels. Blue for her dad. Green for her mom. Each month an ocean. She made no move to get up and look. No one really cared anyway. The only relevant detail was that they were not here.

"Do you want us to call them? Just to let them know we checked everything out?" Leon picked up his pencil, as if suddenly remembering he was supposed to be on duty. He'd been comfortable on the stool, taking a load off after a long day. Paige bet he was itching for that beer she offered and that he'd refused.

"Nah. It's okay. I don't want them to worry."

"My guess is the house was settling, or maybe something fell somewhere—that happens sometimes, nothing scary. No signs of forced entry, and like you said, all the doors were locked, the alarm was on. I think you're safe here," he said, getting up to leave. He took a last wistful look at the iced tea.

"You *think* I'm safe?" Paige asked, again with fake panic.

Of course she was safe. This house was a fortress. At night, when the alarm was set, the downstairs was zigzagged with crossbeams of yellow light, like something out of the *Ocean's 11* franchise. And the fortress was set inside a gated community. So many barriers to entry.

Paige wasn't ready for them to leave yet. Obviously nothing was going to happen between her and Chase, at least not tonight—there was no scenario she could imagine where that was possible—but this didn't feel over. She felt alert, and excited, like when she was little and would sneak a matchbox to the bathroom to flick lit matches into the toilet.

She had done something naughty and would not be caught.

"Of course you're safe," Chase said, and he put his hand on hers. From the outside, it looked like an innocuous, comforting gesture—Leon was busy guzzling his drink anyway, not looking at them, a man eager for caffeine—but Chase's pointer finger lingered, traced hers from tip to knuckle. She looked up, drew in her breath, her stomach somewhere near her toes. Chase was staring right at her.

Paige could feel the blood rushing through her veins, cold and active, alert, alert, alert. This close up, Chase looked older than she thought he was. Maybe he was closer to thirty, or even thirty-five. Too old for her, too old, even, for her older sister.

What was Violet doing right this second? Paige imagined her high at a party, dancing with her eyes closed, not a care in the world. She certainly wasn't thinking about Paige, probably hadn't thought about Paige once since she'd left three years ago.

Chase had the tiniest bit of silver at his temples. A line across the middle of his forehead like an em-dash. She wanted to trace it.

Why would anyone snort Adderall when they could do this instead? Paige thought, and her insides shivered.

CHAPTER THIRTY-ONE

Arch

Arch couldn't stop looking at his phone. Jackson had sent him a gif: a baby giraffe slipping in mud. No message. Only the gif playing on repeat, over and over.

He wrote back: funny

Delete.

He wrote back: hey

Delete.

He wrote back: it was fun laughing with you today

Delete.

He wrote back: you

Delete.

He wrote back: I should slip in the bathroom more often

Delete.

He wrote back: I hope I looked half as cute as this giraffe when I fell

Delete.

He wrote back: what are you doing right now?

Closed his eyes. Hit Send.

Jackson responded immediately, as if he too had been looking at his phone, watching that poor giraffe slip again and again. God, Arch hoped not, because then he would have seen the three dots appear and disappear. How could Arch have forgotten about the three dots?

Jackson: My brother was here playing Xbox but just went home, since he has an 8:30 bedtime. Wild Friday night. You?

Arch: Even more wild over here. Reading in bed

Jackson: Sounds nice, actually. Not fair that you know what my room looks like but I don't know about yours. Describe it to me

Arch hesitated. Jackson was always so comfortable, so forward. Of course, Jackson had kissed Arch and not the other way around. Jackson had no problem writing something like *Describe it to me*. The command wasn't even preceded by some three-dot waffling.

> **Arch:** I sleep on a bunk bed. Share with my sister, which I realize is the least cool thing I could have written
>
> **Jackson:** Cozy
>
> **Arch:** We have a small two bedroom apartment, so

He didn't know why he did that. Always put the least attractive foot forward with Jackson. Jackson already knew he didn't have a lot of money. Why feel the need to remind him? Why would it even matter? Just because Jackson lived in a castle not far from Paige's didn't mean he expected everyone else to. Arch could have mentioned the posters on the wall, the books on the bookshelf, the Polaroid photos of Immie and Paige and Arch through the years clipped to the fairy lights that Immie had strewn across the room.

> **Jackson:** Not a bad deal. Your sister is pretty cool
>
> **Arch:** You're right. She is pretty cool

So Jackson liked Immie. Arch awarded him a thousand gold stars on the sticker chart in his mind.

Jackson: I'm jealous. I've always wanted a twin

Arch: Really?

Jackson: Hell yeah. My parents are 🕊 Would have been nice to have someone to walk through it with. Maybe I'd be less 🕊 myself

Arch: You seem pretty well adjusted to me

Jackson: That might have been the nicest thing you've ever said to me

Arch: The only nice thing I've ever said to you

Jackson: That too

Arch: You are welcome to borrow Immie anytime, so long as you give her back

Jackson: Wait, are you top or bottom bunk?

For a second Arch thought this might be a loaded question, and then decided he was reading too much into it.

Arch: Top

Jackson: Have you ever fallen off?

Arch: Once. Immie pushed me

Jackson: Hurt yourself?

Arch: Only a bruised ego. Like today

Jackson: Sorry not sorry I laughed at you

Arch: I feel for that poor giraffe

Jackson: The cutest giraffe! Hey Archer?

Arch: Yeah Jackson

Jackson: We're friends, right? For real?

Arch: Yeah. Course

Just like that, Arch, who had spent the last two months trying to hate Jackson, officially gave up. Of course they were friends. He remembered that one time in chem last year when he cut his finger on a broken beaker and Jackson ran and got paper towels to clean up the blood and then escorted him to the nurse's office, the whole time distracting him with a funny story about the time he went to Comic-Con and had backstage passes, so Arch wouldn't look down and freak out. Arch ended up needing stitches. Jackson had texted him silly gifs then too, though those were of scary wound scenes from horror films.

Jackson: Want to come over and play Xbox sometime?

Arch: Yeah, sure

Arch rolled onto his back and closed his eyes. He thought about Jackson's lips and big hands gripping the back of his neck. He refused to think about Paige, or even Immie, about the mess that moment had made that still hadn't been fully cleaned up. He couldn't bring himself to regret it.

Friends. He could do that.

CHAPTER THIRTY-TWO

Immie

"Wait so you, like, went on a date with Ro?" Paige asked, confused, only the slightest edge to her voice. They were on side-by-side recliners in Paige's backyard. Arch was lounging on a narwhal-shaped pool float. A pizza had been ordered. An almost perfect Saturday afternoon.

"No. It wasn't. I mean, I ran into him at Ralphs. And then his dad sent us to get a bite. No big deal." Immie, of course, wasn't going to mention the hand-holding. Which had been brief and also the best two minutes of her entire life. "I was wearing my overalls that have the paint. Trust me, it wasn't a date."

She shouldn't have said *trust me*.

Immie doth protest too much, she thought.

Things had gone too far. Immie could see that now. She and Ro had texted back and forth all morning. Last night, when she closed her eyes, she thought of his fingertips, the thrill of their intertwined hands. She'd reel it back. Ro might have felt once in a lifetime, but so did Paige. So did afternoons like this one.

Moments when Immie thought she couldn't live another day in her apartment with her father, when she was willing to blow it all up—her life, college, her future—Paige and Arch were the only things keeping her from boarding a midnight bus to New York. She needed this tether.

"What was Ro's dad like? Is he as cute as Ro?" Paige asked.

"No. He was normal-looking. Same charming accent, though."

"I think I like older men." Paige threw this out there, like she threw most things out there. Like a trial balloon.

"Ro's not older." Immie didn't add that he was born in February—February seventh, to be exact—so he was technically one month younger than Paige and three months older than Immie and Arch. She didn't want Paige knowing she was collecting information like that.

"I make an exception for the otherwise perfect for me."

"Fair," Immie said, and thought about how this silly, impossible situation was almost entirely of her own making. She thought of Ro's face with longing—the sharp cheekbones and jawline, his lashes and lips, his unremarkable and yet somehow distinctive forehead. A worrier's brow.

Paige, lying there, in her giant sunglasses and two-piece bathing suit, looked perfect, which was absurd because no one was perfect. After all these years, Immie was still not immune to her best friend's beauty. She stared at Paige, took in her golden, shaved-smooth legs, her toenails recently pedicured and painted a matte black, the way her hair hung as if recently blown out at Drybar. It hadn't been, though—Immie had seen Paige swim in the pool, had watched her hair turn smooth by the sun.

And, of course, it wasn't fair to Paige to reduce her to her looks. She was smart and funny and confident and loyal and determined and honest and independent, and Immie felt an overwhelming surge of love for her best friend. No, she wasn't perfect—Paige could be too aggressive and pushy and entitled. And yet how lucky that Paige had picked them, out of all the kids at Wood Valley. How lucky that they had instantly clicked, and with the notable exception of this summer, had never, even momentarily, unclicked. How lucky that she got to be here on a Saturday afternoon, in this beautiful backyard with this beautiful person and her beautiful brother soon to be eating beautiful pizza. When they left the apartment earlier, her parents had been sitting on the couch watching TV, her mom's feet in her dad's lap, the other day erased into the ether.

All calm on the home front.

In so many ways, she was lucky.

Immie considered pleading her case. Telling Paige the truth. Not about the kiss—that wasn't her truth to tell—but about the fact that she'd developed real feelings for Ro. Maybe she'd beg her best friend to step out of the way, this one time, for this one particular boy. Paige might be manipulative but she wasn't greedy. She would understand.

"Why are you looking at me like that?" Paige asked. No,

the ground beneath them was too shaky. She couldn't risk it. Paige reminded her that her life was bigger than that little room she shared with Arch, bigger than her apartment and her dad's anger and her mom's fear, big enough that she was allowed to be hungry for the wider world. Without her, she might get stuck and suffocate to death in K-town.

"Like what?"

"I don't know. Like you can't decide if you want to kill me or eat me or maybe like you want to kill me and then eat me," Paige said.

"I have been known to dabble in cannibalism."

"I bet I'm delicious." Paige grinned wolfishly, and then licked her own arm. This was another reason Immie loved Paige. When you looked at her, you didn't expect her to have this hidden layer of weird. "Gross. I taste like sunscreen."

"I love you, you know that, right?" Immie asked, and reached out and squeezed Paige's hand.

"I mean, how could you not?"

"We'll be friends forever and ever no matter what?"

"Well, not if you chop me up into a million pieces and eat me first."

"I wouldn't eat you entirely. I'd share you with Arch," Immie said.

"I get her thighs," Arch shouted from the pool.

Paige lifted her leg, held it aloft for both Immie and Arch to admire.

"Wouldn't be the worst way to go," she said.

"Where are you from in London?" Paige asked Ro. She played tennis five days a week and had a trainer on weekends, and was therefore at this point in the hike, unlike Immie and Arch, still capable of speech without sounding winded. Ro was too, apparently, and so the two of them kept up a steady chatter while the twins lagged behind and eavesdropped.

"You know London well?" Ro asked.

"Of course. It's been about a year since I've been back though. I miss it," Paige said, and though Immie usually admired Paige's ability to sound like a world-weary thirty-year-old trapped in a sixteen-year-old's body, she bit back her surge of envy. Immie had never been to London. Immie hadn't even crossed the border to Tijuana. She had been on an airplane exactly three times in her life, to visit her grandparents in Minneapolis. She remembered the novelty of snow on the ground and seeing her breath smoke in the air and how her mom bought them winter coats from Old Navy special for the trip. Last time they went, her dad picked a fight on the plane about whether her mom had remembered to pack his gloves and how she was an idiot and forgetful and could never do anything right. Of course, they found the gloves when they landed, in her father's suitcase neatly folded next to his sweaters. On the flight home, Immie looked longingly at the emergency exit door and wondered what would happen if she pulled the lever.

Immie only knew London from movies and could name exactly one neighborhood: Notting Hill. She wouldn't have been shocked if Ro turned out to be from there, which seemed, at least from the film, like a pastel-colored fantasy, not a real place, and therefore entirely capable of making a Ro.

"I live in Highgate. Lived. Live," Ro said.

"So this move isn't permanent?" Paige asked. "Did your parents get divorced or something?"

"Paige!" Immie said.

Ro was wearing a baseball hat and sunglasses, and Immie suspected he didn't realize he was rocking the undercover celebrity look so common in LA. A hiker did a double take as he passed. When Immie caught a glimpse of herself in the mirror these days, she often did the same thing. *Who's that?* she'd think, an entire beat before recognizing herself. Part of the problem was that in her mind's eye she still looked like a child and not like the almost-woman she had become. But mostly it was that Immie had the strange sense that she wasn't an integrated human being like other people were. She was instead a brain floating through the world, and her body was Post-it-noted on as an afterthought. Occasionally, she'd look down and think, *Oh right, I have nice boobs now.*

Paige, of course, was Immie's opposite. She *lived* in her physical self, so much so that, apparently, shirts were optional. Today, she wore a black sports bra with intricate webbing stretched across her sculpted back, and high-waisted black yoga pants. The three inches below her ribs were on display like a tiny peep show. Immie had never thought about that expanse of skin and wondered what hers might look like. Freckled, probably. She had also never thought of that part of the body as particularly sexy, but glancing at Paige, she realized that it was.

Why? Because it was random and generally unavailable.

Paige had this weird shoulder-less top, and every time she wore it, Arch would point to the holes and say in a mock-scold, *You had one job, shirt. One job.* Immie secretly loved the idea of a body part highlighted like a sentence in a book, and wondered what other parts of the body became sexy by virtue of making an unexpected appearance. She tried not to think about whether Ro was enjoying Paige's below-ribs.

"Sorry!" Paige said to Ro and shrugged, and then turned the shrug into an arm circle, to make the hike more aerobic. "Immie thinks I'm too nosy."

"You remind me so much of my best friend Kaia back home. It's eerie," Ro said.

"I'll take that as a compliment," Paige said.

"It is," Ro said. "She's the best. Though admittedly I'm a little scared of her."

"Write this down, Arch. Those are the words I want on my tombstone: 'Paige Cohen-Chen was the best, though admittedly, I was a little scared of her.'"

"On it." Arch stopped to tie his shoe, which Immie suspected was really to catch his breath. Good. She needed the break too. This was why Immie didn't exercise. She didn't like to feel her heart pounding in her chest, her breath catching and heavy, her skin wet and unruly. Why would she want this reminder of her icky human-ness? She preferred not to think about Kaia, who was probably beautiful and strong like Paige. She preferred not to think about how no one would ever say she was the best, except for maybe Arch, and that's only because they had shared a womb. She hadn't earned it on merit.

She looked at Ro's hands, and then away again. Immie wondered if she had made the whole thing up. Maybe they had never touched at all.

"Let's pick up the pace. You guys are slowing me down," Paige said.

CHAPTER THIRTY-THREE

Arch

"Oh wow," Ro said when they reached the top and were rewarded with a vista of the whole city, clusters of tall building and little houses and the disorganized, smoggy sprawl.

"Oh crap," Paige muttered, and at first Arch thought she meant the view, and her disloyalty surprised him. Though he and Paige loved and belonged to different LAs with the giant exception of Wood Valley, they shared a hometown pride. And then he spotted Jackson, who was standing next to his little brother a few feet away. "Who invited him?"

"Hey. What are you doing here?" Jackson asked, friendly, as if he hadn't heard Paige, as if he was welcome anywhere. His little brother looked like a mini version of him, down to their matching Nirvana T-shirts and fashion sneakers.

"What are *you* doing here?" Paige shot back, though there was no bite to her voice. Her anger at Jackson seemed performative. Maybe even borderline flirtatious. A show probably for Ro's benefit. Was Paige hurt by their breakup? Arch really didn't know. She was too hard to read.

"As you know, Jagger and I usually come here every Saturday morning, but couldn't yesterday. So today it is. I couldn't go a whole week without hiking with my little man," Jackson said and tousled the kid's hair, which was also performative. And, Arch had to admit, adorable. Then he waved at Arch and Arch felt self-conscious. They were friends now. It had been made official by text. Waving was fully allowed.

Arch was wearing track pants and a ratty T-shirt and a beat-up pair of hiking boots that had turned a dusty brown on the way up. He hoped he didn't look as out of breath as he felt.

"How old are you, mate?" Ro asked, crouching to eye level with the kid. "You can make it up the whole mountain yourself? That's amazing!"

"I'm five," Jagger said. "It's not that high. Though sometimes I get worried about falling over the edge. Jack walks on the outside, though, so it's less scary." The boy was serious and intense, one of those old-man little kids, not how Arch imagined Jackson was at that age.

"He's super brave," Jackson said. "Like, epically."

"If I don't whine on the way up, Jack takes me for chocolate chip pancakes," Jagger said. "And then after he lets me play Dance Dance Revolution at his house."

Arch felt Immie watching him. He turned toward the ledge, pretending to take in the view, because for once, he didn't want her to read his face. He hadn't mentioned the texting with Jackson, or even his humiliating fall, which under normal circumstances would've made for a funny story.

"My mom is in the hospital," Jagger said, apropos of nothing. "She might die forever."

"Nah, bud, please don't say that. She's fine. Promise. She'll be home soon," Jackson said, clasping the kid on the shoulder, and then above his head, mouthed to the group the word *rehab*. "She went to, like, a mommy school to become a better mommy. That's all."

"My dad has been married four times, and I'm his fifth kid, and Jack is from his third marriage, so my nanny doesn't have to let me go to his house. But she does anyway because he's my favorite. His mom is only my third favorite of the other moms though," Jagger said.

"Okay, Jag, I think we should probably get going," Jackson said, widening his eyes at Arch, which made Arch laugh, and then took the little boy's hand. "We need to work a bit more on what's appropriate to share with other people, little man."

"TMI again?" Jagger asked.

"Yeah, TMI," Jackson said, and laughed nervously. And then to the group, not to Arch specifically, but to Arch and his friends, he added: "See you later."

Arch had so many questions. He knew that Jackson's dad had a bunch of ex-wives and that Jackson had a slew of half- and step-siblings, and every Christmas his dad rented a yacht for all of them to cruise around the Mediterranean, even inviting any new husbands who might have married into the mix. (Last year, when Jackson had explained this to Arch during chem, all he'd said was *It's so dysfunctional, dude. You don't even know.*) But Arch had snagged on the idea of a yacht, and hadn't given much thought to what it must be like for Jackson to be a part of a constellation of families, to have to find your place among so many randomly interconnected people.

In the second grade, Arch had been assigned the task of making a family tree, and it had taken him ten minutes. He used a single poster board.

"Wait!" Arch heard himself call after them. Not a choice so much as a reflex. "Does Jackson actually play Dance Dance Revolution with you?"

"Of course! He's really good!" Jagger said.

"I'm not just good, I'm inspired," Jackson said. "Tell him!"

"He's inspired!" Jagger called out, and then turned toward Jackson. "What does *inspired* mean?"

"Nerd," Paige said.

Nerd, Arch thought warmly.

"Good to know," Arch called back, and when he turned around to see Immie and Paige and Ro, but mostly Paige, staring curiously at him, he pretended not to notice.

CHAPTER THIRTY-FOUR

Ro

And there it was again. *Fire, fire, fire.* Ro was in women's studies, sitting next to Immie, and in robotic movements that mirrored the robotic voice, they both rose and followed their classmates out the door. Unlike last time when everyone assumed it was a false alarm, this time, everyone assumed the opposite: that they were all going to die.

By the grace of God, or a semiconscientious arsonist, half of the Wood Valley student body was currently off campus for Fall Giving Day, and so they made their way down the halls with plenty of space. No stampede. No pushing. A gentle jog through the already-open doors.

"Do you smell smoke?" Immie asked. She seemed to be the only calm person there—what was it with these American girls being so good in a crisis?—and he wanted to grab her hand again. He did not feel calm. He felt like Ubering to LAX.

"I don't think so."

"Me neither. I bet it will turn out to be nothing." The fire engines roared in the distance, faster this time, Ro thought. The sirens were even more unnerving than the alarm, as if they were the calamity itself arriving.

"Is this an American thing? Schools constantly being set on fire?" They were outside now, and Ro reflexively gulped in the oxygen. They squinted at each other in the harsh sunlight, and the day's heat felt like hands pressing down hard on his shoulders.

"Not really. I mean, we had cancellations last year because of wildfires, but never arson."

"I forgot about the wildfires." Ro was aware that his fear was probably unattractive. If he had won any points with Immie the other night at dinner, he'd likely lost them now. He was a wimp. There was no use denying it.

"Earthquakes too. You knew about the earthquakes, right?" Immie asked.

Ro shuddered, and Immie laughed.

"This time it was near the science labs," a redhead standing behind them said. She reminded Ro of a doll his sister had when they were little—pigtailed yarn for hair, magic marker freckles, button for a nose.

"Arch and Paige have bio now." Immie's voice was low, too calm. Not the same voice as earlier, when she cheerfully led him down the hall. She stood on her tippy toes, put one hand on his shoulder for leverage. She scanned the crowd.

"That's the other side. Come on." For the first time since Ro'd arrived in LA, he knew where he was going without having to consult the map in his mind. The science wing was on the west side; the closest emergency exits—which, yes, he had taken the time to memorize after the first fire—opened onto the senior parking lot.

He grabbed Immie's hand. This time, they ran.

As soon as Immie spotted Paige, she dropped Ro's hand, as if it were something disgusting or embarrassing, maybe both. Ro felt the slight somewhere behind his left shoulder blade, like he'd been hit with a dart.

"Where's Arch?" Immie demanded, panting and bent over.

"I keep telling you that you need to do more cardio," Paige said with a placid coolness.

"Where's Arch?" Immie asked again, making her panic clearer, as if she assumed Paige had missed it the first time. Paige hadn't missed it, of course. Paige missed nothing. Even Ro knew that.

Ro often suspected that there were complicated dynamics at play with his new friends—he knew from experience that groups of threes could be tricky—but he didn't have the courage to ask any of them what the deal was. He could maybe text Immie one day after school and say something like *hey what's up with Paige being all passive-aggressive with you?* But that seemed mean. He didn't want to stoke the flames of whatever minor drama existed between them, especially because he also sensed so much love.

"I don't know," Paige said, again so casual, as if it were neither here nor there. Like the building was not literally on fire and Immie's brother could still be inside. "I'm sure he's fine."

The firefighters had set up a barricade, shepherding the students back a safe distance in case a window blew. Ro didn't see plumes of smoke. He'd heard that Wood Valley had put new sprinklers in the bathrooms. Maybe they had done the trick.

Ro cupped his hand over his eyes and scanned the crowd. Paige was wearing sunglasses, and this pissed him off too. How had she the presence of mind to grab her backpack when they evacuated? Before, her fearlessness felt badass. Now, it felt callous.

"Over there!" Ro pointed to Arch, who was only a few feet away, talking to Mrs. Gibson. Ro had forgotten that the twins' mom was here too, and it made him consider their dad, and what it must have been like for him to get the emergency calls from school. Mrs. Gibson had her arm around Arch and was kissing his head, and Arch looked like he was pretending to be annoyed about it. Immie jumped up and sprinted over to them, and then they were a huddle of three. Ro watched them for a minute, thinking of his own mum and Kiran, and then he looked over at the firefighters, who made him feel claustrophobic in their big bulky suits. He thought of the way Immie had dropped his hand like it was a gum wrapper.

It was only one in the afternoon. If Ro wanted to, he could catch the six-thirty red-eye home.

CHAPTER THIRTY-FIVE

Paige

Of course Paige saw Immie holding Ro's hand. And now Immie was over in that little bubble with her mom and her brother, and she pictured them all at the dinner table tonight talking about the fire and where they had been when the alarm went off and how worried they each were about the other. Paige thought about how her evening would go: she'd reheat the dinner Marta had made for her—four ounces of chicken breast, no more, no less, with steamed broccoli—and eat it alone at the kitchen island. No one would ask if she was okay.

The itchiness under her skin was back. She felt a burning in her throat, and the pressure of water behind her eyes, and she wasn't sure what she wanted to do more: cry or scream. Paige would do neither of those things—Paige Cohen-Chen did not cry or scream, especially without an articulable reason—and she swallowed down the surge. Funny how she felt so numb the other day, and now all of a sudden she was on emotional overload. Disregulated.

Paige tugged at her shirt, which had an outrageous froufrou floppy bow. Why was it always so hot in fall in Los Angeles? Why was she wearing the exact wrong thing? She was sixteen and it was ninety-eight degrees out and still, this morning, when she looked in her closet, she opted for polished and prissy. Who did she think she was fooling?

"You all right?" Ro asked. Her face felt hot, and she wondered if it had gone blotchy like Immie's always did. Her fingers felt swollen and tight, like her throat. Maybe she was having an allergic reaction, but, and this was something she was inexplicably proud of, Paige was not allergic to anything.

"I can't breathe," she said. When the alarm went off, she had picked up her bag and filed outside. At no point had she felt even the slightest prickle of fear, which had been disappointing. Paige liked adrenaline.

"Asthma?" Ro asked. Paige shook her head. Of course she didn't have asthma. Paige was still young and lucky and stupid enough to believe that her strong constitution was a sign of virtuousness, as if it was something she had earned, like her good grades.

Ro took her by the elbow and led her to a grassy area away from the crowd. He knew her well enough to know that she wouldn't want anyone to see this. "Sit down. Head between your legs."

Paige was in no position to refuse. The air had turned solid in her mouth, too thick to pass in or out. She closed her eyes and felt Ro gently rubbing circles on her back.

"Just breathe," he said. "If it's really bad, nod, and I'll call over one of the medics."

"No. Don't." So she could speak. That was good. She felt her lungs open, and the first hit of oxygen made her dizzy. They sat that way for a few minutes, Paige breathing with a deliberateness breathing didn't usually require.

"I'm okay. This just happens sometimes," she said. Paige didn't really know what happened sometimes, and whether *sometimes* was overstating things. This had happened twice. She was *fine*.

"Panic attack," Ro said. He squatted next to her, capable and handsome. He had the brow of a character from one of her mom's vintage romance novels. The men on those covers were always on high alert. A captain on the high seas.

"Yeah, no," she said, and Paige watched as Ro tried to deconstruct this. If she weren't currently malfunctioning, she'd have laughed.

"So . . . no?"

"No. Not a panic attack." Paige didn't say what should have been obvious. She didn't suffer from allergies or asthma or, God forbid, panic attacks. At least thirty minutes had passed since the alarm had gone off, which means that she should have been changed and ready for PE. She pulled out her phone, stared at the empty lock screen—not even a text from her mom checking in—and put it away.

"These fires are scaring the crap out of me," Ro admitted.

"You're such a cinnamon roll."

"A what?"

"Nothing."

"Seriously? This doesn't scare you? Not even a smidge?"

Ro asked. *Smidge.* Paige smiled at his old-lady word. Unfolded herself to standing.

"No." And it was true. Paige wasn't afraid of fire or of home intruders or whatever else normal people seemed to be afraid of. She looked over at Immie and Arch and Mrs. Gibson again. Immie was talking with her hands, like she always did, and Arch was listening to whatever she had to say, rapt, like he always did, and Mrs. Gibson couldn't stop touching them. Smoothing Arch's hair, squeezing Immie's shoulder. Paige's stomach lurched in a toxic stew of envy and the certainty that one day soon she would lose both of her best friends. "Anyhow, I don't even think there was a real fire. Just some smoke in a bathroom. I heard someone left a lit match in the garbage can."

"There's no smoke without fire," Ro said, and Paige wondered for the first time if maybe he was a little slow. She wasn't into slow. "That was a joke."

"Oh."

"Come on. Looks like they're letting us go back to class."

"Wood Valley lives another day," Paige said.

"What?"

"Nothing," Paige said again, though this time she didn't try to hide the disappointment in her voice. Why couldn't anyone keep up with her?

CHAPTER THIRTY-SIX

Arch

Arch: Why would anyone want to burn down the school?

Jackson: Honestly, I get wanting to burn down the school, but next time I'd prefer if they'd wait till I wasn't in the building

Arch: I don't think they meant to hurt anyone

Jackson: Of course you don't think that

Arch: No seriously. This last one was right under the new sprinklers so it was out before it even really got started

Jackson: Maybe

Arch: If you really wanted to burn the place down, you'd do it behind the auditorium where they store all the drama stuff

Jackson: So you've thought about this

"Who are you texting?" Immie asked from the bunk below.

"No one," Arch said.

"I can hear you smiling."

"You cannot hear me smile. That's not a thing."

Immie craned her neck to get a better look.

"Fine. I'm smiling. Just a random TikTok." Arch didn't know why he lied. He was allowed to talk to Jackson. He was even allowed to be friends with Jackson. This wasn't a secret so much as a private savoring.

"Whatever," Immie said, and went back to her phone. She was tapping her screen. Who was she texting? Probably Paige.

Arch: Were you scared today?

Jackson: A little

Arch: Me too

Jackson: I would have saved you

Arch: You were in econ

Jackson: So you have my schedule memorized

How quickly they had moved from friendly banter into flirting. Because that was what this was, wasn't it? Flirting? Arch closed his eyes and imagined the kiss. He put his finger to his lips, and then wondered if Immie could hear this too.

Arch: Nah

Jackson: You were in bio, which you have before PE

Arch: I see what you're doing here

Jackson: And after school, you had a shift at Espresso Yourself

Arch: Um

Jackson: Am I creepy yet?

This was flirting. Even Arch knew that. His body felt warm and light. A giddiness surged through him, and he shook once with it. Immie surely felt it below him, and he wondered if she'd be able to decode this message: Arch bursting with joy.

Arch: No not creepy. Cute

Jackson: Oh shit. Just got an email. School canceled tomorrow

Arch: I thought the fire wasn't that bad

Jackson: It wasn't. Apparently there's another one?

Arch: WTAF?

Jackson: A giant wildfire in the canyons, spreading fast

Arch: Are you in evac zone?

Jackson: Not sure. Gotta go check. Be safe

Arch leaned over the side of the bed, where his sister looked back at him, always ready.

"Yeah, I saw it. I'm calling Paige right now to make sure she's okay. I bet her parents aren't home, and she's not too far from those hills," Immie said, and then a moment later: "No answer."

"You think she'll come stay with us?" A couple times a year, the twins saw firsthand one of the big benefits of living in Koreatown, which was in the middle of the city: no wildfires, because there was nothing wild to burn.

"Nah. I bet she'll check into a fancy hotel."

"Sounds lonely," Arch said.

"Sounds like paradise," Immie said.

CHAPTER THIRTY-SEVEN

Ro

"I promise you have nothing to worry about," Immie said. She'd surprised Ro by picking up his phone call. He'd figured she'd send him straight to voice mail, where he assumed she hadn't even bothered to set up an outgoing message. "The fires never reach our side of town. They can't."

"I knew there were wildfires in California, but not like this. I can smell the smoke."

"The whole city can smell the smoke. This happens pretty much every year. It's weird and scary and we don't go outside for a day or two and then we pretend like it never happened."

"But people die, yes? And lots of animals? And trees?" Ro asked.

"Yup."

"I do not understand California."

"It's seventy-five degrees every day and we have beautiful beaches. And celebrities. Can't forget the celebrities."

"And yet you are always on fire."

"Not me personally. I have never tested my own flammability, thank God."

Ro laughed out loud. "You speak as though you are a pair of toddler pajamas."

"Huh. Interesting that's where your mind goes. I think of candle wicks. You think of kids burning in their beds. Maybe you're a sociopath after all," Immie said. "Can I tell you a secret?"

"Of course." Talking on the phone felt intimate. The place to whisper secrets. He rolled onto his back on the bed, kicked his feet at the pink canopy. It reminded him of the forts he and Kiran used to make when they were little. Blankets draped across chairs, the two of them beneath and looking up, as if stargazing.

"That first day of school. For about two minutes, I thought you might be the arsonist," Immie confessed. Ro wanted to ask where she was. He guessed in the bedroom she shared with Arch. She'd described it to him over dinner, how she'd calculated she'd spent millions of hours in her bunk bed, alternately feeling crushed and cozy, depending on the day, though lately mostly crushed.

"And then you discovered I'm a huge wimp, and I'd be way too scared to do something like that," Ro said.

"Exactly."

Ro liked the feeling of his phone up against his ear, Immie's voice close. He should call people more often.

No, he should call *Immie* more often.

"But seriously, why is everything always on fire here?" Ro asked.

"*Sometimes* on fire. More on fire lately. But the real reason for this one: climate change."

"London is almost never on fire. It's getting even wetter and we have these horrible heat waves in the summer, but it hasn't ever felt, I don't know, apocalyptic like it does here."

"Do you miss it? London?" Immie asked.

"Usually. But right this second? No."

CHAPTER THIRTY-EIGHT

Paige

The hills were on fire and her mom was in D.C. and her dad was in Vancouver, and so Paige stood on her back patio and watched the flames lick the horizon. She'd packed her to-go bag—Rochelle had booked her a room at the Beverly Wilshire hotel—and now all she had to do was get in the car and drive three miles south. The air was already smoky and her lungs felt tight, in much the same way they had at school earlier today. The fire was beautiful, if you didn't think about the destruction, which Paige chose not to. Instead she thought of its power, its furious relentlessness, how it wouldn't need to sleep or eat, how it reduced its enemies to ash.

The fire was single-minded in its focus: *burn, burn, burn.* An echo in a children's book.

Security had done its patrol, had stopped at every house and made sure the residents were packing up. When the doorbell rang she was disappointed it was Leon and not Chase. Shouldn't he have wanted to check on her personally? No, of course not. They were practically strangers. Paige knew that flirtation did not equal obligation.

Being alone is not the same as being lonely.

And yet, why did she wonder what would happen if she stayed right here and waited for the fire to come? It was unlikely, despite the evacuation order, that her house would be engulfed in flames. Possible, but unlikely. She thought about what it would feel like to watch it move closer and closer, to play that game of Russian roulette. She felt a shiver up her spine, like the moment Chase touched her palm, like a match struck against the side of its book, the delicious flick of a lighter.

Ironic that the possibility of death made her feel most alive.

Paige felt her phone vibrate in her pocket. Immie, making sure she was okay. Immie, not accepting radio silence as an answer. She was not alone. Not really.

Okay then. Paige grabbed her backpack and her to-go bag, and left.

CHAPTER THIRTY-NINE

Ro

School was canceled for three days, and all Ro could think about was Immie. And the fires too, of course. You couldn't avoid thinking about the fires. The air smelled even in the city, miles from any burning brush, a constant reminder that even if things felt normal in your little corner of the world, they were not, in fact, normal. Not at all.

But really he was thinking about Immie, and how it felt like she was right there with him all the time even if he hadn't seen her. They'd been texting constantly, which allowed him to stop thinking about that moment when she abruptly dropped his hand. Actual messages seemed to have superseded that mixed one.

> **Ro:** The entire city of Los Angeles feels like the underground right now
>
> **Immie:** I've never been on the underground

Ro: In the summer it's too hot and crowded, and in the winter there's always a hint of mustiness in the air, but no matter the season there's always soot and some smelly bastard who doesn't wear deodorant who puts his armpits right at your nose level

Immie: No joke why does that sound amazing to me?

Ro: Cause it is. I think you'd love London

Immie: Can I ask you a question?

Ro: Course

Immie: Have you ever told a big lie?

Ro stared at his phone for a moment. He had the feeling Immie was trying to tell him something important, but he had no idea what it could be. What could she have lied about to him? Maybe she did have a boyfriend. Maybe they met at one of those cultish-sounding American camps that some of the Wood Valley kids talked about and were dating long-distance. Maybe she didn't mention it—a lie by omission—because she wanted to hold his hand for a minute in a dark restaurant but not in the light.

Ro: Not really. I mean, I've lied to my parents I guess, but never about anything major

He waited a beat.

Ro: Why?

Three pulsating dots. He held his breath.

Immie: Too long a story for text. Actually not my story to tell at all. But I think I made a mistake

Was the mistake holding his hand? Please let it not be that. At night, under the pink canopy, he thought about Immie's fingers and her sad brown eyes. How, when she came out of the bathroom the night they had dinner, her shirt was only tucked halfway into her overalls and he caught a peek of the flesh on her hip.

Ro: Well I've made plenty of those. I'm here if you are ever ready to tell me about it

Immie: I know. Thanks. Maybe one day

Ro: Ok

Ro wanted to tell her about the signs for package vacations in the Underground, how he had all sorts of ideas for "maybe one day." He could imagine them holding hands as they bungee-jumped off a cliff in New Zealand. Then he remembered that there were wildfires there too. His phone beeped again, though this time it was Kaia.

Kaia: WHERE HAVE YOU BEEN?

Ro: LA is on fire. No school. Been weird here

Kaia: Saw on the news, but your mum said you guys weren't too close

Ro: You saw my mum?

Kaia: Arun called her. He was worried when we hadn't heard from you

Ro: How'd she sound? Did Arun say?

Kaia: Cheery. Maybe this time apart has been good for her?

Ro: Hope so

Ro's dad hadn't gone into work for the last three days. He'd stayed in his pajamas, feet propped up on the coffee table, and had watched CNN for hours, marveling at the exuberant, Botoxed anchors and the wildfire images, his newly mustached lips open in a surprise O. On-screen, the trees were lit up orange, like the bad guy in *Thor*. A dead cow with his tongue lolling out his mouth lay splayed on charred grass. Angry blazes ate houses whole.

It was apocalyptic.

This time apart did not seem to be good for Ro's dad.

Immie: You still there?

Ro: Yeah, sorry. Was also texting Kaia. She says hi

Immie: 👋

Ro: I know I've said this a million times, but you guys would really like each other. Maybe one day you could come to London with me

Immie: Maybe one day

CHAPTER FORTY

Paige

At three a.m. in the business center of the Beverly Wilshire hotel, Paige printed off the first draft of her *Paige for President* flyers. Of course she'd have a real banner made professionally, and she wasn't even sure she had the nerve to use this one, but she wanted to see what it looked like translated from screen to paper. She'd woken up in the middle of the night with the idea, and couldn't wait till morning to execute it. Paige had superimposed her head onto that famous Elmo meme where his hands are thrown in the air and he's engulfed in flames. Underneath, she'd typed in fourteen-point Helvetica: *VOTE FOR PAIGE. SHE'S FIRE!*

As she sat in a padded leather chair enveloped by the crisp spa scent that wafted through the hotel (she assumed it was pumped in through the AC system), the fire was ten percent contained. Paige was wide awake. Her house was fine—the vast majority of residential neighborhoods had been spared and cleared for reentry—and her parents' only concern was about air quality and whether exposure might impact Paige's tennis season.

Everyone was a disappointment. Her family. Ro. Immie. Jackson. Even Arch, though she couldn't say why. Maybe something about the way he leaned into his mother's shoulder the other day, like a dog getting his belly scratched. She did a Google search for Chase Donahue, but the guy didn't have much of a digital footprint. Only a defunct Twitter account that seemed a little overinvested in women's soccer. She hit Print, and then held the feed up to the light, as if it would reveal more than the fact that Chase had a thing for Megan Rapinoe.

Nah, nothing here. She took her lighter out of her pajama pocket, flicked it, and set the paper alight. She blew it out almost immediately. Hotel alarms were sensitive, and the last thing she needed was to find herself detained by security, like that one time she got caught stealing a lipstick from Saks. No one knew about that, except her sister, Violet, who hadn't been disappointed about the shoplifting, only the getting caught. She had considered telling the story to Immie when Immie had confessed about the kiss—in a *see, sometimes I do bad things* kind of way to make Immie feel better, but then she realized that it wasn't her job to make Immie feel better. At least not then.

Paige stuffed the charred remains into the trash bin, again riding that now ever-present wave of disappointment. This time, it was because she didn't get to watch anything burn.

CHAPTER FORTY-ONE

Immie

They had been back in school for a week and already the kiss and the fires were starting to feel like distant memories. The air had cleared outside, the east wing girls' bathroom had been cleaned and repainted, and the school had put up *No Smoking* signs all over campus. Apparently, they believed that a rogue smoker was a more palatable scapegoat than an arsonist, though everyone seemed to have agreed it was the latter. The number one suspect was still Katy Flore, who was sporting a neck tattoo—real or fake, no one knew—that said *I didn't come here to make friends*. Paige's campaign was in full swing, and Immie's dad had an interview lined up for a job that seemed promising. The mood had shifted or lifted at Wood Valley, as if the fires that had burned and ravaged and charred in retrospect had the same consequences as a good rain. They were able to forget about the lost homes and the dead cows and the inevitable future uninhabitability of their city. Instead, they celebrated what felt like an unexpected clearing.

Immie tried to hold on to this lightness when she met Ro after school at a Starbucks on Ventura to work on their women's studies project. She intentionally did not take him to Espresso Yourself, because she didn't need Arch watching them. Though Immie and Ro still texted and, of course, she saw him multiple times throughout the day, this would be the first time they would be alone since their dinner.

When Immie arrived, Ro was already sitting at a table by the window, his fingers looped around a cup. He spotted her, his face lit up and expectant. Perhaps he too felt the shift in the air, like some page had been turned.

"You look cheery," she said, dropping her backpack and sitting across from him.

"Just happy to see you," Ro said, and she felt a squeezing in her chest, like someone had pinched her heart. Did he have to be so perfect? True, he had a poppyseed stuck between his front teeth, and he wore that mohawk chicken T-shirt at least twice a week, if not three times, and still somehow she found each of these details endearing. She'd looked hard for the one thing that would make it easy to walk away. So far she'd come up empty.

Did Paige even like Ro? And not in a "it would look good to date the new hot dude with the British accent after Jackson cheated on me" way? Immie had no idea. When Immie was honest with herself, she knew it didn't really matter. Paige's wishes on this, whatever motivated them, reigned supreme.

"So listen," Ro said, and her heart pinched again. "I think that I've been a bit of a wuss, and I'm sorry, and what

I'm trying to say, quite badly, is: I really like you. I think you are cool and interesting and smart and beautiful and would you like to go out sometime? Like on a date? Just the two—"

"Wait, no," Immie said. Or heard herself say. She didn't remember forming the words, or pushing them out of her mouth. Only that they were out there now, literally stopping the best moment that had ever happened to her. *Cool and interesting and smart and beautiful. Cool and interesting and smart and beautiful.* It echoed like a melody.

She tasted bile at the back of her throat. She wondered idly what would happen if she threw up right there. That would be worse than passing out in the produce section of Ralphs. And then she wondered why she was cursed with a brain that always went straight to the worst-case scenario. She wouldn't puke or pass out. Heartbreak was more subtle than that.

"Oh," Ro said, and his eyes dropped to the table, shy. "I guess I misunderstood. I thought . . ." He didn't finish his sentence, left it dangling out there, what he thought, as if she should already know.

And she did.

She had thought it too, even if she wasn't supposed to.

"No, it's not— I mean, you didn't misunderstand. I just, I can't." Immie reached across the table to grab his hand, and then decided against it. What was she doing here? She should never have texted him. Never have paired with him on this project.

No, she never should have lied to Paige in the first place. *Sometimes things are set in the beginning.*

"I thought there might be someone else." Ro looked up at her then, eyes wide and disappointed.

"There isn't someone else. I mean, there is, but it's not what you think."

"What is it, then?" he asked. Ro didn't seem angry, which perversely made her angrier. Not at him. Never at him. At herself. At her tiny, suffocating world. *You can't always get what you want* echoed in Immie's head. Another melody. This time she heard it in her dad's voice singing the Rolling Stones to her as a kid.

"It's Paige." Ro looked like how his father had approached the vegetable aisle in Ralphs—confused by the possibility of a purple cabbage. Did they not have purple cabbage in London? Immie thought they had everything there that she had here. Plus brown-eyed boys with thick lashes and strong jaws who could fell you with a single sentence: *Cool and interesting and smart and beautiful.*

"You and Paige are together?" he asked.

"No," Immie said. "Not like that. But she's my best friend, and she called dibs on you."

"I can't decide if I'm flattered or insulted," Ro said and laughed, though it wasn't his usual laugh. This one was bitter. Coffee-flavored. "Still. That's why you don't want to do this? Because Paige called 'dibs'?"

He said the word *dibs* with a dripping disdain, like it was a gross word. Like *moist*, or *diarrhea*.

"It's more complicated than that." Immie felt the tears gather in the corners of her eyelids and streak down her face. She'd read once that disappointment was one of the hardest emotions to deal with. And she understood that now. She had come so close.

Tears were better than vomit, she told herself. At least this way, he'd know that it was her, not him. A cliché . . . and yet.

Ro nodded. He wasn't going to make her tell him more, which was one of the things she liked most about him. He didn't push. Everyone else in her life was so pushy. Her dad, of course. Paige too. But also Arch and her mom, in their own ways. They never gave her room to be anything other than who they expected her to be. No room for growth or change. No acknowledgment that it was okay that she was still very much a work in progress.

"I'm sorry," Immie said.

"Me too," Ro said.

I think you're cool and interesting and smart and beautiful too, she thought.

"Can we still be friends and text and stuff? I mean, it's been really great getting to know you." Immie used her sleeve to wipe away her tears. If she were Paige, she'd have pulled a folded tissue from her bag, dabbed under her eyes. Immie wondered if her nose was running. *Dear God, let my nose not be running.*

"Of course," Ro said, and tilted his head to get a better look at her. No, she did not have mucus on her face. If she did, there's no way he'd look at her like that. Like how, on that very first day he walked into class, she'd dreamed he'd one day look at her. Like she had something to offer. "And I'm not just saying that because without you, and of course your brother and Paige, I'd have no one to hang out with."

"I wish I could explain," she said.

"Me too," Ro said. "Maybe one day."

"Maybe one day," she said.

CHAPTER FORTY-TWO

Paige

Her sushi had arrived hours earlier, and she wasn't expecting a package, so when the doorbell rang at eight-forty-five p.m. on a Tuesday night, Paige grabbed her phone and immediately dialed security. She peered through the peephole and abruptly hung up on the dispatcher.

Holy crap.

Chase.

Chase was here.

"One second," she called, and checked herself in the mirror above the couch. She fluffed her hair, let her shirt drop off one shoulder. Rolled the hems of her shorts so they showed off more leg. Better.

She wondered whether Chase knew she was home alone, and whether she wanted him to know.

Yes, she decided. Yes.

She pulled open the door and he leaned against the wall, still in his guard uniform.

"Hey," she said, and blasted him with her smile. The one that had set her parents back ten grand. "Everything okay?"

Paige decided to keep up with the fiction that he was there on some official business, even though it was clear immediately—by the fact that he'd opened a single button on his shirt, by the way he was resting his arm up on the doorjamb, by his sly smile—that he was not. She knew she was playing with fire.

"Yeah. Is now a good time? I thought I might take you up on that beer," Chase said.

"The beer I offered you two weeks ago when I thought someone was breaking into my house?" Paige asked, and she felt a shiver when she realized she was good at this. She sounded mature and flirty. A woman in control of her evening. A woman being coy just for the fun of it.

"Exactly. That beer. Whaddya think?" He asked this lazily, the *what do you* rolling into one word, ever so casual. Paige wondered if he visited any other houses in the neighborhood after dark. Maybe the divorcée down the block who was rumored to have had affairs with a handful of the famous Chrises.

Paige pretended to think about Chase's offer, as if there was any chance she would close the door on him. According to her Google stalking, he was thirty-five years old. She didn't know if he was married or had children. Maybe that was none of her business.

"Come on in," she said, and led him to the kitchen, feeling his eyes on her backside as she walked ahead of him.

Paige felt powerful and focused and unafraid. Sure, she heard her mom in her head remind her of all those traps set for women and girls in this unforgiving world. She tuned her out. She thought about the homework she still had left to do—at least eight fifteen-minute intervals—and tuned that voice out as well.

Paige felt . . . alive.

Chase perched on a stool, and she went to the fridge to grab him a beer. She knew nothing about beer, but figured whatever her dad had on hand had to be good enough. Paige handed it to him with a bottle opener and then leaned across the counter opposite him, resting on her elbows. This seemed seductive without being obvious. She could only guess how much he could see down her shirt, but she knew she was wearing a pretty lace bra—because she always wore a pretty lace bra—and hoped it was doing its job.

"So," she said, searching for something to say. Now that they were face to face, she had no idea what they could talk about. The community she lived in? The fact that he was twice her age? The security guard industry?

"So," he said, smiling. "How was your day?"

Okay, this was easy enough.

"Good," she said. "Yours?"

"Good." He smiled. She smiled back. Was this how adults did it? Just flirted with their eyes.

"Good," she said again, and hoped it sounded cute.

"Wait, what's that?" Chase asked, pointing to her fridge. She turned around, a grin on her lips. She figured he was looking at the photograph on the wall that used to embarrass her but that she had recently come to love. A black-and-white nude of a woman whose name Paige did not know by a photographer whose name she did. But that wasn't what he was looking at.

"Um, it was a joke," she said, but she felt her cheeks grow hot. She had pinned her *VOTE FOR PAIGE. SHE'S FIRE!* flyer on the fridge door with a Wood Valley magnet so her mom could see it when she came home. A way of announcing she was running for class president that would let Paige avoid her mom's obvious disinterest.

"Are you in high school?" Chase asked, already on his feet, his beer left where she put it.

"No. Of course not," Paige said, though even she could hear the lie. Her voice came out strangled. She didn't need to look in a mirror to know her face was betraying her like Immie's always did—red and splotchy and giving everything away.

"I've got to go. I didn't know. I mean, I thought, UCLA, maybe even graduate school. But Jesus, high school?" Chase didn't seem to be talking to her. He seemed to be talking to himself.

"Wait," Paige said, and then he turned and looked at her. Her eyes stung. She set her jaw in that stone-cold empty way, let a smoothness take over.

"I almost . . . We could have. Jesus, you're a baby," Chase said, this time obviously talking to her.

I am not a baby, she wanted to call after him as he walked out the door. But it was already too late. He was gone. And anyhow, she was crying like one.

CHAPTER FORTY-THREE

Arch

Lunch was awkward. Arch had seen Paige hang her official *Paige for President!* banner that morning, right across from Jackson's, and though he and Immie were of course Team Paige (despite Arch's traitorous heart), no one had said a word about it. Ro was being weird and quiet, rubbing the top of his head and looking away longingly at other tables. Only Immie seemed to be trying to keep the conversation going, with a forced cheer and brittle singsongyness that reminded Arch of his mom the mornings after fights with his dad.

"I heard they searched Katy Flore's locker and didn't find anything," Immie said. "And she had an airtight alibi. She was already in the principal's office in trouble when the last fire happened."

"It wasn't Katy Flore," Paige said, definitively. "I think it was Jackson."

"It wasn't Jackson," Arch said, and when Immie shot him a glance, he wished he hadn't said a word.

"I'm betting it was one of the seniors freaking out about college admissions," Immie said, and handed half of her Snickers bar to Arch. "The pressure is enough to make anyone break."

"You are betting what was who?" Jackson said, coming up from behind them and perching on the side of Immie's chair. Seemed a bad choice of seat, but then again, all the choices were bad. "Nice poster by the way, Paige. Not sure fire puns are funny right now, but we'll see."

"I plan to win, Jackson. Might as well start getting used to the idea now," Paige said.

"You people are ridiculous," Ro said, his accent crisp, and without explanation, he jumped up, tossed his half-eaten sandwich in the trash, and walked away.

"What's up his ass?" Paige asked while Jackson moved to Ro's empty chair. Immie shrugged like Paige was asking her. Arch eyed his sister.

"So, P, I come here in peace. I wanted to say that even though stuff went down between us, I hope you know I honestly think you are dope as hell, and I'm honestly happy you're in the race. I needed to sharpen up a bit. I was getting lazy," Jackson said. He didn't look at Arch, though Arch could feel him actively not looking at him. Like this speech was as much for him as it was for Paige. Arch wondered if his "entitled" comment all those weeks ago at Espresso Yourself had stung more than he realized.

"Um, thanks," Paige said, sounding uncharacteristically flustered. "But that was a lot of *honestly*s."

"You make me nervous," Jackson said, like that wasn't

a big confession. Paige made everyone a little nervous, though until the kiss, she had never made Arch nervous. She'd made him laugh, and made him frustrated, and made him jealous, and made him feel lucky, but she'd never made him nervous. Paige was the most reliable person he knew, next to Immie. There was never any reason to be nervous around reliable people. It was the unreliable, the ones who switched on a dime, who you had to be worried about.

"I'll take that as a compliment," Paige said.

"You should."

"We were a good team," Paige said, and then brought her hand to her mouth, as if she surprised herself by saying the words out loud.

"We were," Jackson agreed. "I'm sorry. Anyhow, you deserve more than a teammate."

Arch watched Paige's face fall. Had she not wanted a sincere apology? Had she hoped that she and Jackson would get back together? No way. Paige held grudges against everyone except Immie. He tried to read her, but she had zipped it all back up again. Paige was again steely.

"You're right," she said, and closed the lid to her lunch, her avocado rolls still uneaten, and tucked them into her backpack. Paige got up and followed Ro out the door without so much as a wave goodbye.

CHAPTER FORTY-FOUR

Ro

Ro knew it wasn't fair to be angry. He wasn't one of those boys who thought that girls owed him their devotion or something. It was just that he and Immie had a real connection, didn't they? And in his almost seventeen years on the planet he'd never felt this way about anyone else before. He heard his sister in his head: *You have this backwards, bruv. What matters is how she feels, not you.* Ro couldn't believe he had said it out loud: *I really like you. I think you are cool and interesting and smart and beautiful.*

The whole thing was humiliating.

Ro had emergency-texted Kaia and Arun afterward, and the three of them hashed it all out even though it was the middle of the night in London. God, he missed his real friends. The ones who knew him when he was small enough to play with Matchbox cars and Lego. Still, hours later, they hadn't figured it out. Paige had called dibs and that meant what, exactly?

He'd walked down the hall and out the rear doors of the school and kept walking, though he didn't know where he was headed. The yard, maybe—the tree he secretly thought of as Immie's and his tree. He was hopeless. *Immie's and his tree.* He had the distinct experience of being embarrassed by his own thoughts.

"Hey, wait up," Paige called from behind him. His heart sank. He liked Paige. She was also, by all accounts, cool and interesting and smart and beautiful. She wasn't Immie, though. He'd hoped, against his better judgment, that Immie would follow him outside. Give him an explanation, at least. "You okay?"

Ro turned then and wondered how much Immie had told her, if anything. Did she know his heart was currently decimated?

"Fine, yeah," Ro said.

"Is 'fine, yeah' like California 'no, yeah' or 'yeah, no'?" Paige asked.

"I have no idea," he said. "I still don't speak American. Or Californian." They were facing each other now, and he saw, beyond her shoulder, Immie and Arch and Jackson through the window. Were they watching?

"You're cute," Paige said, like they were having a totally different conversation. She smiled flirtatiously and took a step closer. She leaned forward, touched her fingertips to his cheek. "You have an eyelash. Make a wish."

Paige held her finger out to him, and he closed his eyes and blew. He didn't wish for anything in particular, only a feeling. He saw Immie's hand across a table, that sudden rush of relief that he was finally, finally, for once in his goddamn life, in the right place.

"How'd you get your scar?" Paige asked, again touching his face, the tiny knot between his brows. He took a step back.

"From a very mean rock when I was six," Ro said.

"I think you should kiss me," Paige said then, apropos of nothing.

"Excuse me?" Ro asked, at a total loss at how this was happening. Everyone had it all wrong. America was upside down. He felt enraged. He imagined Immie watching through the window, Paige setting him up for a show.

"I think you should kiss me," Paige said, again, oblivious to the anger soaring through Ro, hot and blinding.

"You don't get to call dibs on a person," Ro said.

"What?" Paige asked, confusion wiping away her flirty smile.

"You don't get to call dibs on a person. Immie said you called dibs on me. I'm a real person!" He was yelling now, and heads were probably turning, and he couldn't stop himself. He thought of his father and his ridiculous goatee and his mum in a totally different country and that twenty-two-year-old graduate student. He had looked up her Facebook profile and she looked almost creepily normal, like the person you'd queue behind at the Tesco's or stand next to on the Tube and not take a second look. It was extraordinary that someone so ordinary could ruin your life.

Paige was cool and beautiful and smart and interesting and the thought of kissing her made him want to cry.

Ro thought of Immie's dad, and how if he could he'd smash his face in.

Ro thought of Immie watching right this second.

Ro thought of the person who had lit a match, and felt a surge of empathy so vivid, he almost buckled at the knees.

"Sorry, sorry," he said now, getting hold of himself, hands up in the air, as if he thought Paige might take a swing at him.

"Immie said what?" Paige asked, angry now. Her white teeth flashed bright in the sun, and he thought about *Little Red Riding Hood* and the Big Bad Wolf dressing as Grandma.

"Nothing," Ro said. "Immie said nothing." The air had gone out of him, and he was suddenly too tired to fight. Also, he didn't even know what they were fighting about.

"You and Immie? Are a thing? Like, for real?" Paige's lower lip quivered and her eyes filled and she looked him straight in the eyes. He wouldn't lie. Ro was many things, but a liar wasn't one of them.

"It's real for me. I can't speak for her," Ro said, and then he saw that Immie and Arch and Jackson were now here too, behind Paige. They had come running when he had started yelling. His eyes caught Immie's and she looked at him, shell-shocked. He didn't know what to do. If he should go to Immie and explain or comfort Paige, whose feelings he'd so obviously hurt. Or if he should turn around, call an Uber, and borrow his dad's credit card for a last-minute transatlantic flight.

"Immie?" Paige turned around, her face white and drawn, and Ro remembered her panic attack after the last fire. He wished he had a paper bag to hand her to help her breathe. Arch's mouth had fallen open, and he clasped his sister's hand. "Again? What the hell? You're supposed to be my *best friend.*"

Ro's brain snagged at the word *again*, and the word *hell*, which seemed wrong coming out of Paige's mouth, and the way Paige looked back at Jackson. Immie and Jackson? Jackson, who he had long ago figured out was Paige's ex-boyfriend? Ro couldn't picture Immie and Jackson together. It didn't make sense.

"I *am* your best friend. Nothing happened with Ro. I swear," Immie said, and this hit Ro straight in the gut. Something *had* happened. Maybe not something you could point to like a kiss, but something *had* happened.

"Paige," Arch said.

"Don't you dare defend her, Arch. I swear to God," Paige said.

"I wasn't . . . She didn't . . . ," Arch said. "It's not like that."

"Paige," Jackson said, and looked at Arch and then back to Paige.

The bell rang in the distance. Lunch period was over.

Ro stood frozen, unsure what to do. He understood suddenly he was mixed up in a larger drama that he did not in any way understand.

But then Paige turned on her heels and walked away, head held high, and she reminded Ro of someone but couldn't quite think who. It wasn't until seventh period, when it hit him: Paige reminded him of the Queen.

CHAPTER FORTY-FIVE

Paige

Paige didn't go back to class. For once in her life, she skipped school, ignored all the waiting boxes to be checked in her planner, and drove home even though it was only one in the afternoon. Her hands shook as she kept them on the steering wheel, her heart thumping so loud she couldn't even hear the music playing on the radio.

Immie and Ro.

The betrayal felt like déjà vu. What was that expression? Fool me once, shame on you; fool me twice, shame on me? She pictured Immie's face—all innocence and *I am your best friend* as if this is what best friends did: stabbed each other in the back. And to think of all she'd done for Immie through the years. The sharing of her SAT worksheets, her swimming pool, her innermost fears and secrets. Only Immie knew that Paige's sister had done a stint at an eating-disorder clinic, that Paige once had a babysitter slap her across the face when she was seven and when she told her dad, he hadn't believed her, that Paige still slept with her Binky from toddlerhood. That Paige had, only one time, but still, tried cutting just to see what the fuss was all about.

Paige almost didn't see him when she pulled up. But of course, because today was the absolute worst, Chase was there in the little security hut. She didn't wave her hand. She didn't even look up. She paused and waited for him to pull up the gate.

"Paige," Chase said, and she didn't wait to hear if there was a note of apology in his voice. Instead, she pressed down hard on the gas pedal, shot forward so fast, Mrs. Parker with the walker and the six Pomeranians yelled at her to slow down.

At home, in her bathroom, Paige looked in the mirror. She had peeled off all of her clothes. The white shirt with the ruffles down the front, the royal-blue tweed miniskirt, the boots from that place on Rodeo. Her bra. Her underwear. Lacy and matching. She stared at herself, wondering why she couldn't see what was wrong with her. Shouldn't it be obvious? A gash down her stomach? A scar somewhere?

She was broken. That was the only explanation for Jackson, for Ro, but really for Immie. Paige opened the medicine cabinet. She had no idea what she was looking for. Xanax, maybe. Instead, she happened upon an electric razor. She picked it up, stared herself straight in the eyes.

I want to be like Katy Flore.
I'm tired of pretending to be fine.
I'm tired of pretending.

I'm tired.

I'm.

She held the razor to her widow's peak and began to shave. Her hair fell in long, dark ribbons onto the floor. It looked beautiful like that. Piled up like a cloud. Paige went in straight lines—she never did anything haphazardly, and certainly not this—and in a matter of two minutes, her hair was all gone.

She was completely bald.

There, she thought. *Now they'll have no choice but to see.*

Paige got into bed. Left the hair for Marta to clean up tomorrow. She turned on her side, pulled the sheets up and over her shoulder. She stayed that way and slept through the next forty boxes on her planner.

CHAPTER FORTY-SIX

Arch

Since Paige jumped ship, Arch sat by himself in bio, and texted Jackson under the table.

Jackson: You have to tell her

Arch: I know

Jackson: She'll understand

Arch: Which part? The kiss or the lying?

Jackson: Both

Arch: No she won't

Jackson: She will

Arch: You like to make everything seem easy when it's not

Jackson: You like to make everything seem difficult when it's not

Arch: What are you talking about? Life is complicated and messy. Things might be easy for you but they've never been that way for me. I can't buy my way out of life

Jackson: You don't get to do that. Belittle my problems because I have a trust fund

Arch: You know what I mean

Jackson: No I really don't. My world is just as complicated and messy as yours. Have you asked me even once about Jagger's mom? Did you know that she not only OD'd but it was on purpose? She left a note blaming my dad for leaving her

Arch: That's awful. I'm sorry

Arch thought about writing *My dad sometimes gets so mad he punches holes in the wall*, but he didn't. He wasn't ready for follow-up questions.

Jackson: All I'm saying is I know complicated and messy. A stupid kiss at a party is nothing.

Arch looked up to find the whole classroom staring at him. Apparently he hadn't been paying attention to the lecture, and now Mrs. Spalding had sidled up to his table, as if she were a cowboy walking up to a bar in a Western.

"Mr. Gibson, you know we have a zero-tolerance policy about texting in class." She held out her palm as if Arch should drop his phone into it. He refused, gripping it so tightly he felt his hand cramp. Jackson's last text was sitting there, inside, like a bad fortune in a fortune cookie. Once when they had gotten takeout from Shin Beijing, Immie's fortune had said *Soon you will be set free* and Arch's read *Enjoy yourself while you still can.* They'd all laughed, but later that night, he wondered for the first time if maybe he was doing his life backwards, that later wasn't guaranteed.

"I'm sorry. I'll put the phone away," Arch said. Mrs. Spalding gave him a long, searching look, and he was surprised when she backed down.

"Okay, in your backpack. Now." He felt something wet on his cheek. A single tear had snaked its way loose. No wonder Mrs. Spalding had let him off the hook. He stared at his bio notes, but couldn't read them. Instead, he heard it repeat in his head, in Jackson's strong, confident voice, and he felt himself shrink into himself under the weight of the words: *stupid kiss, stupid kiss, stupid kiss, nothing, nothing, nothing.*

CHAPTER FORTY-SEVEN

Immie

Paige wouldn't answer her calls or her texts, and when she didn't show up for school the next day, Immie officially got worried. She considered calling Paige's mom, but she didn't have her number. Or Marta's, which would have been the smarter way to go. Instead, she and Arch called in sick to work and drove to Paige's house. Of course, they had forgotten all about security, because they didn't live in a gated community or even a house. In order to get into Immie and Arch's building, you were supposed to press the intercom, which had been broken for more than a year. So the residents of the Moonrise kept a brick in the doorway to keep the swinging glass door from ever closing shut. The system worked just fine.

"Name, please," said a guard, mid-thirties with a slightly sleezy vibe. He wore a name tag that read *Chase*, but he didn't look like a Chase to Immie—it was the sort of name that conjured up boats and polo shirts, but his uniform was rolled up at the sleeves and half a size too small, as if to say, *I work out.*

"We're here to see Paige Cohen-Chen," Immie said, and channeled Paige by giving him her most dazzling smile. The guard didn't say anything for a beat. Only stared at her and Arch. Immie's smile slipped a bit.

"We don't have any visitors on the list for the Cohen-Chen residence. I'll call her to see if she's expecting you." He stepped back into the little hut, and then stepped out again.

"She's not picking up," Chase said.

"Okay, listen, we're worried about her. Please let us through. It's sort of an emergency," Immie said.

"What kind of emergency?" the guard asked. Immie pictured Paige in her bathtub, ribbons of blood pooling on the floor. No, Paige would never hurt herself, not for real—would she? Absolutely not. For one thing, Paige was not the type to ever leave behind a mess.

"Come on, man, do we look even a little bit dangerous?" Arch chimed from the passenger seat.

"It's a personal emergency. But we're her best friends and she needs us," Immie said. She wondered if that sounded silly to this guy, who was probably married with children, who watched football on Sundays and carried a gun and by four o'clock already needed another shave.

"I'll make you kids a deal. I'll let you through if you tell me one thing," Chase said.

"Sure," Immie said without hesitation, though she

couldn't imagine she had anything to say that he'd find at all interesting.

"Tell me the truth: how old are you guys?" She had no idea why he winced at her answer and cursed under his breath. There was no shame in being sixteen.

CHAPTER FORTY-EIGHT

Paige

Paige was on the couch eating ice cream out of the container, something she had never done before. Actually, make that two things she had never done: she'd never eaten on the couch either, since it was custom-made and her mom would kill her if she stained it. She felt like a heathen. Or a rom-com heroine in her dark night of the soul. Sloppy and unraveling. Her hand kept absently touching her head, each time a shock that her hair was no longer where it was supposed to be. Only a prickly stubble that felt soothing to rub.

No one had seen her yet. According to the calendar, her mother would be home tomorrow. Marta had called to say she wasn't coming in, that her daughter had the stomach flu. Paige knew Marta had a daughter, but in all the years Marta had worked for their family, Paige had never met her, had never even imagined what she looked like. Was she petite like Marta? Did she wear her hair pinned back in that same way, tight enough that Paige wondered if she ever got headaches?

The doorbell rang, and Paige ignored it. There'd be no good reason for her doorbell to be ringing. Packages were collected by security and delivered to the back porch at six p.m. The doorbell rang again, more insistent this time, like someone was leaning against it. Then banging.

"We know you're in there. Let us in!" Arch yelled, his voice muffled by the oak, by the long distance between couch and door. "Paige, come on."

"I'm not home!" she yelled back.

"Paige! Please!" This time Immie. Paige pictured her best friend in her mind's eye—she'd bet good money Immie was wearing a black T-shirt and jean shorts, that her hair was pulled messily back in a ponytail. She wondered what it felt like to be her—to have Arch, to have her parents, so solidly in her corner. A backstop. If Immie ever ate ice cream out of the container on the couch, which Paige guessed she did as a matter of course, it would not be some big act of defiance or a slippery-slope release. It would be Wednesday. It wouldn't mean anything at all.

"I'm very busy!" Paige called back, and laughed to herself. A semi-real laugh, though she had to admit it sounded slightly maniacal. Was she having some sort of mental breakdown? No. It was only ice cream and her hair. When she'd looked at herself in the mirror that morning, all freshly shorn, she thought she looked badass.

"We need to talk to you. Seriously," Arch said.

"Seriously?" Paige asked back.

"Paige, this isn't funny. We're worried. Open the door," Immie said, and this was what finally got Paige off the couch: she wanted to see Immie's and Arch's faces when they saw her new hair. She wanted to see their jaws drop. Wasn't that the point, after all?

Shock and awe.

Paige made her way to the door, leaving her ice cream and spoon on a side table. A tiny bit pooled on the granite. She ignored it.

"I'm fine," Paige said, opening the door wide, her arms up in the air like she'd just won a prize. She felt a buzzing in her ears, an unfamiliar heat on her cheeks, a clench as she waited for their reactions. She knew it would be fast: their eyes would widen, then they'd cover their reactions with big smiles. She expected them to tell her she looked like Charlize Theron in *Mad Max: Fury Road*. She expected to feel triumphant—shocking people had always been fun.

Paige hadn't expected this. To see Arch's and Immie's faces simultaneously fall. They didn't smile. They didn't say a word. Instead, they moved so quickly it was almost a tackle. They surrounded Paige in a hug, and after a while her face felt wet, though she wasn't sure whose tears were whose.

CHAPTER FORTY-NINE

Arch

Arch and Immie bounced questions back and forth silently over Paige's bald head. Things had obviously moved to DEFCON 1. Should they call her parents? Could they tell her the truth now, like they had planned? Would that make her feel better or worse? They decided nothing in those five seconds. They only shared a moment of panic.

Arch steered them to the couch and produced a pack of Kleenex from his backpack and they all wiped their faces.

"So I take it you don't like the hair?" Paige asked, and somehow this managed to break the tension, and they laughed. So like Paige to be in command, even now, when she seemed to be the most broken. Arch knew how scary this must be for her, to always grip life so firmly and to finally feel things slip a little. He understood. He had felt the same way lately.

"Honestly, I think you look badass," Arch said.

"Like Charlize Theron in *Mad Max*," Immie said.

"I knew you'd say that," Paige said.

"But . . ." Arch paused. "I mean it, I love how you look, I think you'd look beautiful with a mustache, but this was a big move. We're . . ."

"Concerned," Immie finished.

"Ha," Paige said, and Arch heard the bitter note creep back into her voice. He nodded at Immie, a signal that he was ready. They'd discussed it in the car. Time for one hundred percent honesty. A shaved head didn't change a thing.

"I didn't kiss Jackson," Immie blurted, her delivery not as smooth as they had planned, but effective enough. "I did hold Ro's hand, and I really like him, and I'm sorry. But I never kissed Jackson."

"What? I don't understand," Paige said. She rubbed the top of her head, and Arch already knew that later, if they managed to recover their ground, he'd ask if he could feel it too. Or maybe that was rude, like asking a pregnant lady if you could touch her belly.

"I did it," Arch said.

"I'm not following," Paige said. "Immie, you called me and told me you kissed him. You cried on the phone."

"I kissed Jackson. It was a betrayal of our friendship to kiss your boyfriend. It was also a betrayal to let Immie lie for me. I'm so sorry," Arch said, and then he held his breath. He didn't know what her reaction was going to be. She had every right to be furious with him.

This wasn't how he imagined coming out, if you could call it that when you were only telling your best friend who you already knew deep in your bones wouldn't care about the you-being-gay part. He had long ago imagined this particular moment to be filled with hugs and acceptance and, maybe later, if Paige was feeling silly, a balloon. It was supposed to be only good.

But now it was rolled up with dishonesty. This wasn't so much a coming out as a coming clean.

"You kissed Jackson?" Funny how the new hair changed the angles of her face, like it unpeeled a layer. It turned the inscrutable, scrutable. Recognition dawned. Maybe even a hint of relief. "That makes so much more sense."

"It does?" Arch and Immie said at the same time.

"You're not mad?" Immie asked, her voice betraying her hopefulness. Arch's heart leaped toward his sister, to protect her from inevitable hurt, and he marveled how this instinct on her part—to protect him—is what had gotten them in this trouble in the first place. Maybe Immie was right to want to move somewhere far away, to experience life without that beautiful tether.

"Oh, I'm so pissed," Paige said. "But at least this makes sense. Immie kissing Jackson? So weird. You kissing Jackson, I totally see. So are you gay, bi, exploring, haven't decided on a label yet?"

Paige said this casually, like it was the least relevant part of their conversation. Which Arch knew it was, and still it felt deeply important to him.

He wanted—no, needed—Paige, his second-favorite person in the world, to know who he was. Specifically.

"I'm gay," Arch said.

Paige nodded. "You know what sucks? I want to hug you and tell you I love you and I'm so happy you told me, but

I also want to punch you in the face for everything else, so I don't know what to do." Her eyes filled with tears again. Arch's face, he noticed, was wet too. He smiled at her.

"I love you too. But please don't punch me in the face. If you break my nose, I can't afford to fix it."

Paige laughed, and Arch risked a glance over to Immie, who was also crying. Of course. He felt her warmth all around him, like he was wearing a cozy winter coat.

"I kind of want to get you a balloon," Paige said, and Arch reached out his hand and grabbed hers and squeezed. "And then kick you in the balls."

Right. Still, he didn't let go.

CHAPTER FIFTY

Ro

The ticket turned out to be the easy part. Nine hundred fifty dollars on his father's credit card, saved on the laptop, one way, LAX to Heathrow, in two days. After what he and Arun and Kaia called the "Paige Incident," Ro had texted Immie: *did you know that tampons only cost £1.90 for 20 in England?*

He thought she would take it as a funny change of subject and a way to clear the air. Immie had written back almost immediately, like she didn't want to keep him waiting: *I'm sorry.*

He'd sent her more texts after that, at first thinking they could have a conversation, because he wasn't sure exactly what she was sorry for. But soon it became clear *I'm sorry* was her final answer, and he found he couldn't stop himself reaching out. He sent texts, one more pathetic than the next, so many that Kaia had told him that if he didn't stop, she'd find a way to confiscate his phone from halfway across the world. Ro didn't doubt she could pull that off.

Immie stayed silent, and he found he missed the ding in his pocket, that rush of endorphins he felt every time he saw her name on his screen.

The ride to school in the morning, which had once felt comfortable, had turned awkward and sour. Immie spent the whole time looking out the window, lips pursed, like she was trying not to cry. He wanted to ask if she was okay, if he could do anything to help, but Arch turned up the music too loud to speak. That's how they made their way to school: listening to some terrible local band Ro'd never heard of and never wanted to hear again.

The girl that no one knows, a warbling boy sang, as if it were a gift not to understand someone. Mystery wasn't sexy. Mystery was torture.

Ro was no longer angry, which was a new feeling, since he'd been angry since he'd arrived on American soil. Instead, he was heartbroken, which turned out to be way worse. He wondered if this was how his mother had felt at his father's betrayal, and then felt foolish comparing his non-romance with Immie to a twenty-year marriage. For the first time he understood his banishment, why his mother would want to grieve alone. Why she'd want to insulate him from seeing her pain.

He lay on his canopied bed with Blue Bear, only eating when his dad forced him to swallow down some tacos from the place around the corner with the fluorescent cactus sign. When Ro hit Purchase on his ticket, he'd had a momentary flush of joy, and he imagined that's what the arsonist had felt upon lighting a match. He said a silent prayer that his dad wouldn't get a credit card alert. It felt good to imagine burning this American life down to the ground. Like taking a shower after a run.

But then he'd picture Immie and her fingers and the way her face lit up when he said she was *cool and interesting and smart and beautiful.* He had no doubt that leaving meant that he'd never see her again. He wondered if he'd even get the chance to say goodbye.

CHAPTER FIFTY-ONE

Immie

"This is all my fault," Immie said. She felt swollen with guilt and, if she was honest with herself, rage too. Her entire life felt like taking one for the team. Are you allowed to be mad when you're the one who decided to play martyr?

"I'm not going to disagree with you there," Paige said. "Though I think Arch also sucks for, you know, kissing my boyfriend."

Paige's sarcasm sounded hollow. Immie looked at Paige's newly sharp, angled face, so much more obvious now that Immie wasn't distracted by her shiny hair. She looked at Paige's Wood Valley Tennis T-shirt, which had something chocolate-like smeared across it. She looked at the way Paige held one hand over the other to hide their trembling. The old Paige had molted and revealed a fragile new being underneath.

Immie had always assumed the opposite would happen to her one day—that Immie would molt and a more Paige-like Immie would appear: strong, capable, polished.

"But what I don't get is, why? Why lie?" Paige asked. And there it was, the question no one seemed able to answer.

"I don't know," Immie said, eyes filling again. "It was a middle-of-the-night split decision. I wanted to protect Arch, I guess."

"Because Arch's feelings always come first," Paige said. Immie didn't deny it. Of course Arch's feelings always came first. Once, when they were about seven, their dad was on a rampage, chucking pans from under the kitchen counter. He was pissed he couldn't find the one he wanted, or maybe he was pissed at his boss, or maybe he was pissed at some imaginary slight by their mother. Though there was little risk of getting hit, Immie still jumped in front of Arch, held her arms out wide, like she was a mom reaching out to protect her kid in the front seat of the car when she was driving and stopped short.

That arm did nothing to stop the impact. It was a reflex born from love.

And though she couldn't say it out loud to Paige, she realized that was why she had jumped in front of the kiss too.

Another reflex born from love.

"What were you protecting him from? From me? I really don't get it."

"I shouldn't have let her. It's my fault," Arch said.

"How adorable. Each of you trying to take the blame again. Were you really that worried about what I would say if I knew you kissed a boy?" Paige asked Arch.

Immie watched her brother, though she didn't need to.

She could feel his steely mix of pride and regret. She wanted to hug him. He was tougher than she gave him credit for, even tougher than her. His willingness to consider staying near home was a sign of strength, not weakness.

Someone needed to be around to keep an eye on their mom. Immie wasn't willing to make that sacrifice.

"It wasn't just any boy, though," Immie insisted. "It was Jackson."

Paige shrugged, like that was irrelevant.

"Also, it's my dad," Arch said, and Immie felt her stomach drop. They had not discussed this in the car. In fact, they had never discussed this out loud. It went unspoken between them that their dad—more accurately, their shared shame about their dad—in any way factored into this decision. He was too undeserving.

"Seriously? This is about your dad? We live in LA," Paige said. "And it's not like I would have told him."

"It's not. He's just. I mean," Arch said. Empty words. Immie understood. No one had armed them with the vocabulary to describe how it felt to live with their father's undulating moods. She remembered the feeling of recognition when she read this line from *Anna Karenina* in English II last year: *Happy families are all alike; every unhappy family is unhappy in its own way.* At the time she thought of the Cohen-Chens, who she knew weren't perfect, no family was, but they were happy and unremarkable except for their remarkable careers and wealth. But Immie's family was unhappy in such a specific way—pancake breakfasts and thrown vases. Her father had named Ernie the plant. It seemed impossible that that same person would knock him over.

Looking around at the empty house, at Paige's bald head, she wondered if she had the Cohen-Chens all wrong. She thought of Ro and his dad, banished to America.

"Our dad is . . . ," Immie said, as lost as Arch. Neither of them had ever allowed the word *abusive* to creep into their heads. That word meant they were *victims*.

They were not victims.

They both got straight As and did extracurricular activities and ate bountiful meals with vegetables. They were loved by each other and their mother and even their father. They were thriving as best as one can thrive within the confines of high school, weren't they?

Immie thought of the arsonist. The unrelenting desire to watch a flame lick their world away. She understood exactly how it must have felt to light the match.

CHAPTER FIFTY-TWO

Arch

"Our dad's an asshole. And I'm not planning on coming out to him until after high school. And if he found out before and not from me somehow, it would be, it could be, really bad," Arch said. He didn't feel better when he said this out loud. There was no relief or lifting, despite the fact that he sounded calm and definitive. It shouldn't have been so hard to say such a simple sentence: *Our dad's an asshole.*

Two years felt a long time away.

Arch would wait. He was patient and smart and careful.

It wasn't fair, but life wasn't fair. Ironically, one of his dad's mantras. Nothing was going to change now. His mom and dad were inexplicably tied together by guilt, by irrational forgiveness, by finances. By love as much as fear. Not everyone's story got tied up with a bow.

"Oh," Paige said. "He seems cool."

"He is. Sometimes," Immie said. "And sometimes he's not."

"I've always thought your family was perfect," Paige said,

and the twins simultaneously huffed out air. They were always in sync. "What?"

"We thought the same about you. It's so quiet here. Peaceful," Immie said.

"And lonely," Paige added.

"Well, good thing you have us, then," Arch said, throwing his arm around her.

"Some friends you are," Paige said, but she was half-smiling.

An hour later, they were still on the couch, faces dried out from salty tears. They had talked and then paused and then talked some more. Paige's head was in Immie's lap—Immie pet her spiky hair—and Paige's long legs were draped across Arch's. They were back to a shape all three recognized, even if Paige felt lighter to Arch. She'd turned from a solid into something more slippery. Like they needed to hold her down or she'd slide away.

"I wouldn't have told your dad. I wouldn't have told anyone," Paige said after they'd lapsed into another thoughtful silence.

"I know," Arch said. "I was embarrassed. We don't talk about it. The stuff with our dad."

"Have you ever done something that makes no sense?" Immie asked. "Or it makes a little sense, and at the time makes total sense to you, but you can't really explain it? Like, even if Ms. Lee made us write a three-thousand-word essay in which we had to answer the question, you don't think you could do it? But once you started down that road, there was no going back?"

"Duh," Paige said, pointing to her hair.

"It was kind of like that," Immie said. Arch thought about the morning after the kiss, how resolute Immie was to take the bullet for him. How a small part of him wondered if this was her goodbye gift. She'd do this for him if one day soon, he'd let her go. An unspoken quid pro quo.

"What if we spend more time here, P? I know you are married to that calendar, so what if you scheduled us in for a weekly sleepover?" Arch asked.

"God, it would be nice to get out of our apartment," Immie said.

"And spend time with your best friend," Paige said, smiling up at Immie.

"That too," Immie said.

"I like Jackson for real," Arch blurted out of nowhere. Might as well rip off all the Band-Aids at once. Tell the truth. He held Paige's legs tight, kept her in place.

"I like Ro for real," Immie added, almost an echo. "I'm sorry."

"Screw you both," Paige said, but she made no effort to move.

CHAPTER FIFTY-THREE

Paige

Of course her friends went home that night. It's not like Paige expected them to move in. And for once she needed the quiet. Her brain felt oversaturated. Too much to parse and unravel. Too many revelations at once.

The twins hadn't wanted to leave. Paige could tell they were worried about her. Arch joked about setting up a nanny cam and made her promise not to touch her eyebrows. Immie had already texted before they'd reached the front gate. And yet they were off again, now with Paige's blessing to run after the boys they wanted.

She wasn't losing anything, Paige told herself. She already had let go of Jackson. And Ro, well, Ro had never been anything more than a lark. To be honest, she found him a little basic.

Let the twins be happy, she thought, even if Paige herself hadn't yet figured out how to do that. She liked soaking in her own generosity. Maybe she needed to get used to losing.

Soon they'd all be off into the world. Soon she'd be shedding more than her hair.

She rubbed her prickly head. Channeled Furiosa from *Mad Max*. Flicked her lighter. Felt a tiny bit badass.

And like with everything else, the feeling passed, and a sad desperation crept back in. Paige knew she needed help. Life couldn't be fixed by a single conversation and with only the unsnagging of truths.

She picked up the phone. Who to call? Marta? Security? Her parents? The twins again?

Paige thought about what her mom would do, and followed her lead.

"Can you get me the number of a good therapist?" Paige asked, without even saying hello.

"Sure thing," Rochelle, her mother's assistant, said, as robotic as ever. It was a relief when, as Paige had suspected, she didn't ask a single follow-up question.

CHAPTER FIFTY-FOUR

Ro

The text came in at nine p.m. Ro had spent the evening packing up a duffel with only the essentials. He didn't want to tip off his dad.

Blue Bear, his vitamins, his new sunglasses. He'd wear his lucky mohawk chicken T-shirt on the plane.

Immie: Can we talk tomorrow?

Ro wondered if writing back quickly would make him sound too eager, which was ridiculous because he'd already sent Immie eight unanswered texts. Too late to play it cool now.

Ro: ?

Immie: Arch is going to catch a ride in early with my mom. Can we talk on the way to school?

Ro hadn't planned on going back to Wood Valley. What was the point? His flight was at ten p.m. tomorrow. He'd imagined disappearing into the ether, a smooth exit, regaining at least a tiny bit of the dignity he had lost the second he gulped that stale recirculated air on the plane to LA. He'd send a text to Immie once he landed in London with some sort of iconic selfie—standing in front of the Tower of London or a red telephone booth or possibly Borough Market (Immie would love Borough Market)—and then that would be that.

Ro's fingers were quicker than his mind.

Ro: *YES*

CHAPTER FIFTY-FIVE

Arch

"Buckle up, buttercup," Arch's mom said, and Arch shifted in his seat. He couldn't remember the last time he was alone with his mother. Immie was always there too, though not today. Today, she'd planned to declare her love to Ro in the front seat of their Toyota Corolla.

Arch's mom's car smelled like Arch's mom. Patchouli and lavender oil. An evil eye and a crystal hung on yellow yarn that dangled from her rearview mirror.

Apparently she needed all the protection she could get.

"Do you ever think about what it's going to be like when Immie and I graduate?" Arch asked, and he watched a range of emotions play over his mom's face. First, a flinch, a reflex like any other, and then a sort of pre-grief. She was feeling the loss before the loss. Arch had been there too—had test-run the goodbyes so many times in his head, a solid two years in advance. Imagined what his right side would feel like without Immie sitting next to him. What he would do with the other half of his Snickers bar. Whether he'd be able to sleep knowing his sister wasn't in the bunk below.

"Of course. Though I'm hoping you guys get into UCLA," she said. "It's an amazing school and you would be a quick drive away."

"No way Immie is going to UCLA. Actually, I don't think Immie's going to want to go to the same school as me."

"You're probably right. That one is ready to fly away on her own." Arch's mom turned right onto Highland, away from Hancock Park, taking Arch's favorite pre-Ro route.

"How about you?" he asked.

"How about me, what?"

"Are you ready to fly away on your own too?" Arch asked. Based on the look she shot Arch, it was clear she understood his subtext. This was the closest Arch had ever come to giving his mother permission to leave their father. Not that she needed it, or even wanted it, necessarily. But sometimes needs and wants are irrelevant. It was time he made clear whose side he was on, that he saw that there were, in fact, sides to take, even if his mother wasn't ready to see it that way yet.

Every other day they pretended their family was functional and happy. Every other day they pretended their dad knew best. Arch was too tired to play their usual *everything is fine* game. "Maybe it's time for you to make a change."

Arch's mom's features tightened inward, a pursing from forehead to lip. The air in the car felt drier, like they'd taken a wrong turn and ended up in the desert. All crackle and static.

"Sweetheart," his mom said, her voice warmed by love, and wary of land mines. "I . . . couldn't. You don't understand. I have responsibilities. Bills. And your dad means well. He takes good care of all of us."

"Mom, you could, though," Arch said, ignoring the "takes good care of us" part. He too had thought that for years, for almost his entire childhood, a drumbeat brainwashing until he'd crossed over into clarity. Perhaps this was what it meant to be an adult: being able to see your parents clearly for the first time, to allow yourself also to see all the damage they had wrought.

Arch's mom had worked steadily at Wood Valley for the last twenty years. *She* took good care of them.

"Do you know what two households cost? How hard it is for a woman of my age to start all over? I don't want to be alone." Her lower lip trembled, the slightest of wobbles, until she flattened it out again with her fingertip.

"You will never be alone, Mom," Arch said, though even as he said it, he realized it wasn't exactly true. Immie was leaving. He would too, in his own smaller way.

"I love him, Arch. And he loves all of us," his mom said with just enough edge to warn him that the conversation had gone too far. That Arch had crossed the line into disloyalty and betrayal, that she intended to keep to the rules of the Gibson family. Arch didn't say what he wanted to say: *love isn't always enough.*

"Okay, Mom," Arch said, careful to keep his voice kind and devoid of sarcasm. He would take a step back from the brink, move them back into safer territory. She wasn't ready. Maybe she'd never be ready.

He checked the time on his phone. "I bet Immie's still in bed."

"You know how we always joke that Immie pushed you out of the womb?" his mom asked. Her hand found Arch's on the passenger seat and they linked fingers. He looked up at the crystal, rough-edged and unpolished. Either a tchotchke or a talisman, depending on your perspective. Despite all the mistakes his mother had made—marrying and then sticking by their dad—Arch had never once doubted he was loved. He thought about Paige alone in that big, beautiful house and felt a well of sadness open for his friend. Had her mom even seen her new hair yet? Did she even know to be worried? Again, it was all perspective. A shaved head on one kid would simply be a healthy form of self-expression; on Paige, though, who was only sixteen and already owned four pink tweed blazers, it was something altogether different.

"Yeah," Arch said.

"Know what I think? I think it was the opposite. Starting that very first day, you've always led the way in this family. You cleared the path for Immie. Put your toe out first, took the temperature, and told her it was safe to say hello to this bananas world." His mom kept her eyes on the road, and Arch watched in awe as her features slackened again. Arch had never thought of it that way before.

Some things, he had assumed, were set in the beginning.

Immie pushed. He followed.

"You know why your sister feels so ready to launch? Because she knows you have her back."

"She has mine too," Arch said. He thought of her jumping in front of that kiss, of a Kind bar thrown from the bottom bunk, of their lives running in tandem.

"When I was your age, I was convinced one day I'd be famous. Have my face on a billboard like that one." Arch's mom motioned to a giant poster overhead, an advertisement for a new series on the CW. A blond woman in a blue latex superhero suit shot a ball of fire from her hands. "My life hasn't turned out exactly according to plan, but I have done two things I'm truly proud of. I made you and I made Immie. And when I look at you guys—how much you take care of each other—I feel like the luckiest person in the world." She grabbed the crystal and kissed it.

"Let's not get all dramatic," Arch said.

"Hazard of the profession."

"You better not make me chant now," he said.

"Seriously, Arch. I know I haven't been a perfect mother, and I don't always make the choices you think I should make, and I'm sorry about that. Sometimes I wish I were stronger."

"Mom." Arch felt his eyes fill. His mom was the strongest person he knew. And also, it was true, one of the weakest.

"Let me say this, please. I am so proud of you. And I love you. And I think you are perfect. You hear me? I think you are perfect. Every single thing about you." Arch's mom was crying now, and he absently thought about the makeup pouch she kept in her schoolbag, how later she'd stand in front of the mirror in the bathroom off the teacher's lounge and fix her mascara. He thought about the times she wore long sleeves in summer, another form of makeup.

"Mom," he said again, because he didn't know what else to say. He wanted to hug her and kiss her cheek and tell her he thought she was perfect too, even if she wasn't. No one was. He thought about when he came out to Immie, and she said the exact right thing at the time: *Of course you are*.

He looked over at his mother.

"Jackson's a good egg, by the way," his mom said. "I like him."

Arch closed his eyes, let the moment wash over him. He locked it into place.

"I love you," he said.

"Love you more," she said.

Arch thought about how amazing it was that everything and nothing could change in the exact same moment.

CHAPTER FIFTY-SIX

Immie

Immie wore jeans and a T-shirt and smelled vaguely of fear and desperation despite multiple applications of antiperspirant. *Too much?* she wondered. Ro had never before sat in the front passenger seat. The car was small. Their arms would likely brush. He'd be looking at the right side of her face, which she had examined extensively in the mirror before leaving. Thankfully her stress breakout was mostly on the left.

When she pulled up in front of his house, Ro was there, waiting on the curb like he did every morning. She felt equal parts relief and panic. Every day she wondered if today would be the day when he skipped town. She knew his escape plan would involve an airplane, not that bindle that Arch liked to joke was her dream, and yet that's how she imagined him running away. Ro on the side of the road, holding his belongings in a bandanna hanging from a stick, hitchhiking his way across America. She could picture him stopping at the Grand Canyon. Looking out at its open mouth.

Today, Ro wore his mysterious mohawk chicken T-shirt. He looked like Ro.

His face still made her want to cry.

"Morning," Ro said, slipping into the car. The doors automatically locked and she felt the click deep within. He couldn't go anywhere now.

"Morning," she said. Could she do this while driving? Her hands were shaking. She turned off the engine. Turned to look at him. "I owe you an apology. Maybe a million apologies. That's all I've been doing lately. Apologizing."

"Oh."

"I'm sorry. I should have been honest from the beginning," Immie said.

"Are you with Jackson? Is that what this is really about?" Ro asked. Even now, he looked at her with those clear, open eyes. The confusion still there three months later. Like the world was a Rubik's Cube he was unable to solve.

"Jackson? No," Immie said. "Never Jackson."

"But Paige said—"

"It was complicated."

"Was?" Ro asked.

"Was. I mean, it's all still a little complicated. Nothing ever is simple, right? But I don't know. I think. The thing is . . ." In her head, she had the words ready. She'd practiced in the shower, even though her dad was banging on the door to *hurry up already*, and practiced again on the drive over here. *I think you are cool and interesting and smart and beautiful. I like you.*

"I'm leaving for London tonight," Ro blurted. She turned

her entire body toward him then. She thought about the locked doors. How all he had to do to walk away was press a button and board a plane.

"Oh." Immie felt the telltale shaking of her lower lip, and she bit into it to steady herself. She would not cry. Cool and interesting and smart and beautiful girls did not cry, at least not in front of the boys who took up excessive real estate in their minds. They tossed their hair back, like Immie had once seen Alexandra Cohen do live on the air with Anderson Cooper, a moment later turned into a meme with the words *just try me*. "Yeah, no, I get it."

Immie looked down at her hands. She kept her nails trimmed and short, no polish. She thought about painting them black and glittery. She wondered if Ro would like that, if it would seem mohawk chicken-y. She realized when he left tonight, she'd most likely never see him again.

"I bought the ticket yesterday. I thought there was no reason to stay anymore," Ro said. He had shifted in his seat also, and now they were facing each other. No room to hide. "You didn't return my texts."

"I told you I had a lot of apologizing to do," Immie said, and she coughed out a fake laugh. Ro closed his eyes and opened them again. He didn't smile.

"You don't have to apologize for not wanting to do this," Ro said and waved between the two of them. She wanted to catch his fingers between hers and still them.

"But I do. Want to do this, I mean," Immie said. "I hadn't factored in the you-going-back-to-London part, though. When you say tonight, you mean *tonight* tonight? For real?"

"Ten p.m."

Immie felt that certainty again, the same one she felt in the middle of the night that had led her so far astray. Words tumbling without control. Decision made without thought or reason. Was this another mistake? Shouldn't she take a minute, weigh the pros and cons in her head?

Nah.

"Stay," Immie said. "Please stay."

She didn't wait for him to respond. Instead, she leaned in, cupped her cold hands around Ro's warm cheeks, and kissed him.

And all of a sudden she understood what Arch had been talking about: this was spontaneous combustion.

CHAPTER FIFTY-SEVEN

Paige

Paige opted not to wear a hat, and as she walked down the hall, various people held their hands up for high fives. She was right to wear her skinny khaki pants and her sister's old army boots. It added a certain edge to the look. The only teacher to comment was Ms. Lee, who asked Paige to stay after class, and once the room had cleared, asked, "You okay, honey?"

"Never been better," Paige answered, lying straight to Ms. Lee's face. Paige felt her toes flex as if to tighten her grip on the floor. This was the question she had most wanted to hear from her mother, who had insisted on FaceTiming from D.C. last night after Marta had dropped off dinner and seen her new look.

"Why would you do that to yourself?" Paige's mom asked instead, putting on her glasses and getting closer to her computer screen to take a better look. "You were so beautiful."

That *were* reverberated in Paige's brain for hours afterward. Paige had never considered the fact that she might no longer be beautiful. She had a nice proportionally shaped head and sharp cheekbones. Today, she'd charcoaled her eyes to make them pop.

"I don't understand you," her mom continued, a coldness seeping into her voice. She wasn't the type to get hysterical. She had grown up in a household of loud women, a mother who was prone to screaming and swatting with a broom, sisters talking over each other. Paige's mom loved their big, quiet house. How, on the rare occasions she was home, she could find a multitude of corners to hide in.

"Mom, it's just hair," Paige said, another lie. At night, she used to untangle her long tresses with her Mason Pearson brush, counting out one hundred strokes. Paige special-ordered conditioner and bond strengthener to keep it shiny. Shaving felt like some sort of offering.

"Well, the good news is, you can probably grow it back before your Yale interview next year. Turn it into a cute pixie cut." Her mother, always problem-solving. Paige pictured Rochelle standing next to her, checking *worrying about Paige's Yale interview* off on a running to-do list. "We have made you an appointment with a Dr. Simon next week. She's apparently very good with rebellious teenagers."

Paige did not think she was a rebellious teenager. She was likely going to be valedictorian. She played tennis. She had never been arrested or caught drinking or smoking or vaping. She had no hidden tattoos.

"Great," Paige said, her voice flat, like it had been run over.

"Got to go, baby. I'm live on *Maddow* in two minutes.

We'll talk more about this later," her mom said, and then clicked off. Paige put on the television, and there she was, arguing about Title IX sports. Her mom looked beautiful and shiny-haired. Unflappable.

"You don't seem like the type of person to shave off all your hair," Ms. Lee said now. Her voice was kind, which was always worse. Paige wasn't going to cry, certainly not here in her English III classroom, in the five minutes between periods.

"I guess I'm full of surprises," Paige said, and forced herself to smile. "I'm going to be late for math and we're having a quiz. See you later, Ms. Lee!"

Paige sprinted from the room and reached her hand into her pocket. She felt for her lighter, and rubbed her thumb gently against its spokes. She should wear pants with pockets more often.

CHAPTER FIFTY-EIGHT

Ro

Immie had kissed him. *She* had kissed *him*. Grabbed his cheeks and brought his lips to her lips and the whole thing hadn't been in his head. It was nothing like kissing Kaia near the Tesco. This was fiery and passionate and when Immie finally pulled away, she whispered again, *Stay*.

He thought of those ads in the Tube station, the bungee jumping and the air-balloon ride, the man astride a camel in the desert. They couldn't feel any better than this: kissing Immie in Los Angeles. They arrived late to school, ten minutes into first period, their faces flushed from making out in Immie's Corolla. Ro had been ready to leave, had said goodbye to California in his mind, had imagined his dad coming home from work to an empty flat. His mum on the other side of the Atlantic, exasperated but proud when she'd see the dent he'd made in his vitamins. Arun's bedroom, roast chicken-flavored crisps, a school where people looked and sounded like him.

Ro snuck a look at Immie in English III. She was doodling

in her notebook, obviously not paying attention to Ms. Lee, one hand resting on the back of her neck. She kept glancing up at Arch's empty seat, as if expecting him to appear. Ro hadn't made any promises to stay. He'd said they'd talk later, and Immie said, *Yeah, no, that sounds good*, and he almost laughed but then didn't. Ro wasn't naive enough to think that he could leave and they could make a go of it. It was one kiss, or, more accurately, a series of kisses, and he felt unmoored thinking how much a kiss could change things. That it could so fundamentally redirect his life plan.

In one world, he returned home, with Los Angeles left behind as a failed experiment, and a girl who would eventually dim in his over-exercised memory. In another, he stayed and possibly continued kissing Immie. He'd spend the next two years in a flat with his father in front of the television, robotically eating tacos from the fluorescent cactus place.

Ro looked at the back of Immie's head, at the white of the part in her hair. Such a vulnerable spot. He wanted to kiss it.

Signs came in all forms. Maybe this was his. A jagged line. An overwhelming urge. The impossibility of saying goodbye.

CHAPTER FIFTY-NINE

Arch

Would it always be like this? The twins living life in tandem, their biggest moments arriving almost simultaneously? While Immie was kissing Ro in her car, Arch waited for Jackson by his locker. Arch no longer had to pretend he hadn't memorized Jackson's schedule, but that didn't mean he knew how to stand. He leaned against the aluminum, casual, and then felt like the jock villain in an eighties movie. He stood straight, jiggled his foot, realized that made him look like he had to pee. Before he could come up with a third position, Jackson was there, the goofy far-off smile Arch had only seen once before, in the middle of their stolen midnight kiss, stretched across his face.

"Hey," Jackson said.

"Hey," Arch said. So he was doing this today. He was puffed up with all kinds of courage this morning. "Can we talk?"

Jackson nodded toward the abandoned girls' restroom, the one still marked off with caution tape after the first fire.

How long ago that seemed now, when they all stood outside watching the east wing burn. An unsolved mystery. They ducked under the tape and turned the corner and then, suddenly, they were blissfully alone. True, they could still hear the muted chaos of a high school hallway, but that seemed a wholly different world to this surprisingly lovely restroom, which was spotlessly clean despite its charred walls. This time there would be no slipping in urine.

"You want to play Xbox after school?" Arch asked, unable to keep the hopeful lilt out of his voice.

"That's what you wanted to talk about?" Jackson asked, and Arch felt all of his muscles clench with nerves.

"No," Arch said. Jackson waited but Arch had lost the ability to talk. He was looking at Jackson, straight in the eye, while Jackson walked closer and closer. Arch, in response, found himself part of the dance, and he stepped farther and farther back, until his spine was pressed up against the wall. Were they doing this?

Yes, thought Arch. *Yes, we are.*

Jackson leaned into Arch, so close Arch could feel the heat of his breath, his hard chest against his own. Jackson did not kiss him. He stayed there, suspended, frozen in place, body to body. Was Jackson asking permission first? Arch wondered. No matter. Arch would be brave and strong and perfect.

Arch grabbed the back of Jackson's neck and brought their lips together. Finally. Things between them turned frantic and desperate fast. Hands and hot breath and unleashed desire. Arch might have dropped to his knees right there in the girls' bathroom if the first bell hadn't rung and shaken them out of their reverie.

"I've been wanting to do that for so long," Jackson said, tracing his fingers along Arch's lips. Arch couldn't hide his grin. He now had a second kiss to relive during the long nights on the top bunk and, even better, the promise of more to come. "Shall we get to class?"

"Wait. I have to tell you something," Arch said.

"Are you about to come out to me? Because I think you already did," Jackson said, laughing.

"Well, sort of. I need to come out about something, but not about me being gay. I'm pretty sure you've known that for a long time. I need to tell you about my dad." Arch watched the surprise bloom on Jackson's face. Whatever Jackson thought he was going to say, it wasn't this.

"Okay," Jackson said, linking his hands with Arch's and stilling them.

"You might not want to be with me after what I say. And I'll totally understand. It's sort of a big ask." Arch's knees felt weak, an embarrassing cliché, though he wasn't sure if it was from the kiss or his fear.

"I think that's highly unlikely, but keep talking."

"I'm not out-out. I mean, I am—the people who deserve to know already know—and I am not ashamed. Let me be clear because I think it's important: I have *never* been ashamed. I told Im a million years ago, and recently Paige, and my mom knows—she's a big Jackson fan, by the way—but not everyone in my life knows and not everyone can. Some people don't deserve to know."

"What are you saying? Your dad is a raging homophobe? So no playing Xbox at your house." Jackson shrugged. "I think I can live with that."

"Actually, it's more complicated." Arch took a breath. This was way harder than coming out had ever been so far, though he wasn't naive enough to think coming out would always be that easy. Arch knew he had a long road ahead of him on that front, that it didn't end here, kissing a boy in the bathroom. That the opportunity to come out may present itself almost daily in adulthood. That he'd have to make continuous choices about how much he wanted to reveal about himself and to whom. "My dad's not a raging homophobe. At least, I don't think so. But he is prone to raging. If I told him, he'd pretend to be totally supportive, but then he'd freak out about something else, like not being able to find the kitchen scissors or some other nonsense, and lose his shit. And I know it would be my mom who would bear the brunt."

Arch didn't have to say the quiet part out loud. He could tell from Jackson's gasp that he understood the subtext. Arch wondered if he had overplayed his hand—surely his dad wasn't that bad, that this was all a gross exaggeration—but then Arch thought of his giant headphones, his emergency audiobooks. None of that was normal.

"I'm sorry if that means we can't be together. I know it's not ideal to have a boyfriend who isn't, you know, out-out," Arch went on. His hands felt warm weaved into Jackson's. He steeled himself for the inevitable rejection to come. Someone like Jackson couldn't settle for limitations. He had the guts to wear eyeliner and a skull ring. He lived his life in full color and at full volume.

Now when he looked at Arch he'd see a victim. Arch felt sick, ashamed, considered sprinting into a nearby stall.

"Boyfriend?" Jackson said, his smile now at full wattage, his eyes closed for a moment, as if he were savoring the word. "I want to be with you, Arch. And I'd never ask you to do anything that would make you or your family unsafe."

"Really?"

"Of course. I want to clock your dad, though. Is he a big dude? Can I take him down?" Arch laughed shakily and Jackson tugged him closer. Not for a kiss this time, but for a hug.

"He's about three times the size of you."

"Crap."

"I think we need to get to class," Arch said, but neither of them moved. This scorched bathroom felt like the safest place in the building.

CHAPTER SIXTY

Ro

Ro came home to find his father waiting for him in the flat and pacing the old wooden floorboards.

"You were just going to leave?" his dad asked before Ro even had a chance to drop his backpack. "You weren't even going to say goodbye?"

Ro's dad looked old. He'd shaved that morning, finally cleared his face of that disgusting facial hair, and new lines that looked like pleats on a skirt had taken residence on his chin.

"Dad," Ro said, a nonanswer.

"You stole my credit card." There was surprisingly little anger in his voice. Instead, only raw hurt. If Ro had been given a choice—and with all things with his family lately, he hadn't been given one—he would have picked rage every time.

"I know."

"Nine hundred and fifty dollars! That's over seven hundred pounds!"

"I know." Ro sniffed the air. Something was burning.

"Oh, damn." His dad ran to the toaster, pulled out two pieces of charred bread. *Ro's London dad*—that's sometimes how Ro thought of him, as if when his dad cheated on his mom he'd severed personas—would have cursed at the toast and then spread some Marmite and eaten it anyway. Ro's *Los Angeles dad* threw it into the sink and collapsed into a chair at the kitchen table. He dropped his head into his hands and started to cry.

Ro had never seen his father cry.

As the moment stretched and his father's back stayed bent, Ro was at a complete loss. He felt himself shift to a clinical, observational distance: *he cries like I do, folded in like a turtle.* And then back to a piercing vulnerability and guilt: *did I do this?* And finally landed here: *make it stop.*

Ro's dad lifted his head, used his sleeve to dry his face. Looked back up at Ro.

"I got a fraud alert on my card. If I hadn't, I would have come home tonight and you would have been gone. I can't stop thinking about that. You not being here. Me not knowing where you were."

"Dad," Ro said again. He didn't know what to do. If he should hug his father or yell at him for ruining their lives. Though Ro's life hadn't been ruined, exactly. Of course, he was furious at his father for hurting his mum, mad at both of his parents for making this LA thing not optional, but Ro saw the truth with sudden clarity. This morning he got to be the Tube bungee jumper. Maybe LA was the best thing that could have happened to him.

"I didn't cancel your ticket, by the way. I needed to look you in the eyes one more time before you left. I'm going to miss you so much." His father's eyes filled with tears again, and Ro felt his insides shrivel in terror. Parents were supposed to be the strong ones, immovable, the people who held steady and never changed. They were supposed to have the answers, not pose the questions.

"So I can leave?" Ro asked. Not that he had been acting like he needed his father's permission. Still, now that it was on offer, everything felt different. He wasn't in exile.

"I obviously don't want you to go, but I won't stop you. I'm sure your mum will be thrilled to have you home."

"But mum wanted me to come here."

"Are you serious? She misses you like mad! But you've been talking nonstop about leaving London for the last few years and it was obvious you were so itchy. She thought this would be good for you, and for us." He signaled between them. "You and I needed time to patch things up. And if you stayed and I left, we'd likely never live under the same roof again."

Ro felt a rush of blood to his head and an opening in his lungs. Another first: processing this new information physically, as if he had eaten these new facts and they were now winding their way through his system as he digested them. He felt them stick somewhere near his small intestine.

"What happens if I don't go?" Ro asked.

"You mean, the money?"

"I guess. Maybe. All of it."

"I'm not bothered about the money. I'm sure I can say

that it was an unauthorized charge by a minor or something. Or not. It's a small amount to sacrifice if you'll stay. The rest—us, you mean? I don't know. I think we do what your mum wanted us to do in the first place. Figure it out. Together."

"I don't know how to do that," Ro said. When he thought about staying he thought only of Immie's face, her hands, even that women's studies project they had yet to finish. He hadn't thought of his father as unfinished business. He thought of him only as *Los Angeles Dad*. The one who slept with his twenty-two-year-old graduate student and no longer deserved his sympathy or attention.

"I don't either. But we could start by eating tacos at the fluorescent cactus place together, instead of us doing takeaway and sitting in front of the TV every night. We could drive to the beach sometime—I can't believe we've been here three months and haven't seen the ocean. And let's hike to the Hollywood sign. It's practically around the corner. And the Walk of Fame."

"You think playing tourist will fix everything," Ro said, and though he hadn't meant it, there was an unmistakable bite to his voice.

"No. Not really. But I think it can't hurt. I did something terrible, and one day I might be able to explain it to you or maybe I won't. But I love you, Rohan, and I want us to be better. I'm not asking for forgiveness. I know you may never be able to give that to me. But I hate feeling like we are strangers."

"We're not strangers, Dad."

"We used to talk about everything. Remember that? Now you haven't even mentioned this girl you so obviously like. Did the dinner go well? I thought it was suave of me to slip you a couple of fifties, sending you to that fancy romantic restaurant next door."

Ro felt his stomach settle. He had no idea his Dad had set that up, though in retrospect it seemed highly unlikely he'd mixed up the exchange rate. Money was not something their family had ever taken for granted, which is why it also felt like an unusual gift that he could take or leave the ticket.

"Well, you still have a couple hours to decide if you want to go. Let me make you something to eat. Your sister sent us a care package with a couple of jars of Pasta Bake. We got crisps too."

"Roast chicken–flavored?"

"Of course."

Ro grabbed the familiar Walkers bag from the pantry, plopped down in the seat next to his father, and opened it. The smell wafted up, and with it a new form of homesickness. A sweet sentimentality replaced the painful ache. He offered the bag to his dad. After everything he had put him through today, the least he could do was give him the first crisp.

CHAPTER SIXTY-ONE

Immie

They were parked along the curb of Ro's street again. The smog was bad today, probably because of the soot from a fire burning two hundred miles away. Not close enough to check the air index, or even to register in Immie's mind. As hard as she tried to read Ro's face, she couldn't tell what he had decided. Things could go either way.

She realized it hadn't been fair to ask him to stay. In retrospect, it sounded like an empty plea, the Immie equivalent of a terrible pickup line at a bar. They barely knew each other. Arch had been by her side her whole life, and he'd never be so selfish. If anything, when the time came for her to leave, she'd bet he'd take his Espresso Yourself earnings and put them toward buying her a ticket.

It was the kiss's fault, of course. She thought back to that first day of school, how she hadn't understood how a single moment of two lips touching could change everything. Now that she was on the other side on her own epic kiss, after her chin was chafed from this morning's shenanigans, it all made so much more sense.

"I brought you a present," Ro said, holding out a red bottle. She wanted to ask if it was a goodbye gift, an *hasta la vista nice knowing you have a great life* gift.

"What is this?" she asked.

"Lucozade. The nectar of the gods. Take a sip."

She opened the top, sniffed. "It smells like cough syrup."

"Exactly."

"But it's not cough syrup?"

"No. Try it. It tastes like London." Her heart squeezed. Ro was leaving, of course, which Immie had already known was the most likely outcome. A boy wasn't going to change the course of his entire life because of one beautiful morning making out in her Toyota Corolla.

She took a sip.

"Well?"

"It tastes sort of like Gatorade that's gone bad."

Ro grinned, as if this was exactly what he'd expected her to say and her observation delighted him. That was the thing about Ro: he always seemed delighted by her. To have that sort of layered attention was a new and heady feeling. That's all this was. She'd survive the heartache.

Still, Immie knew without a doubt that she'd remember their morning forever. Some kisses were indelible.

"I'm staying," Ro said, and Immie felt the words climb up her spine, a chill like a vibration from a bell.

"You are?" Immie whispered. She didn't want to speak too loudly, in case he spooked easily and changed his mind.

"I realized today I actually like LA, and I obviously like you." Ro looked at her, straight on, the way she had imagined so many times, like he was an airport X-ray machine and he could see all her components. Her swollen heart. "Maybe it will be good for me and my dad to work some stuff out. I've been wanting to see a different part of the world for so long, and now I'm here. This is not the time to wimp out. I should give it at least a year."

"Great," Immie said with faux nonchalance. "I'm glad."

"You're glad," Ro said, leaning in closer. "That's all I get is an *I'm glad?*"

"I was trying to play it cool," Immie said.

"Please don't," Ro said, and there it was, another kiss, the simple miracle of two people's lips coming together and somehow changing everything.

CHAPTER SIXTY-TWO

Paige

Paige wore the army pants and combat boots again, this time with a tight pink T-shirt. She aced her AP Bio exam, of course, but when her teacher handed back her paper, Paige had felt nothing. Not her usual thrill, not even the endorphin rush when she mentally recalculated her GPA and her raised chances for valedictorian. At lunch, both Immie and Ro and Arch and Jackson were on their best behavior, obviously careful not to flaunt their new obvious coupledoms. Again, Paige felt nothing—not happy for her friends, not lonely that their pairings meant she was the odd one out.

The numbness was overwhelming and terrifying, like those nightmares when you scream but you can't get the words out.

Her first therapy appointment was set for tomorrow. Paige had no idea if it would be the answer, the vital thing that would resurrect her, but she knew enough about herself to know it was necessary. Some pits couldn't be climbed out of without professional help.

   Paige excused herself from the table and headed toward the west wing. The bathroom was empty. She knew it would be. Most of Wood Valley was on the other side of campus, in or around the cafeteria, flirting over tater tots. Paige bent close to the mirror, examined her face from every angle. This was a new hobby now that she had shaved her head: taking notice of all the things she now showed that she had previously kept hidden. Hollows under eyes and cheeks. It turned out the pull of her mouth was sad, not pouty.

   She reached into her pocket and took out her lighter. This was her favorite part: the feel against the pads of her fingers. The knowledge that something was about to happen. That internal spark before the literal one. Last time, she'd lit the paper towels, enough to get a real fire going, not enough to hurt anyone. Paige was not a sociopath.

   This time, she'd leave her mark, let the evidence trace back to her. It was, after all, what she deserved. She took out her planner, held it up, thought about all the fifteen-minute increments in which she had previously measured her life, all the work still left undone. So much time ahead, already divided and allotted. Would she wear a pixie cut for her Yale interview? Would there still be a Yale interview after this?

   Paige didn't know.

   Probably not.

   She flicked the lighter and set her calendar aflame.

CHAPTER SIXTY-THREE

Immie

Later, Immie would think it was some sort of sixth sense that led her to the west wing. That maybe there was such a thing as a connection that went deeper into the cellular level. She'd always resisted the idea that she and Arch had some sort of twin intuition, despite all the evidence to the contrary. When he hurt, she hurt, and vice versa.

Now it was Paige, with whom she had not shared a womb but an adolescence. As if Paige had left a trail of bread crumbs for her to follow. Immie thought of Hansel and Gretel. Were they twins? It had been a while since her mother had read them fairy tales, but Immie remembered this: the bread crumbs led to a witch who wanted to eat the kids whole. And suddenly, it felt vital that she catch up with Paige.

Immie began to run.

When Immie opened the bathroom door, her first thought, even ten days after Paige had shaved it, was *Where is Paige's hair?* Which was silly, because it was only hair. The next thought, of course, once her brain kicked back into gear, was that Paige was on fire. No, that wasn't right. Paige's calendar was on fire, in Paige's hand, and Paige was watching it burn.

"Stop!" Immie cried, though her friend didn't even turn her head. She was mesmerized by the billowing smoke, the way the flames ate the pages, the same slack-jawed way the two of them had once sat together in front of a screen watching TikTok videos. Immie had been right that this was a version of Hansel and Gretel after all. "Paige, stop!"

Paige finally turned to look at her. Eyes wide, spell broken, she glanced at the book in her hand and then at her best friend.

Horror dawned.

"This is not. I didn't," Paige said while Immie grabbed the burning calendar and threw it into the sink. She turned on the water, and the fire went out with an unsatisfying hiss. There was no alarm in the distance, nor the roar of trucks. Not enough smoke yet.

Immie turned off the faucet, and handed the soaked book back to Paige.

"Please don't tell," Paige said. Her entire body was shaking. Immie thought she should be able to hear the rattle of Paige's bones. *Click, click.*

"It's been you the whole time," Immie said. A statement, not a question, because of course it had been Paige. Now that she knew, it seemed obvious. Like that time she caught her mom sticking money under her pillow from the "tooth fairy," and how she had cried at her own naïveté. Of course fairies didn't deliver money when you lost a tooth. How bizarre that she had ever believed it in the first place. "Why, why would you do this?"

Paige held herself in her own arms, as if suddenly cold. Immie waited.

"You know that feeling you get when you hear the song 'Hallelujah'? How it always, always makes you cry?" Paige asked.

"I still don't understand," Immie said.

"You play it all the time anyway."

"So?"

"That song makes you feel something, right? That's why you listen. To hurt a little. This—and I know it's horrible and terrible and I need to stop—but this makes me feel something, Im. The rest of the time, I don't know, it's like I'm numb or I'm sleepwalking," Paige said, tipping over into tears, her normal cool, neutral face long gone. With her bald head and sunken eyes and chapped lips, she looked cracked, like a long forgotten, neglected doll fished out of storage.

Immie pulled Paige into a hug, tried to still her shaking, crying friend with the tight embrace. Already the smell of smoke was lifting, so faint that when Immie closed her eyes she wondered if she imagined the whole thing.

"I'm scared," Immie said.

"Me too."

"Promise me you will never do this again. Promise on

your life and mine and Arch's. Promise me, Paige," Immie said, stepping back and grabbing Paige by the shoulders. "You need to get help."

"I promise. On all of our lives. I promise," Paige said. "This was going to be the last time, for real. The plan was to get caught." Her voice was hoarse and tired and sad. Immie looked at the wet, charred planner in Paige's hands. The leather-bound book that every single person at Wood Valley could take one look at and know who it belonged to. A perverse form of confession. "This will never, ever happen again. I swear."

Immie's eyes stung wet and hot. She thought about the girl who had sat next to her that first day of middle school who was so full of the good kind of fire. Vibrant and assured. This Paige felt unrecognizable. She grabbed her for another hug, desperate to let Paige know how much she was loved. How their friendship was not conditional on Paige staying any one version of herself.

"Do you want me to report you? Is that what you need?" Immie asked. "We can go to Principal Hochman together. Tell me what you need me to do, Paige."

"I'm done. For good. Please don't tell anyone," Paige whispered, and then folded over with a whimper, as if she had been socked in the stomach. "Oh God, please don't tell Arch."

"I won't," Immie said. And just like that, after she had rid herself of the old secret, a new one had bloomed. A fresh tether between her and Paige. She knew, without weighing the options, that she would not tell, would never tell, that she would carry Paige's secret forever. She would do this for her best friend, even as she knew it to be dangerous and wrong, that it could at any moment turn out to be the worst decision of her life.

"Give me the lighter."

Paige dropped it in Immie's palm.

"No more," Immie said, and Paige nodded.

"I already made an appointment to talk to a therapist. I promise I'll get help," Paige said.

Would a promise be enough? Immie didn't know, though it turned out she believed in second chances. And anyhow, there weren't any grown-ups to turn to for help. Not Paige's mother. Nor her own.

Immie made a decision: She would drive Paige to therapy. She would check her bags for lighters. She would be there for her, day in and day out, until Paige became the next, better reboot of herself, whoever that turned out to be.

That was what you did for family.

Immie felt the weight of the secret, the seriousness of the responsibility, the feeling of jumping off that rocky cliff from childhood to adulthood. But she was already bound, she remembered. To Paige and to Arch. That way, tied together in their infinite webs and to their infinite versions of themselves, she knew they'd all, somehow, land safely.

Maybe.

CHAPTER SIXTY-FOUR

Immie

Six Months Later

The crowd made Immie blush. Arch and their mom—thank God their dad had to go to work at his new job and couldn't see her off—Ro's dad, Paige, even Jackson, who stood behind Arch as if to hold him up.

"Guys, it's only six weeks," Immie said out loud. In her head, though, that six weeks meant something altogether different. Six whole weeks of waking up in a new bed with a new roommate, a girl named Linnea from Sweden, and to Ro only a building away. A summer program at University College London, a scholarship covering everything except airfare, an opportunity for that first taste of freedom. It felt like a gift from the universe, when really it was the result of Ro suggesting they both apply to every single summer opportunity available for sixteen-year-olds in the U.K. They had sent out hundreds of applications. One came through.

"We'll WhatsApp every day, right? Morning here, night

there?" Paige asked. Her hair had grown out a little, and she had gelled it up into a mini-mohawk. Of course it looked amazing. Paige had quit both the tennis team and her trainer and had become obsessive about yoga instead. She had started taking medication. She talked about balancing her chakras and kept an essential oils collection in her bedroom where her lighter once lived. Most promising, Paige had bought a new calendar, one that didn't divide her days into tiny increments, and left whole blocks empty. She still wobbled, and when she did, she called Immie and her therapist, in that order.

"Don't take this the wrong way, but I am so happy for you and so sad for me," Arch said, and grabbed her into a hug. "I can't believe you are going to be halfway around the world."

"It's only 5,437 miles away. I googled it last night," Immie said.

"We expect lots of cheesy selfies in front of all things London," Jackson said.

"Take care of Mom," Immie whispered to Arch.

"I'll try."

"And take care of you," Immie added.

"I'll try that too."

"And Paige."

"Got it," Arch said. "Now get out of here before I start to cry in front of my boyfriend."

A few more hugs—Ro and his dad; Immie and her mom; Jackson, Arch, Paige, Ro, and Immie all together, like a team huddle—and then the goodbyes were over way too soon and Ro and Immie found themselves catapulted into the line for passport control. The crowd who had come to see them off were now on their way to the parking lot. Immie gripped on to the moment, as if she were already crossing over to a new land—no longer here but there—and needed to process the simultaneous rush of homesickness and thrill of independence.

Immie felt the invisible strings tethering her to Arch and to Paige pull tauter. Like a clip at her back before bungee jumping. No matter how far she went, they'd keep her from floating away.

Ro handed their passports over to the security agent, and then smiled back at Immie. They were really doing this. Immie pecked Ro on the cheek, and then she couldn't help herself, she was allowed to do things like this now: she sniffed him. Ro always smelled to her the tiniest bit singed.

"Ready?" he asked her, like going through the metal detector was the major step forward. Not the sending of applications, or the buying of tickets, or the hours of making plans.

This single step. This was it.

"Of course I am," she said. Immie passed through first, on her own, and waited for him on the other side.

A border crossed. A new, heady expansiveness.

In six weeks, when they would return from London, it would be August. There would be, again, passport control.

Then, of course, a new school year.

The start of fire season in Los Angeles.

ACKNOWLEDGMENTS

First and foremost, thank you so much to Beverly Horowitz and Jennifer Joel! Forever thank you to Elaine Koster and Susan Kamil.

Special thanks to the entire Random House Children's Books team, including Barbara Marcus, Jillian Vandall, Emma Benshoff, Rebecca Gudelis, and so many others.

Much of this book was written during the pandemic, and I am so grateful for my writer crews for helping me get through. Special thanks to Charlotte Huang, Kayla Kagan, and Amy Spalding, who are always down for finding the perfect joke or the perfect word. Huge shout-outs to Rose Brock, Max Brallier, Stuart Gibbs, Gordon Korman, Sarah Mlynowski, James Ponti, Melissa Posten, and Christina Soontornvat. A hug to the FWC. And thank you to my oldest and closest friends and family for always being there for me. You know who you are.

And finally, I'd like to say a giant thank you to the readers who have picked up my books throughout the years.

You have made my wildest dreams possible and I am eternally grateful.

Last but not least, a shout-out to Indy Flore, who I still not only love but also like even though we've spent the last year locked in a house together. You are so handsome when you take out the garbage. And extra special thank-yous and love to Luca and Elili, who make everything better. ILYTTMABABABAI.

MORE FROM JULIE BUXBAUM...

You're right. This place is a war zone, and I could use some help.

Jessie has just started her junior year at an ultra-intimidating LA prep school where she knows no one except for her new stepmonster's pretentious teenage son. Just when she's thinking about hightailing it back to Chicago—to her friends who understand she's still grieving the death of her mother—Jessie gets an email from a person calling themselves Somebody/Nobody (SN for short), offering to help her navigate the wilds of Wood Valley High School.

In a leap of faith—or an act of complete desperation—Jessie begins to rely on SN, and SN quickly becomes her lifeline and closest ally. Jessie can't help wanting to meet SN in person. But are some mysteries better left unsolved?

★ "The desire to find out whether Jessie's real-life and virtual crushes are one and the same will keep [readers] turning the pages as quickly as possible." —*Publishers Weekly,* starred review

"Fans of Rainbow Rowell are sure to adore." —*PopSugar*

"You'll eat up this book about a new girl at a prep school."
—*Seventeen*

A teenage girl's privileged life is shattered when her family's lies are exposed.

It's good to be Chloe Wynn Berringer—she has it all—money, privilege, and a ticket to the college of her dreams. Or at least, she did, until the FBI came knocking on her front door, guns at the ready, and her future went up in smoke. Now her B-list-celebrity mother is under arrest in a massive college admissions bribery scandal, and Chloe might be the next one facing charges. The public is furious, the headlines are brutal, and the US attorney is out for blood.

As everything she's taken for granted starts to slip away, Chloe must reckon not only with the truth of what happened, but also with the examination of her own guilt. How much did she really know—or guess? Why did her parents think the only way for her to succeed was to cheat? And what does it really mean to be complicit?

"[Buxbaum's] assessment of the entitled 1% feels spot-on."
—*Publishers Weekly*

"A gripping, thoughtful exploration of contemporary themes."
—*SLJ*

"Whether or not readers are familiar with the real-life events that inspired the story, they're likely to find it captivating; the novel goes behind the headlines to add humanity and complexity to a juicy national scandal." —*The Horn Book*

"An absorbing and topical novel." —*Booklist*